Ph.Dead

_____

JP Bloch

_____

PEGASUS BOOKS

Pegasus Books
3338 San Marino Ave
San Jose, CA 95127
www.pegasusbooks.net

First Edition: June 2016

Published in North America by Pegasus Books. For information, please contact Pegasus Books c/o Christopher Moebs, 3338 San Marino Ave, San Jose, CA 95127.

This book is a work of fiction. Any resemblance to actual persons, living or dead, events, or locales is entirely coincidental.

Library of Congress Cataloguing-In-Publication Data
JP Bloch
Ph.Dead/JP Bloch– 1st ed
p. cm.
Library of Congress Control Number: 2015959201
ISBN – 978-1-941859-44-5
1. FICTION / Satire. 2. FICTION / Ghost. 3. FICTION / Mystery & Detective / Amateur Sleuth. 4. FICTION / Humorous / Black Humor. 5. FICTION / Thrillers / Supernatural. 6. FICTION / Fantasy / Contemporary.

10   9   8   7   6   5   4   3   2   1

Comments about *Ph.Dead* and requests for additional copies, book club rates and author speaking appearances may be addressed to JP Bloch or Pegasus Books c/o Christopher Moebs, 3338 San Marino Ave, San Jose, CA, 95127, or you can send your comments and requests via e-mail to cmoebs@pegasusbooks.net.

Also available as an eBook from Internet retailers and from Pegasus Books

Printed in the United States of America

To Tristan, who does not need a Ph.D.

"Truth is the name we give to the choices to which we cling."
Paul Veyne

"To know, is to know that you know nothing. That is the meaning of true knowledge."
Socrates

ACKNOWLEDGEMENTS

Unless it is your intention to live a solitary life, you must carefully choose a few people along the way to take your journey with you. Writing a novel, a series, is no different. In this case though, I was blessed to have with me on this magical journey, some very enchanting people. It is with humble appreciation that I now bestow my thanks.

A writer's best friend is her editor. I'm fortunate that my main editor for this series was indeed one of my dearest friends. Pam Newberry graciously took time away from her own writing pursuits (check them out at www.pambnewberry.com) to be the voice of reason for my words' earliest drafts. Her ability to simultaneous be an editor and reader by asking the hard questions is an immense help in keeping my creative mind on track to get to the true heart of the story.

My dear friend Marcella Taylor does not just read books, she inhales them. Because of this, she has some keen insight into what will hold a reader's attention. In my case, it also helps that we have been friends for over twenty-five years. She can almost "think like Rosa," which is a scary thought for her. It is a comforting one for me though, as she often realizes where my thought process has gotten ahead of my typing speed.

Trained journalistically to limit punctuation, commas are a weakness of mine. Donna Stroupe is my compassionate reader who carefully checks "all things grammar" and keeps my commas on their toes. Her love of a story is evident in the thoughtful comments she makes during her review.

After having been sidekicks for the creation of the Legends of Graham Mansion series, Mary Lin Brewer has probably read my writing more times than anyone. I am very appreciative that she has taken the time to cast her eyes on this journey and give me some "delicious" feedback to consider.

The final person who reads my stories before I undertake the last edits is Carole Bybee. Despite the many reads that the story has undergone by then, Carole's keen skills find a few more errors or raise much needed questions of clarity. She also looks at the "big picture" of the story and helps to surmise if there are missing links which might confuse a reader.

Some say, you should not judge a book by its cover. I disagree! The wonderfully colorful and captivating covers for this series were designed by Cassy Roop of Pink Ink Designs (www. pinkindesigns.com). Even though Cassy and I have never met in person, she quickly understood what my vision was for this series and made the covers come to life. Her talented fingers are also behind the formatting of these books.

Every girl should be like Tremble and have her own Protector. Mine agreed to do that over twenty years ago. His patience during the writing process is very much appreciated as there are probably more "sandwich nights" than he would like.

Many thanks to all those wonderful readers who will take this journey with Tremble. I appreciate your feedback and loyalty. You are the reason I write.

ABOUT THE AUTHOR

Rosa Lee Jude began creating her own imaginary worlds at an early age. While her career path has included stints in journalism, marketing, hospitality & tourism and local government, she is most at home at a keyboard spinning yarns of fiction and creative non-fiction. She lives in the beautiful mountains of Southwest Virginia with her patient husband and very spoiled rescue dog.

The Enchanted Journey is Rosa Lee's second series. She is also the co-author of the award-winning time-travel series, the Legends of Graham Mansion. Learn more about her writing life at RosaLeeJude.com.

www.ingramcontent.com/pod-product-compliance
Lightning Source LLC
Chambersburg PA
CBHW020634260626
47157CB00008B/2730

Forensic psychologist and perpetual loner Dr. Bentley Gamble is murdered, and becomes a ghost. To move on to the next realm, he must find out who killed him. His is but the latest in a series of murders to occur at his dysfunctional college campus, the Elmer Butte (pronounced "byoot") College of the Liberal Arts. Offing people isn't even the half of it.

A series of campus sex crimes may have something to do with who gets bumped off. The sex crimes also lead to blackmail and various permutations of insanity and mayhem. Small wonder everyone calls the college Elmer Butthead.

The ghost detective gets it all sorted out, but not before he has ghost sex and pulls his fair share of pranks to get even. Ghosthood messes with his DNA, and he finds it increasingly difficult to act human when instead he can be haunting people and taking possession of their souls. He is as misunderstood in death as he was in life.

The novel's dark humor and satire of eggheads are used to make a very real point about the problem of sex crimes on campuses across the nation.

Ph.Dead

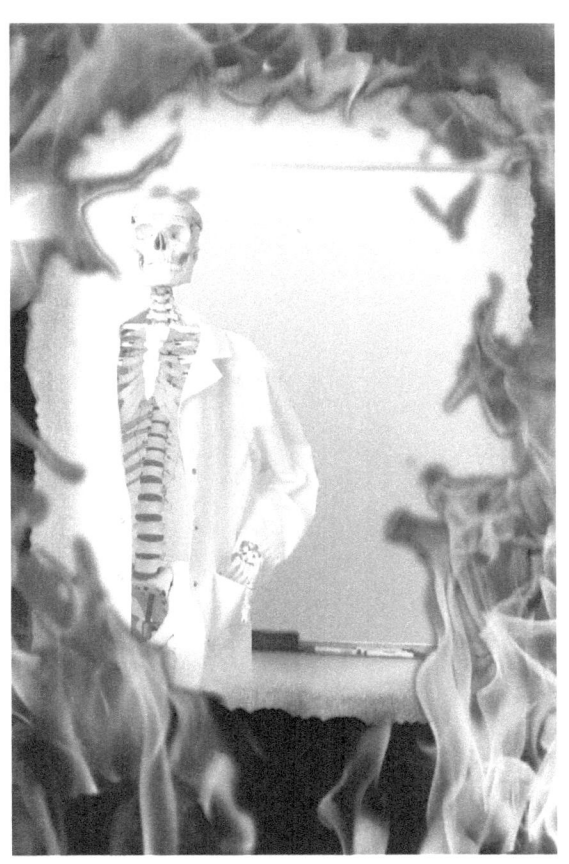

EBCLA Break-In Baffles Police

July 7 – Over the July 4 weekend, offices of EBCLA's psychology faculty were, according to police Sergeant Candy MacDougal, "defaced with profanity and sick, inappropriate jokes," pertaining to the May 25 murder of forensic psychologist Dr. Bentley Gamble.

A live skunk was discovered in the department's library, and skunk odor could be detected in all the offices. The department's sign was smeared in dog excrement, and comical glasses and goatees were drawn on the photos of faculty outside the main door. "This hardly seems a time for such juvenile sarcasm," remarked Sergeant MacDougal, who added that much of the graffiti was too obscene to print.

The psychology office showed no signs of break-in. None of the faculty were on campus during the incident. The police have taped off the department as a crime scene.

According to an inside source, handwriting analysis revealed a match to the penmanship of the late Dr. Gamble. Sergeant MacDougal stated, "Clearly there must be some other explanation" for the incident, though she did not elaborate on what it might be.

Dr. Gamble's murder is the seventh on the EBCLA campus in as many years, inspiring the regional hit songs, "Eggheads Be Dyin' Like Flies," and "Same Murder, Next Year." Sergeant MacDougal stated that Dr. Gamble had been working closely with police on the case, and was on the verge of solving it before his untimely death.

Photocopies of a news item from seven years ago were scattered about the department: the death of EBCLA student Kimberly "Wicki" Kulwicki, who jumped to her death from the Shuck Library roof after what the coroner ruled was a "history of mood swings." When asked what the connection was between the student suicide and the series of murders, Sergeant MacDougal would not comment.

Ghost 1

Yeah, I did it. The vandalizing, the doggie doodoo, the debonair skunk, everything. Wicki couldn't speak for herself, so I did it for her, just as I had for seven years. Suicide my ass. Mood swings? She was a normal kid. She told she me had a fear of heights, so why would she jump from the roof? I said this a million times, but nobody listened. No surprise there—it had long been all but illegal to take me seriously. Most everyone at school acted so goddamn smug. They thought I was crazy. Not that they said it in so many words. But I *knew*. "Give it a rest, Bentley." I must've heard that a thousand times. "Get a life," which proved ironic under the circumstances. Well, finally I'd get someone to listen. What could they do, fire a ghost? Deny me my ghostly retirement benefits?

I didn't wear a halo myself. Though I assisted the police, I never said boo about several potential murder suspects. I figured the victims asked for it, and singing like a choirboy would've ruined the lives of some essentially good people. If you want to split hairs, I suppose it's wrong to murder even the jerkiest of people, but no one ever said preserving academic integrity is easy. I realized, even at the time, I made life-and-death decisions that were way out of my depth. This may explain why I didn't die-die but instead got plunked down in spirit form in the exact environment that caused my untimely demise. Well, you deal with the hand you're dealt, as they say. If I was stuck as a ghost I might as well make it count for something.

Besides, my pranks on the psych department gave me something to do. It's not like they have self-help books for ghosts on how to be your own best friend. "Rest in peace"— talk about a sick joke. I could only guess what wondrous surprise the universe had in store for me next.

The truth is, being a ghost is not all it's cracked up to be. For one thing, you see everything in opposite colors, which is disconcerting to say the least. It's as if someone applied the Photoshop invert function to the world. Light-skinned people are Smurf blue, while dark-skinned people are closer to turquoise. Smiling teeth are dark brown to black. Roses are green, violets are yellow, and they both have red leaves. The sun is purple. Blood is also green. It's like a bad acid trip. A total bummer.

This answers the age-old question about why ghosts tend to prefer the night. For us, it looks like daytime. I'd long been a morning person, so now I prefer what is for you pitch darkness. If you wanted to get philosophical, this raises questions about reality versus illusion, etcetera and so forth, but I find such discussions unproductive.

By the way, in case you wondered what "EBCLA" stood for, I lived, taught, and died at the Elmer Butte (pronounced "byoot") College of the Liberal Arts. The dear old institution was called "Elmer Butthead" by most of the faculty, plus a sizeable number of students and staff. Nerdy people called it the peppier EBCLA, or as people said aloud, "Ebbclah." Elmer Butte himself was some rich prick that made a pact with Satan to construct a living Hell on Earth.

Supposedly psychologists didn't believe in ghosts. Countless case studies concluded that "seeing a ghost" meant you suffered from deep-rooted cognitive problems or a lousy childhood and all that garbage. Yet I always believed that ghosts existed. It's pretty hard to be an atheist about these things when you had your first acid trip at age thirteen. I didn't talk about my Drug Years with other faculty, but a long time ago I came out of the closet as interested in the supernatural. At a department meeting I presented a proposal for a new course entitled, "Psychology and Metaphysics," and it went over like a lead balloon. Dr. Dumont Dungworth in particular went on about how only crazy people believed such nonsense. Dumont was the last person on earth qualified to pronounce what constituted normality, and by this time I couldn't keep smiling and nodding my head like a jack-in-the-box clown.

"Well, Dumont," I said, "I believe in psychic phenomena. I think there are spirits and that it's possible to predict the future and read people's minds. Am I crazy?"

His beady eyes vibrated for a flash, and I knew it perturbed him that I disagreed with his lofty, magnificent self.

"Bentley, we've had enough of your contrary nature," he said. "You say irremediable things just to be vexatious. It's extremely puerile on your part." (Translation: I was an asshole.)

"Can't we all behave like adults?" Dr. Henry Zwieback, our nincompoop Department Chair, added. Everyone applauded, which pissed me off.

"Ha! The supernatural is real, and one day I'll prove it."

Me and my big mouth. Flash forward to May 25 of this year. There was a tempting, thick slice of banana nut bread in the break room with a post-it from Boris, our male secretary, which read: "Reserved for Dr. Bentley Gamble." Little did I know it was laced with enough potassium chloride to wipe out the entire Elmer Butthead community. (Not a bad idea, incidentally.) As I keeled over in pain, I knew it meant curtains.

Boris, as a contemporary man, saw nothing wrong with being the sole male secretary on campus. He more than fulfilled his testosterone quota through two tours of duty in Afghanistan. The virtuous Boris took one night class per semester to become a history teacher, and in the meantime endured working in the psych department to support his wife and two kids. My unexpected death gave him a twinge of PTSD, and he shouted out, "Medic, medic!"

"I'd love to keep talking, but to do that I need a pulse," I managed to say to Boris, not a speech destined to end up on those websites for famous last words.

Adding to the absurdity of my spirit incarnation, I have on the same clothes as when I died: sandals, jeans, and a T-shirt that reads: *Question Everything.* The T-shirt took on an ironic meaning, seeing as how I knew that Boris didn't drug the banana bread. It irked him when I turned in my schedule after the requested deadline, but surely his rancor in these instances paled after what he lived through in the army. Somebody else did me in. And since it made no sense that they would've been the person who I suspected did everyone else in (more on that later), I had a shitload of questions. But when you're a ghost, you suffer a lot of distractions. You're like a drunk driver trying to follow traffic lights. There's no use pretending you are who you were—alive only dead.

My inability to journey beyond the Elmer Butthead campus and a few surrounding blocks did not help matters. I could walk through walls—trust me, it gets old fast—and jump kind of high, as if the ground were a trampoline. But after landing on my butt a mess of times, I deduced I could not fly. When I tried driving my car or climbing into the back of a truck, a strange force plunked me back to Square One, Elmer Butthead. Not my idea of an inspiring setting.

When I got bored I said to myself, *Time to rock and roll.* I approached people walking in a nearby park at night and made them see me for a flash of an instant. They screamed like there was no tomorrow. I don't know why it gave me such a kick, but it did. It reminded me of being a kid, when my buddies and I set off firecrackers in the woods. So many people suffered from phasmophobia, the fear of ghosts. By virtue of being a phobia, if you were normal, you wouldn't be afraid of me. So if I scare you, that's your problem, not mine. Go lie on a psychologist's couch and get your act together.

The other night this guy really-really saw me, and tried to beat me with his briefcase. I kind of goofed up and grabbed it from him, and the guy fainted or maybe had a mild heart attack. To my credit, I stayed with him until the paramedics arrived, even though it was his fault.

"You're a prick," he whispered to me, as they slid him into the ambulance like a pizza into a brick oven.

"It takes one to know one." I shot him the finger.

"Who's he talking to?" asked a medic, to which query the other medic replied, "Nobody, you numbskull, he's delirious."

Sometimes I slipped into people's houses to see what was on TV. If classic rock music played, so much the better. I loved getting my groove on. But when I got recognized, the living humans shrieked like someone shoved dildos up their asses. I found this insulting, so I struck back any way I could. Hence, the breaking of objects and the like. Well, they started it.

Yet when people weren't scared to death of me (no pun intended) things got ever weirder. Suddenly some idiot scratching his beer gut became this religious zealot. With a TV commercial in the background for aerodynamic cars or anti-depressants, the person in the room said, "Away with thee, foulest of creatures, go forth unto the evil darkness from which thou comest." Either that, or some New Age numbskull wanted to know everything about me—who I was/am, and did I have a special message? I'd say something lame like, "You are gathered here to love each other," or, "It is up to each of you to work for world peace." I said these things with my fingers crossed behind my back.

I had no idea why some people could see or sense ghosts, while others couldn't. As a psychology professor, I'd hazard a guess that it had to do with how they were raised. I couldn't stand people who didn't realize how fucked up they were, but that's a whole other story.

The sickest thing of all was that about five minutes after I croaked, the department received a swarm of applications to take my place. Eggheads were so hard up for work that they figured a few years of employment before getting bumped off was better than nothing.

Thank goodness for dogs. I heard somewhere that when a dog sensed a ghost it barked as if it had rabies. But dogs were crazy about me when I was alive, and they acted the same after I died. They lay on their backs in ecstasy while I rubbed their tummies and the humans in the room thought

Fido went doggie-psycho. Even if people at Elmer Butthead didn't get me, dogs did. If I'd been born a cocker spaniel, none of this would've happened.

In my obsessive, ghoulish way, I counted the milliseconds until the first day of the fall semester. I planned to make it an occasion to remember.

Human 1

One of the many perks about being a ghost (and yes, I'm being sarcastic) is that you remember everything that ever happened to you. And I mean everything, even things you had the good sense to forget years ago. So in a way you're the one who's haunted, not everyone else.

I view my life in terms of BEB (Before Elmer Butthead) versus AEB (After Elmer Butthead). With one glaring exception, the former memories are good, while the latter are bad. In this respect, I lived a simple existence. Frankly, the annual murders were but the tip of the iceberg.

One of my all time favorite recollections has got to be the first time I tripped on LSD. I was thirteen, on a Boy Scout camping trip, if you can believe it. With no one watching, an Eagle Scout handed me a tab of sunshine acid that he said he stole from his older brother. It may sound strange that an Eagle Scout turned me on to acid. But all my life I had this peculiar magnetic force that led me straight to the fun, dirty secrets.

"You haven't lived until you've done acid," the Eagle Scout said with a wink. "It's like it draws out all the stuff inside you. And there's awesome colors and shit."

"Are you tripping now?" I asked.

"You bet your sweet ass I am, Squirt."

"Why give this to me, out of everyone here?"

"My inner armadillo told me to."

In that case, how could I refuse? I'd yet to smoke pot or even take a sip of wine, but I figured, *What the hell?* and thought maybe nothing would happen. (In a way, that summed up my life.) I went to the creek to rinse out a fry pan, and looked up at the sky. It was a huge, beautiful sunset, all orangey-purple, and the clouds moved and flowed and burst open in a way they never had before. All I could do was look up with my mouth hanging open. Later that night, I snuck off to an icy mountain lake, took off my clothes, and as I dove in I felt bathed in starlight. I jerked off for the first time, and the orgasm made me weightless. I discovered that the moon made people climax, which made me the only person in the world who knew this secret. I uncovered the fundamental spirit in all things.

I earned two merit badges from the campout.

Eventually, tripping got weird and scary, the way everything in life did. But I mention this episode to contrast my carefree, aesthetically rich BEB life to my ruinous AEB technical existence. The nonstop catastrophe began ruling my life the first day I taught at Elmer Butthead. It happened seven years before I got murdered. And what a day it was.

My brain turned into calamari from about a zillion different drugs ingested the previous evening. I did not intend to get loaded the night before my first day teaching, but I received an upsetting series of emails from this couple I met a couple of times. When you tell people you're a psychologist, they assume they can milk you for free insights. People confided all sorts of bizarre things to me over the years. You'd be surprised what goes on behind closed doors with what seems to be perfect suburban couples.

The realtor who located my apartment invited me to have dinner with his wife and three kids. After a wholesome meal of Sloppy Joes served with tall glasses of milk, the kids fell under the hypnotic spell of TV while Mommy and Daddy shared their real reason for inviting me over.

"So, Bentley," said Harvey the realtor, "do you swing?"

"Er . . . I'm guessing the answer is no?"

Madge the stay-at-home mom said, "You should try it. We have three-ways like they're going out of style. Which, by the way, I can assure you they are not."

To contextualize the conversation, Elmer Butthead was situated in a quirky hamlet in the northern Midwest, where kinkiness blended with a bland, *Lawrence Welk Show* politeness. Everyone was so busy minding their own business that people got away with all sorts of weirdo stuff. Having lived in this region all my life, I can't say Harvey and Madge caught me off guard. That they were less than one-hundred-percent-missionary-position-monogamous didn't phase me, either. Excepting my parents, every couple I knew had at least one extracurricular episode in its history. I just wasn't into it, thanks anyway. More to the point, even if I did three-ways I would not have been into Harvey and Madge, who were like a derelict Barbie and Ken. When cool people had exotic sex lives it seemed only natural, but Harvey and Madge were so bland they made it creepy-crawly.

"*Viva la ménage à trois.*" Harvey smiled while giving the thumbs up sign.

"The only French we need to know," added Madge with a wink.

I forced a slight laugh.

"Whatever rings your chimes."

"Doing me is optional, if you don't fly in that helicopter," Harvey said. "But Madge is one frisky little poodle."

Madge said, "You should talk. You want it even more than I do."

"It sounds like you have a vital marriage," I said in my nonjudgmental psychologist way.

"What about role play?" asked Harvey. "If you don't mind my asking, are you S or M?"

"SMBD is bigger than ever," Madge elaborated. "Everyone's doing it."

"You'd find me pretty boring," I assured them, hoping to dodge the question.

"We're all adults," said Madge. "There's nothing to be ashamed of."

"Let's put it this way," Harvey said. "If someone was going to shoot your mother in the throat unless you declared yourself S or M, which would it be?"

The oddness of the question caught me off guard.

"Gee, I dunno. M, I guess."

"Well, just call me Madame S," said Madge. "When you need a dominatrix, you know where to find one."

"And I'm M for man, and for . . . well, you know. Sounds like we have a little something in common." I found it of passing interest that Harvey needed to assert his manhood when telling me of his submissive nature. But for the most part, I wanted to go home and finish unpacking. PS: And forget I met Harvey and Madge.

"You're a psychologist," Madge informed me. "Tell us if you think this is weird."

With that, they led me into their bedroom, unlocked a dresser drawer, and took out a deluxe strap-on dildo with shiny metal studs on the belt.

"My, isn't that something." Mom raised me to be polite to your dinner hosts.

Madge pointed the rubber contraption in the direction of Harvey.

"Take that, you little Mama's boy," she commanded.

"Please," said Harvey. "You're turning me on. I swear, sometimes I shoot my load the moment it goes in, without even touching my you-know-what. I have a highly sensitive prostate."

When you get right down to it, there are two kinds of information: Things you're glad you're told, and things you could've lived without ever being told.

We talked for a few minutes about one thing or another—winter snowfall predictions, the Vikings versus Green Bay—before I made my excuses to leave. I expected this to be the last I heard from Harvey and Madge.

I should be so lucky. The night before my first day of teaching, I received the following email:

Dear Bentley,

Our strap-on has been missing for days. The only explanation is that you stole it. If this is your idea of a joke you are a loser. Return our personal property IMMEDIATELY or face legal action.

Harvey and Madge

First of all, I never stole anything in my life. And second, why on earth would I want this neurotic couple's strap-on? I emailed back:

Dear Harvey and Madge,

So sorry item is missing, but I did not take it. I was never even alone with it. I have my own whatsits, and while it may not be as impressive as your rubber one, I resent the implication that it is inadequate (ha-ha, just kidding). Are you sure you've checked everywhere? Maybe it's under the coffee table.

Bentley

To which they responded:

Of course we've checked everywhere, we even looked in the refrigerator, and it's gone. We have bent over backwards to be nice to you about this, but unless you return it tonight and take a solemn oath in our presence that you will never blackmail us we will meet with our attorney. We also will contact EBCLA and tell them you are a pervert. We are good friends with Dr. Henry Zwieback, your department chair.

I thought of acerbic responses to the part about bending over backwards, and with all due respect to absentmindedness, I found it hard to believe that someone would put a strap-on dildo in the refrigerator by mistake. But they CC'd the message to an attorney. While other new profs got a good night's sleep before their first day of teaching, I had to fend off a lawsuit that might as well have come from outer space. The terrible twosome didn't have a legal leg to stand on, but this made their message more threatening. Attacks from irrational people scared the crap out of me.

Worst of all, I knew my department chair was dead set against hiring me, and my teaching contract contained a morality clause. I did not view anything I did as immoral, but I was a non-tenured new faculty member, which is like being Daniel in the lion's den, only there is no God. And I did not know the morality clause mattered diddly-squat. Case in point Henry Zwieback, though I didn't know that yet, either.

I replied to Harvey, Madge and the attorney:

Am starting new job in the morning. I truly do not have the object in question but would be happy to take a solemn oath tomorrow night.

Yours very truly,
Bentley

I waited for a reply, and each second I did not receive one made me anxious. From the distance of time I realize it makes for a droll anecdote, but in the moment I could not have been less amused. When still alive, I was quite prone to panic, especially in my younger years.

As the night grew longer I found myself pacing the floors, feeling like I could not bear another instant of limbo. I experienced Liticaphobia (fear of lawsuits) with some Dikigorosophobia (fear of lawyers) thrown into the mix.

In my irrational, panicked state of mind, all I could think to do was find a way to lessen my anxiety. After all, I needed to be at my best the following morning. It was too late to call my mom or any of my college friends, and I hadn't smoked pot in years. So I turned to my medicine cabinet for succor. I had Vicodin left over from a knee injury, Percocet from a root canal, and some Oxycodone that was just sort of there for some reason. I also remembered some Xanax that a fellow grad student gave me as a good-by present. My better judgment said to take one pill at the most, but as often occurred, I rebelled against my better judgment. (A Freudian would say I had superego issues.) I took two or three of each pill. Finding some mushy powder in the bottom of the Xanax vial, I decided to snort it.

Bad timing became my new best friend. No sooner had I finished doping myself to the gills than did the couple finally email me back:

Never mind, we found it behind the dining room buffet. Our cat, Shnookums, must have hidden it. She likes to hide things.

Harvey and Madge

They didn't apologize, or wish me good luck at my new job, which I found incredibly rude. But they knew Henry, so I had to be careful.

Still, I felt a tremendous weight lift from deep inside me. I had my life back. For about forty-five minutes, I could've been king of the world. I played *Led Zeppelin IV*, dancing to it in my spiffy new apartment, and playing air guitar.

Then I passed out. I had a dream in which I could not see, speak or hear, yet insisted on teaching my classes without any special accommodations.

Through sheer dumb luck, an ambulance or cop siren woke me at 5 a.m., at which time I crawled on all fours to the bathroom. My head pounded and I had mild hallucinations, but I managed to shower and shave and put on my T-shirt and jeans.

When I arrived in the prison-like main building, called Phineas T. Labrador Hall (a/k/a Lab Hall), I couldn't find the psych department. I kept going in circles that led me back to the English Department, like the kids in *The Blair Witch Project* coming back to the tree. I thought I entered one of those impossible drawings by M. C. Escher.

"You look lost."

I heard a friendly-sounding woman's voice, and turned to see a professorial type in a business pants suit with black high heels. She wore her hair in a tight ponytail. "Are you a student?"

"No, I'm a new professor. In psychology." I hoped my out-of-it-ness didn't show.

"And do you have a name?" She laughed, as if I were an entertaining child.

"Oh, sorry. Bentley Gamble." I waited to see if she wanted to shake my hand since Mom taught me never to shake a woman's hand first.

"Cecilia Puff. English." She did not offer her hand, but I thought she seemed an okay person. I also once thought that a woman got pregnant by the man pissing up her ass. As Cecilia told me how to find the psych department—which resembled being told how to get from the Milky Way to the Andromeda Galaxy—I'm sure neither of us had the faintest idea of how our destinies would intertwine.

Boris the psych secretary took one look at me and said, "When push comes to shove, eat a lot of Chinese food."

Everyone made a huge deal over the fact that our secretary was a guy, as if this made our department the embodiment of gender equality. Boris was built like a football player and had a deep, drill sergeant voice, as well as a rhinestone stud in each ear. He wore crisp business shirts with a tie and sweater vest, as if a dress jacket would've been inappropriate to his subordinate station in life.

"I don't know what you mean, Boris." I also wondered if I heard him wrong, seeing as how I felt so wasted I had trouble remembering what planet I inhabited.

Boris gave a scowl that communicated I should cut the crap.

"Detoxing from drugs. It's not as effective as rehab, but the rice absorbs the toxins, and the soy sauce makes you drink tea to wash out your system. There's a twenty-four hour delivery place. I'll call them for you."

"I never heard of a twenty-four hour Chinese restaurant," I said, attempting to deflect attention from myself. I didn't want Boris to regard me as some pathetic druggie.

So there I was, preparing for my 8 a.m. class in forensic psychology by scarfing down three orders of General Tso's chicken with extra chili peppers. I even ate the broccoli. As my mind wandered I pondered why vegetables had such onomatopoeia-like names that signaled how disgusting they were. Broccoli. Cauliflower. Brussels sprouts. Cabbage. Maybe it was the power of suggestion, but the Chinese food did ground me somewhat.

Dummy that I was, I left my office door open, so my department chair, Dr. Henry Zwieback, stopped in to say hi. He knocked on the doorframe as he always would, that thing where there are five beats, a pause, then two more beats, like the end of the song, "Turkey in the Straw." As if one of Pavlov's dogs, I became conditioned over the years to associate his knock with a sick, sinking feeling in my gut.

Henry looked like a nightmare version of Humpty-Dumpty. His skin was so pink it appeared to be fluorescent. I could tell by the look on his face that he regarded someone eating Chinese take-out first thing in the morning to be the oddest damn thing he ever saw. I didn't yet know that Henry had far worse peculiarities, and in academe it didn't take much to seem like the strangest creature in the world. Since I knew Henry tried to stop me from getting hired, I assumed he already started composing a mental list of reasons not to renew me for a second year.

"I didn't know you could even get Chinese food in the morning," he said, with his horrific grin. Even without knowing he was a sex offender, he gave me the heebie-jeebies.

"There's a twenty-four hour place," I said.

"So I see," said Henry, increasing my paranoia.

"I like dinner for breakfast," I lied, which caused me to feel worse instead of better.

"Huh, you don't say. My wife has a brother-in-law like that. Drives his wife crazy."

"Huh, you don't say."

"Oh, by the way. I heard you had dinner with my good friends Harvey and Madge."

Holy shit. I could only imagine what they told him.

"Yes, I did."

"They said you were very nice, which needless to say didn't surprise me at all."

So they told him I was a pervert creep, and this was Henry's smiling way of telling me without telling me. In my experience, men are bitchier than women, or at least in academe.

I can tell when someone is fucking with my mind, and I try to fuck theirs right back.

"Thank you, Henry. I hope to make a positive impression with everyone."

"Don't let the students bully you. If they think you're peculiar, that's on them, not you."

I emitted a hollow laugh.

"I'll do my best."

When someone doesn't like you, and when that person is in a position of power, it's upsetting to talk to him at all. I experienced relief when Henry resumed walking down the hall, as if a cop pulled me over for speeding but let me off with a warning.

I all but crawled my way to class. As it turned out, I had little to worry about since most of the kids had their heads on their desks, trying to deal with the night before same as I.

"Howdy, folks," I said to the debouched students. "Welcome to Psych 21875-LXC."

A student raised his hand.

"Yes?" I asked in a tone of voice intended to create an impression that nothing in the world compared to the pleasure of answering student questions.

"Is this Botany 43916-NKZ?"

"Why, no. This is forensic psychology."

"Oh, okay."

It took forever for him to gather up his book bag and skateboard to leave the room. The entire time I thought to myself: *I so want to be someplace else right now.*

An eternity later, I continued where I left off.

"Forensic psychology is quite different from how it is depicted on TV. As you'll see, it is a complex science. First we will—"

A student raised her hand.

"So this is like TV, when the cops profile the crazy killer?"

"Well, sort of," I replied with a judicious smile. "The reality is that there are many schools of thought as to why people kill."

I went to the board and drew a diagram of various factors—personality development, cognitions, and so forth—that might be considered.

"Does this make sense?" I asked the girl.

"No, not really."

"Well, feel free to see me during my office hours. As I started to say, we'll explore a number of models. Thrill kill, murder by design, algebra of aggression, neutralization theory—"

Another student raised her hand. "Will we get to leave early today?"

It felt like a punch in the stomach, but I tried not to let it show.

"We'll see."

Having taught as a graduate student, I managed to deliver a wobbly first lecture about how homicide is defined, as opposed to other forms of killing that are seen as quote-unquote normal. More and more heads fell onto desks, and I got shakier and shakier, but I survived.

As students got up to leave, a girl asked, "Can I talk to you about something?"

Fuck. Just when I thought I was in the clear. I didn't have to teach another class that day, and couldn't wait to go home and crash.

"Sure!"

"Gee, thanks," she said. "I need to graduate in May, but I have to take Psych 32266-LXC and Psych 49017-LXC, which is cross-listed with Anthro 45128-GMY. I also need another free elective. So can I take 49017-LXC as 45128-GMY, to fulfill my free elective as well as my core requirement? And can I get a waiver on the prereq for 32266-LXC, because Psych 21085-LXC is not being offered this year? Or would I have to arrange an independent study through Psych 44488-LXC? Can I even do that, since I already did an independent study as 22288-LXC?"

All the while she spoke, her face kept fading into a blur, as if she were headless. I widened my eyes to keep them open.

"Tell you what—stop by my office tomorrow at noon. We'll talk then."

"Sure, I can do that," said the student without a head. "I'll bring my degree audit and my Minor Declaration Form and my Blue Sheet for requesting three credits of field experience. Do I need a Yellow Sheet for that as well? Can the copy of the Green Sheet be on white paper?"

"We'll get it all straightened out tomorrow," I said.

"Great. I'm Kimberly Ann Kulwicki. My friends call me Wicki. Like Wikipedia."

"And I'll bet you're just as smart."

Wicki laughed. "I wish. I'll see you tomorrow. My research assistanceship with Dr. Dumont Dungworth starts today. I'm so excited to be an RA."

"Sounds great," I said, not yet knowing the truth about Dumont. And Wicki didn't know she had about twenty-eight hours left to live.

Ghost 2

They say bad things come in threes, and a short time
after I became a ghost I saw proof of this phenomenon.
Being a ghost doesn't mean you never have One of Those
Days. If anything, ghostliness strips away the BS, and when
things go wrong you experience it all the more.

The first disaster was that Boris got arrested for my
murder. They found a bottle of potassium chloride in his
desk. I couldn't comprehend the flakiness of the local cops.
As if whoever offed me would be dumb enough to leave the
potassium chloride in an unlocked drawer. Even if Boris
hated my guts for reasons unknown to me, the six other
murders were supposed to be linked to mine, and he had no
reason to kill these other people. True, my murder was the
sole charge against him, but it made no sense when you
looked at the big picture.

I wondered who set him up. Any one of the creeps in
the psych department could've done so; it might've been a
conspiracy. Why not pin it on the lowly secretary so that the
cops would leave the Very Important Professors alone?
Though he had no criminal record and served in the army,
Boris got denied bail. As far as I could tell, the department
did nothing to help him.

It must've baffled Boris to come home from the war
only to be put in jail for something he didn't do. His poor
wife, Jamie, had to explain why Daddy went away to their two
kids, Something and Something. (I heard their names many
times but never paid attention.)

This development so unnerved me that I walked in the
park without bothering to scare anyone. That was when the
second crummy thing happened. I saw our current president,
Kingsley Shufflebottom, and some piece of slime from the
Board of Directors whooping it up in the sitting area by the

rose garden, each of them clutching a beer like they'd won the Oscar for Best Bromance.

"There must be a God," Kingsley said. "No more Bentley Gamble. I can breathe again."

"But Bentley can't," said the witty board member, and they both found this remark hysterical. President S. gave new meaning to the word nondescript. You could've rendered his portrait by drawing a single oval. The other dude could've been his twin. Big shots in academe all look the same.

"What if they figure out Boris didn't do it?" Kingsley asked.

"The case will go cold," answered the board guy. "Like all the others. It's pure synchronicity. Right place, right time, right murder."

"You sound like you willed it to happen."

"Your honor, I plead the Fifth Amendment. I play hardball with the best of them, but I draw the line at murder. Still, when a pain in the ass is no more, all you can say is hallelujah."

I decided to grab their beers and pour them over their smug little heads, just to scare the crap out of them. Then I'd shove them into the oncoming cars and leave the rest to fate. I figured if I harmed or even killed someone as a ghost it wouldn't count. But as I lunged at them some invisible force stopped me. What was the point of being a ghost if I couldn't do what I wanted?

Maybe there was no point. I had to stay this way—stuck as an undead soul—just because I had to.

The third lousy thing happened when I elected to pay another visit to the psych department. During summer the department saw little activity, and the area got taped off as a crime scene. But I hadn't been back since my last invasion and I wanted to see the police tape for myself. I don't like to brag, but I took considerable pride in the mess I made. My favorite touch was to cross off the word, "Psychology" on each of their Ph.D. diplomas and write in the word,

"Cocksucking." *Doctor of Cocksucking*—I felt better thinking about how it must've insulted their smarmy egos.

Call the word choice ironic, but I found deep satisfaction in seeing the department resemble a ghost town. I thought to myself that it should stay that way—silent and unpopulated.

Naturally the opposite happened.

Two professors walked down the hall. One was a woman I saw at faculty meetings for years, but never knew her name. The other was my acquaintance from my first day at Elmer Butthead, Dr. Cecilia Puff from the English department. Seven years later, she looked the same. She still wore a business pantsuit with black high heels, her hair pulled back in a ponytail.

As they approached the psych department, the other woman said, "Ugh. How depressing. Bentley was an obnoxious loudmouth, but he didn't deserve to die."

Cecilia laughed a little.

"Everything happens for a reason. I never dwell on negative things. I'm an existentialist. I live each moment to the fullest. I choose happiness, not despair."

"But didn't you think he was strange? And overbearing?"

"Sure, but so what? I must've had to know him or else I wouldn't have encountered him. If nothing else, he showed me how not to live my life."

"But don't you feel guilty when someone dies, and it makes you . . . it's almost like you're glad they're gone?"

"Why would I feel guilty? I don't control other people's destinies. From what I understand, it took him all of a minute to die, so it's not as though he suffered. I'd say he got off easy, considering how he treated other people. We faculty need to stick together, and it's hard to do that when people like Bentley Gamble are among us. Really, if the worst thing you ever did is wish someone dead, look at what other people do to make everything as miserable as possible. It was his time to go. There are no accidents in life."

I sure hoped that was true, because as Cecilia waxed enthusiastic over her joyous sense-making existence, she lost sight of where she walked and tripped over the police tape. Her head hit the floor with such force that it knocked her out. The other woman screamed and took out her cellphone, but by the time the medics arrived a few minutes later Cecilia had died.

So much happened in such a short time, I didn't know what to think. I was like: *Well, whatever.* Why should I feel bad about someone who considered me to be so much chopped liver?

Things got more interesting as I watched her spirit self lift up from her body like a cellophane wrapper. For a crucial instant, the apparition stopped moving, as if making up its mind.

It took shape as a ghost. Like me, Cecilia wore the clothes she died in.

Cecilia gazed at her new invisible body with disgusted amazement, like Frankenstein's bride. She looked at me and looked at herself, and back again. She kept blinking her eyes, as if she could make all the opposite colors normal again. When she tried to scream, it sounded like a hyena in need of an exorcism.

"Being a ghost takes getting used to," I said, trying to be helpful. "Actually you never get used to it, but that's how it goes."

Cecilia had a nervous habit of redoing the elastic tie for her ponytail, as if she could never get her hair pulled back tight enough. Death did not cure her of this habit, even though she hadn't anyone to impress. I found mild distraction in watching her ghostly stray hairs undulate as if underwater.

"What the heck is going on?" she said, satisfied with her hair for the time being. "What am I doing here? And with you? This has to be a mistake. I know—it's a dream. I'll be waking up any second now."

She pinched her arm many times, but it made no difference.

"I thought you said everything happens for a reason. And who the hell says, 'What the heck?' What are you going to say next—'Gosh darn it, I'm dead?'"

"You know, if you were a very close friend, I might—notice I say might—let you poke fun at me, but since this has not nor ever will be the case, I'd appreciate it if you'd keep a safe distance from my penetralia."

"Please be assured the feeling is mutual. I could not be less interested in penetrating your penetralia. I had to get fucking murdered to have some much needed alone time, and now Miss Clumsy spoils everything. Assuming you aren't just passing through on your way to . . . to someplace or another."

Something told me Cecilia wasn't going anywhere. Since when did anything work out in my favor? We hated each other's guts while alive, and we could not have been less alike. As a faculty member, she was what we good guys called a Pod, paying tribute to *Invasion of the Body Snatchers*. Cecilia fell for the Elmer Butthead claptrap like the brainwashed drip she was. She was the repugnant sort of person who said things like, "Be an actor, not a reactor," or, "If you're not part of the solution, you're part of the problem."

All sorts of people began arriving at the scene of this newest tragedy: doctors, cops, administrators, custodians, and of course, news reporters.

"C'mon," I said, as the do-gooders stampeded down the hall. "Let's boogie out of here."

"We should sing that *Wizard of Oz* song. You know the one I mean—when they're skipping along the yellow brick road. Or was it purple?"

I couldn't tell if she was being sarcastic or wistful or just being an idiot.

For many, many days to come there'd be rhetorical questions posed as to whether the psych department had been cursed. The media milked every last drop from the tragic irony of Cecilia's freak accident, making for a great deal of maudlin, self-congratulatory sentiment that I'd ignore as much as possible.

Human 2

As I believe I mentioned, in my BEB years I had one super-bad experience, and now is as good a time as any to mention it and get it over with. Speaking as a psychologist, it is relevant to the sordid tale of my wasted AEB years. It made the unbearable all the more unbearable.

I got kidnapped at age three, and locked in a cellar until age six. You might be thinking, *Say what?* But this did happen. While alive, I remembered almost nothing about it. But it remained part of me, like the way your skin tingled when nobody touched you but you knew how it felt to be touched. My dreams were a psychologist's cornucopia of unconscious anxieties. People in some way different saw in me a kindred soul.

I didn't know who kidnapped me until I got rescued, because the person always wore a black hood. The kidnapper also talked through an electrical scrambler so I couldn't recognize the voice. All I did for three years was sit on a concrete floor in the dark; there was a toilet within reach of the ankle chain I had to wear. I lived on scraps of stale bread and tap water. Maybe once or twice a year, the kidnapper removed the raggedy sheet I wore, and hosed me down.

I had no toys, so I made up little games with my fingers on the concrete floor. Ironically, I called one such innocuous pastime "Ghost." The fingers of my left hand would crawl up to my right hand and say, "Boo," making the right hand run out of sight.

From time to time, the kidnapper tickled me beyond the point of endurance—even as a ghost I am extremely ticklish. I also got raped, though until I became a ghost I had no memory of this.

At other times, the hooded weirdo hugged me and seemed to be crying.

"I'll protect you," the kidnapper promised during such tender moments. "I won't let the world do to you what it did to me."

Talk about a whack job. But I never said as much. I knew better than to anger this person, and strange as it may sound I felt like the adult in our relationship.

"I can't go on," the weirdo said on many occasions. "People are so cruel to me."

"I like you," I'd lie. "You take good care of me, and we have fun."

"That's so sweet. You know you're a special little boy, don't you? No one but you knows how to say just the right thing to make me happy."

"Gee, thanks."

Now and then the kidnapper removed my tattered sheet and dressed me in a proper little boy suit with short pants. On command, I'd smile as the crazy asshole took my picture.

At a young age I understood how to be dishonest in order to survive. Not lying about eating a cookie before dinner, but the cheerful, mind-fucking lies adults tell. I lost my innocence as a preschooler, and once it's gone there's no getting it back.

When the cops rescued me at age six, I learned my jailer was a picture perfect PTA mom named Misty Rose. She hid me in a locked, off-limits basement room, unknown to her husband and two kids. Her house was a spanking clean white colonial in an upper middle class neighborhood. It befitted her immaculate make-up and designer high heels. She'd rape me with an organic zucchini, fresh from her garden.

When they cuffed her, she cried, protesting that I was the only person she could confide in.

"You're taking away my soul mate," she wailed. "What we share is heaven on earth."

If that was her idea of heaven, spare me her vision of purgatory.

Misty never offered much explanation for why she did what she did. She saw me playing outside at my pre-school, lured me into her SUV when no one was watching, and that was that. She said she'd never done anything like it before.

After being found guilty on all five counts, her attorneys argued for leniency because her husband and children needed her. Less than convinced, the no-nonsense woman judge sentenced Misty to life in prison plus one hundred years. The publicity from the trial enabled her honor to get her own courtroom TV show.

Misty's husband cried and cried like the wimp he was. Imagine being oblivious to something so awful going on in your own home. Then again, maybe it wasn't so hard to imagine. Watching his old court appearances, it's obvious from his body language that he thought of no one but himself. Probably he cried because he had to learn to operate the microwave. His name was Poindexter, which I thought suited him. Poindexter Rose, Certified Public Dick.

Once back home, my mom and dad all but locked me away themselves to ensure I did not dwell on my ordeal. None of us spoke to the press, and I never had to testify in court. We also never talked about it at home. My wholesome Midwestern parents would've sent me to church and Bible summer camp anyway, but now these pursuits took on a greater importance. I needed *salvation*.

Mom and Dad had cause to be optimistic. After all, how much do most people remember about being three to six years old? And so I put Misty Rose behind me . . . more or less. Looking back, I can see my parents went from treating me like a kid to treating me like a problem, a test case. If I lost my cool, they worried that I'd relived the trauma. When I acted happy and energetic—which I did, most of the time— they thought I showed remarkable fortitude. But I never just *was*.

I'm sure that's why I got interested in psychology, where everything we think, do or feel is drawn and quartered for analysis. By my teen years I called my moments of self-doubt "Misty Attacks." In my twenties I flitted in and out of therapy.

My captor became the subject of three books, and a movie that earned the snooty actress who played her an Oscar nomination. When I read these books as a grad student, I couldn't believe how political the issue became, since I thought it obvious that Misty Rose suffered from schizoaffective disorder. One book told a story of white privilege, depicting Misty as a spoiled, affluent ultra-white woman who thought she could get away with anything. Another author presented a story of male privilege, reasoning that poor Misty had no choice but to channel her life's goals into something perverse, given that she married an abusive control freak. The third author blamed the incident on violence in the media.

By contrast, the film version depicted Misty as a good old-fashioned nut job. There were lots of close-ups in which the actress moved her eyes from side to side, as if watching a Ping-Pong match.

"Illegal serve," I heard myself quip, while viewing the joke of a movie. The kid who played me—though they changed my name to avoid a lawsuit—acted so cutesy wootsy he must've pissed pink lemonade.

But whether the written or spoken word, none of these accounts said much about me. I felt like Jan Brady saying, "Marcia, Marcia, Marcia," only in my case it was "Misty, Misty, Misty." True, I refused to be interviewed, and from a legal standpoint the less said about me the better. Still, the books and the dumb ass movie made me feel like a victim nobody cared about. I bawled for the first time in years, and then got angry, though I didn't know who to be mad at.

I called my mom to tell her about my misbegotten research. Taking a deep breath, I also told her about being in therapy. Though no one ever said it out loud, I knew that it broke with family custom to linger in the woebegone past instead of the bountiful present.

"Ben, why would you do that?" Mom asked.

"Mom, did you really think I'd go my whole life never asking questions?"

"No, because you've always had to know everything. This need to dwell on horrible acts—I've never understood it. Isn't life challenging enough?"

"I didn't know it would hurt so much."

"No, you never think anything will, do you? Of all the things that bitch did to you, that's the worst. She made you believe you had no feelings."

"It never should've happened. Why did it happen?"

She paused and sighed.

"I've always blamed myself."

"Mom, how stupid. The pre-school fucked up."

"I never should've sent you there. I was your mother. I should've been—"

"I've never blamed you. Or Dad. I only meant why in some meaning-of-life way. You know how deep I like to get."

She laughed.

"Darling, if we knew why things happened, life would be even harder than it is. There wouldn't be any wiggle room at all."

"I hate being angry. It pisses me off."

"Yes, dear, I know. You have no patience when life makes you stop and think. Promise me you won't tell your father what you did, it'll break his heart. God, what he went through because of that woman. And then when you were found . . . I have no words for it."

My dad was lucky to be married to my mom, because she gave him a much better life than he deserved. Mediocrity has a way of rising to the top of the bottle. I died without ever once talking to him about the kidnapping, though when I was maybe fourteen he got mad at me and said, "You were a boy, couldn't you have gotten away from her?"

"Obviously not," I replied.

"It's extremely annoying when you say, 'Obviously.'"

"Obviously."

"I don't know how you do it, but you always know the worst possible thing to say. You should go into show biz.

Bentley the Obnoxious. Watch as he pisses you off in two seconds or less."

"It must be genetic."

Dad was a nice enough guy, but hard to communicate with. *Don't disturb your father* became a common chant in my childhood home. It's true that I said my share of annoying remarks while growing up, but even when I got older my dad and I never clicked. Though he'd never admit it, he regarded me as tainted—spoiled merchandise, courtesy of Misty Rose. He didn't abuse me and we seldom fought, yet in her most delusional moments Misty Rose was nicer to me than Dad. If he thought I did anything right, he never told me.

Still, Mom was an angel, and for years after being rescued nothing slowed me down. I acted as if life were a happy ending scene that got caught in a loop in a film projector. The sheer pleasure of being free, of feeling the sun and snow on my skin and running around and climbing trees and making friends and even, yes, going to school—I felt beyond alive. The smallest nice thing made me ecstatic. My Misty Attacks were few and far between.

It's hard to believe, but at one time I was known for my boisterous optimism. I hated no one, and everyone agreed I was destined for something colossal. It wasn't so much that I walked into a room and turned on the charm, but that I believed in the charm. I earned A's and varsity letters. I played bass in garage bands. I diddled around with cheerleaders behind the bleachers, and never forgot to use protection. I got along with the jocks and the stoners. I played video games with the intensity of a barracuda.

Dad remained a mute, non-applauding observer of my triumphs, but Mom made up for it with her over-the-top praise. She didn't know about my R or X rated activities—or if she did, she never lectured me.

Sex and drugs at a young age weren't about being bad. The kidnapping gave me a fluid sense of morality, and I wanted to experience everything. Like many young people I thought myself invincible. I had compassion for Misty Rose, and prayed to God to forgive her.

But guess what? Nothing I accomplished mattered at all. I got swept up in this magnificent tornado that plunked me down in a barren field of nothingness. I went from Oz to Kansas, instead of the other way around. Life turned into one long Misty Attack.

Case in point, I became a college professor.

I did my undergrad work at a small cuddly college in the northern Midwest, where I grew up. I did my graduate work at a gargantuan rah-rah university in the northern Midwest, and then got a job teaching at Elmer Butthead, a clueless liberal arts college in the northern Midwest. I never went gaga over the northern Midwest, but that's how the cookie crumbled.

I saw academia as but another topping on an extra large pizza that included sex, drugs, rock and roll, and playing third base on weekends. I thought by studying forensic psychology I'd understand why people hurt other people. If that wasn't idiotic enough, I also thought so doing would in its small way make the world a better place. But needless to say I emerged more confused about people than ever, and last time I checked, the world kept getting worse. I'm sure on some level I wanted to understand the kidnapping—as if it could be understood—but I don't recall that entering into my conscious drives. Not that it would've made a difference. Once I became a professor nothing made a difference.

My dissertation was entitled, *Spurious Post-Freudian Hermeneutical Correlates in Prediction of Agateophobia: A Case Study Application of Late Criminological Theories of Heathcote Pinch.* Yep, that's right. *Spurious Post-Freudian Hermeneutical Correlates in Prediction of Agateophobia: A Case Study Application of Late Criminological Theories of Heathcote Pinch.*

In case you were dying to know, ageteophobia is the fear of insanity. Looking back, it seems obvious as the invisible nose on my invisible face that Misty Rose made me fear insanity—her own, plus the possibility of mine for having been abducted. Though of course nothing so personal, nothing to do with actual life, found its way into my treatise. I recall staying up nights working on this 300-page piece of tripe, so hyper and excited by my ideas that I couldn't sleep. What world did I live in?

For starters, a world that couldn't care less about the later works of Heathcote Pinch, let alone spurious post-Freudian hermeneutical correlates. The college job market sucked, and I felt lucky to get interviewed at all.

I sensed something peculiar about the Elmer Butthead psych department from the first time it contacted me. It took dozens of phone calls to arrange an on-campus visit, throughout which Search Committee Chair Dr. Phyllis Willis kept saying, "I shouldn't tell you this, but . . ."

"I shouldn't tell you this, but the way our university does job searches is so-o-o dysfunctional."

"I shouldn't tell you this, but our department chair is so-o-o full of male bullshit it makes you want to puke."

"I shouldn't tell you this, but I heard a good one the other day. There's this couple. He never makes her come, and he'll say, 'Is there something wrong with you?' Like there couldn't of course be anything wrong with him. Men are such pigs. But finally she always fakes it and says, 'Oh, oh, oh,' and he says, 'That's more like it.' So this one time they go at it and he says, 'Is there something wrong with you?' Only this time she's hidden a razor blade in her hand, and in one swift motion she whacks off his equipment. He's bleeding all over the place and he says, 'Oh, oh, oh,' and she says, 'That's more like it.'"

From the first time she called me, Phyllis Willis took me into her confidence.

"I can tell you're that rarity among men," she said. "You can work with a strong woman without getting a castration complex. How ridiculous—the last thing women want to do is castrate men."

"Uh, thank you for the compliment."

The first time I visited campus, Phyllis told me things about other faculty that were nobody's business—who was impotent, who was on happy pills—but I smiled and nodded my head and kept my mouth shut. She bore an uncanny resemblance to Sherman from the old Mr. Peabody cartoons, except that she wore mukluks.

At the time I ignored my misgivings, and concentrated on the gratitude I felt for someone wanting to hire me.

In appearance, the Elmer Butthead campus rated an A+. There were fine old brick and brownstone buildings covered in lush ivy, old growth elms and maples that turned splendid in the fall, dogwood blossoms in the spring, and a large, peaceful pine grove, soft underfoot with discarded needles. The campus had a lake with elaborate wrought iron benches, and in winter there were ice skaters that looked like something out of a Grandma Moses painting. The annual ice sculpture contest produced glimmering, imaginative statues.

Before long, I perceived the beauty of the campus to be a Venus flytrap, luring in innocent creatures to devour them. But at first I had to admit it looked like a storybook college.

After maybe a month of phone calls, Phyllis told me that the Committee couldn't decide if they wanted someone who specialized in psychoanalytic treatment of crime-related phobias and neuroses such as myself, or a behaviorist who did the same. The Search Committee consisted of the entire six members of the department, since—as I learned when I interviewed—everyone was a super-paranoid control freak. So, as Phyllis gossiped to me, they were split down the middle three-three between myself and some other poor sucker.

Eventually they were stuck with me, because the behaviorist accepted another job. Over the years, I've wondered what became of her or him. I presumed something less awful than getting murdered.

Since Henry Zwieback, my department chair, lived and breathed behaviorism, he was not thrilled by my hire. In fact, though Phyllis wasn't supposed to tell me this, he tried to block it from happening. Things could only go downhill from there.

At first I thought her parents must've been sadists to name her "Phyllis Willis," but this proved only half right. "Willis" was her mother's maiden name, and Phyllis legally adopted it to distance herself from her father—whom she depicted as a nasty, abusive truck driver, a Stanley Kowalski made flesh. Having survived the ordeal of Misty Rose, I thought Phyllis and I had something in common. But over the years she never remembered the story after I retold it yet again. Maybe she was too self-absorbed to remember anything about anyone else, or maybe the fact that I suffered abuse from a woman did not compute, given her women-can-do-no-wrong view of life.

Phyllis's research concerned building self-esteem amongst adolescent girls. She wrote a book called *Love Yourself First*, a title that made me imagine a scene in a porn movie. But it was about how teenaged girls should stop fucking the football team, and instead prepare for college and a career.

"The key to making the right choices is self-esteem," said Phyllis. "This means they shouldn't turn to boys for approval but instead learn to love themselves, ergo the title."

"It sounds like an important book."

"It is," she replied with characteristic modesty.

High self-esteem is a fine sentiment, to be sure. Yet after spending five minutes with Phyllis the egghead neuter, it became obvious that she herself never experienced any of the hormonal melodramas she wrote about. Steadfastly single, she probably thought "libido" to be a kind of smelly cheese. So unfamiliar was she with human customs such as casual pick-ups that the few teenaged girls she interviewed came across as extraterrestrials. To hear Phyllis tell it, if bikini girl beer commercials were banned, young women would be standing in line to become nuclear physicists. Granted, being a crack whore was unlikely to win you a Nobel Prize, but did Phyllis believe anyone wanted to be like her instead?

Big surprise, few copies of her opus were sold. But, slow to take the hint, she blamed the poor sales on the patriarchy.

"Power-mad men of privilege control all businesses," she said. "And that includes publishing, so that people read nothing but sexist books. It's all connected to the male heterocapitalist plot for global domination."

Phyllis made it sound as if at that very moment, men were holding secret meetings in boardrooms across the nation, intent on keeping her book from destroying their privileged way of life.

"But," she assured me, "I'm not about to let them win. Somehow, somewhere, I'll find a way to reach the next generation, and we'll build a new social order led by women, without all that male egotism."

"Yeah, maybe," I did my best to agree. Since Phyllis saw herself as leading the crusade that would change the world, who was I to interfere with her quest to destroy "egotism?"

Ghost 3

When I conveyed my tale of horror to fellow ghoul
Cecilia, she made Phyllis seem sympathetic by comparison.

"That poor woman Misty Rose," Cecilia said, shedding a
few ghost tears.

I must say that ghost tears are quite lovely, like liquid
diamonds.

"She must've felt trapped, desperate. Did you ever try
reaching out to her?"

For a second I thought I heard wrong. *Did I what?*

"Cecilia, she raped me. She locked me in the cellar. I was
three years old."

"And who would do that besides an incredibly lonely
person? You don't know the isolation women experience."

"Apparently not. But since most child abusers are men,
are they lonely, too?"

"So predictive of what a man would say," Cecilia sighed.
"Taking a woman's lived experience and turning it into a
riddle of statistical probability."

"Have you ever been kidnapped or raped?"

"Not in the physical sense. But men have tried to kidnap
my intellect and emotions all my life. Not a day went by that I
didn't feel intellectually and emotionally raped."

"That's a bunch of shit."

She cupped her hands to her ears.

"I've stopped listening."

To call Cecilia uptight was like calling Lake Superior wet.
Lord only knew why she became a ghost. Maybe just to
torment me. When I first realized we were stuck with each
other's company, I decided to make the best of things and get
to know her. But, as an egghead, she assumed this meant I
wanted to know about her research, which she claimed was
her *raison d'être*.

As I learned *ad nauseam*, Cecilia studied Patriarchal Discourse in 18th Century House of Hanover Rhetoric. Exactly what we've been waiting to know more about.

She called herself a utopian feminist, a fancy way of saying she was a dork. Though like many so-called feminists at my college, her personal life didn't exactly vibrate with liberation. Unless you believed supporting your husband through medical school even after his gay lover moved in to be the height of personal independence. Word had it that she also cooked and did the housework.

In an inexplicable moment of synchronicity, as soon as hubby finished medical school he divorced her to marry his boyfriend. Cecilia claimed she bore no rancor towards her ex, because everything happened as it should, when a door shut a window opened, if you love someone set him free, and all the other claptrap that passed for wisdom among people scared to death of life. I wondered what she used to do for fun. I imagined her idea of a good time to be reading Simone de Beauvoir with one hand while the other hand recycled something.

I shouldn't be too hard on Cecilia and her ilk, as the sicko male professors at my school were a hell of a lot worse. I think it embarrassed her to be a ghost, as if she took a crap in front of the Queen of England. Ghosthood signaled something amiss about your life, or at least according to negative cultural stereotypes. A masochistic perfectionist such as I'm-always-happy Cecilia must've found her current state of being a nightmare—though ghosts don't sleep.

Still, I'm the sort of person who never resists a gag.

"Hey, Cecilia," I said. "Do you have a few extra bucks? I've decided to go to medical school. Is it okay if Whatshisname moves in, too?"

"Shut up, Bentley, or I'll—"

"Or you'll what? What *can* you do?"

"You just wait," she said. "I'll get back at you big time."

"Yeah, yeah, yeah. Big talker."

"How would you understand wanting to give something back to the world?"

When we found nothing better to do we argued about current events. We disagreed on everything. Drug legalization was by far our biggest bone of contention. Cecilia being ruler-up-her-ass Cecilia, she believed that if you took a single hit off a joint they might as well lock you in the loony bin and throw away the key.

She claimed never to have partaken of an alcoholic beverage because her parents were drunks. And like many children of alkies, Cecilia regarded surviving her parents to be the equivalent of climbing Mount Everest.

Jutting her invisible chin to punctuate her holier-than-thou anti-drug stance, she told me, "When you grow up around people who are too out of it to acknowledge your emotional needs, you die inside from neglect. Parents who do this deserve the death penalty, because what they've done is the equivalent of homicide. It took me years to reclaim myself. To find my voice as a woman."

"Well, I never acknowledge your emotional needs, and I'm stone cold sober." I pretended to play a violin in mock sympathy.

"Yes, but you told me you took LSD and who knows what else. Bentley Gamble, you bring recalcitrance wherever you go."

"Oh no, someone accused me of recalcitrance. I must find a way to obnubilate your words."

"Ha-ha, very funny. I am proud of my vocabulary. I am quite content to be one of those nerdy eggheads you speak of with such umbrage. Or should I say 'I was' instead of 'I am?' After all, I'm not alive anymore."

"Exactly. So what difference does it make? Afraid you'll flunk Ghost Grammar 101?"

"Oh, be quiet. I don't know why you need to be so censorious. I'm proud of my scholarly record. I see no reason to turn my back on what I worked so hard to achieve."

"Yeah, well, I was a psych professor, whoop-tee-do. And look where it got me. Nowhereville, the capital city of Nowhereland, at the shores of Lake Nowhere. I'm stuck here, with the same nowhere people that drove me crazy."

"Don't blame other people for your problems," Cecilia said, as if she herself didn't blame everything but global warming on her drunk-O parents. "What good can come of it? Negative energy attracts negative outcomes. People complain they have bad luck, but they do it to themselves."

"'Bad luck?' Bad luck is when you're caught in traffic and have to take a piss. There happened to be much more I wanted to do with my life."

"Maybe you still can in a different way."

"You mean the dead way instead of the alive way? Silly me, why didn't I think of that?"

"Like my granny used to say, 'No use crying over spilled milk.' Personally, I feel sorry for the faculty we left behind. They must be frightened by all the death and violence. I'm praying for them. Especially the women."

"You pray? You're a ghost and you pray? Unbelievable. No, I take that back, coming from you I believe it."

"What's wrong with praying? Given our current existence, I should think you'd be more convinced than ever there are otherworldly realms. It's a matter of attitude. If you see yourself as nothing but. . . well, *dead*, then that's all you're going to notice. I've always been a cup-half-full type of person. Think of all we have. We can see the sun rising and setting. And the beautiful rose garden in the park. We can still hear children's laugher."

"Eat shit, Cecilia."

"I don't know why you have to be so cynical."

As you can see, being ghosts doesn't keep people from getting on each other's nerves. Plus Cecilia was such a prude of a Pod that I enjoyed pushing her buttons.

On one occasion my fellow ghoul and I were standing near the dead-ivy-covered student center. It was a Sunday summer evening, so only a few deranged students came and went. Since they couldn't see me, I thumbed my nose at them, until Cecilia elbowed me in the ribs.

"That's mean," she said.

"Hello? They can't see me."

"It's still not nice."

"I don't see how you can say something is not nice when the person it's happening to doesn't know it's happening."

"I totally disagree. When something not nice happens to someone and they do not know it happens, it still happens. Being nice has nothing to do with whether people know you're being nice. Or not nice, for that matter."

"Such eloquence. You picked the wrong major. You should've been a philosopher."

"I'm ignoring you. I'm pretending you're not even here."

Cecilia stormed off to wherever she went when we had a tiff. We were like a married couple in that we missed each other when we were apart, but the moment we were together again we argued. So go figure.

Never a patient person when angry to begin with, being a ghost multiplied this trait by a thousand-fold. I scared some people in the park, and smashed all the windows in Lab Hall.

Human 3

If Phyllis's in-your-face Political Correctness had been the worst I dealt with at Elmer Butthead, I could've retained my sanity. But she was a cinch compared to the men in my department. There's a funny thing about wishing people dead. When they do die you wonder in some illogical way if it's your fault. And when they don't die you wonder if you're being punished for the ones your mind bumped off.

Take for instance my department chair, Dr. Henry Zwieback. Please, take him. He did these trivial, pompous, outdated behaviorist experiments with rats, one of whom he always named after his wife. At last count he was up to Millie XXI. Millie Rat enjoyed a far more charmed existence than Millie Wife, since all the rat had to do was chase a piece of cheese. Millie Sauerbraten-Zwieback, on the other hand, had to deal with a husband who was a flasher, as in he showed off his thingie to girls in the park. You'd think that would've gotten him fired, if not put in jail, but he said he was in recovery for his condition. I guessed they called it Flashers Anonymous, but was there any other kind? In any event, his elderly father was a bigwig university trustee, so Henry wasn't going anywhere. With pretzel logic the college declared Henry had a condition that needed accommodation. Millie also worked as a prof in our department, and when the local media had nothing better to do, it ran yet another heartwarming feature about hubby and wifey working side by side.

As a behaviorist, Henry pounded on the podium to express his unshakeable position that undesirable conduct could be extinguished through punishment and rewards— that is to say, everyone's but his own.

"We can only study observable behavior," he'd lecture us a dozen times a day, as if the world would come to an end if people failed to grasp his point. "Observable behavior we must then quantify!"

Quantify into statistics, that is. What eating their own droppings was to rabbits, statistics was to Henry.

His grandstanding grew especially tiresome because Henry did the same experiments over and again, just as he used the same textbooks for twenty years. They stood out from a mile away in the campus bookstore, taped and torn and yellowed, as if having survived some epic disaster. From his throne of profundity, Henry claimed no other book ever written contained the information he needed to teach—much of it outdated. But looking up new references would've detracted from his golf game.

With her frizzy long gray braid, gypsy shawls, and gritty New York intellect, Dr. Millie Sauerbraten-Zwieback strove to insure no one ever discussed her husband's icky proclivities. She smoked as if it made you smarter, like some Depression era commie. Smoking was not permitted in any campus building, but people made an exception for Millie, since she had good reason to hide behind a noxious cloud of smoke. She puffed away as she blathered and dithered in a commanding voice that was impossible to interrupt. Once I timed her taking up forty-seven minutes of a department meeting to treat us to a monologue about the mating rites of wombats.

"The point *is*," she said toward the end of her spiel, "the male only mates with the female when he smells pheromones on her droppings. And did I mention that the female knows when it's a good time to release these pheromones? So she's in charge. It's her body. Her decision. The hetero-patriarchal sociobiological notion that males are by nature the aggressor does not hold up when you look at the natural world."

By the time she finished, you'd have thought that N.O.W. stood for the National Organization for Wombats. I pictured these female wombats at a consciousness-raising, with one giving a PowerPoint presentation as the others took notes. I wanted to say, "Ooh la la, pheromones on droppings," or maybe, "Stop it, Millie, you're giving me a hard-on." But of course I said no such thing. I'm glad, though, that Millie practiced what she preached. No pheromones on droppings for her. I couldn't imagine how screwed up a child would've been getting raised by Millie and Henry.

Whether a defense mechanism or typical egghead worldview, Millie claimed that her true love was her research. She charted happiness scales of women through their years of marriage. As academics are wont to do, she declared there were four levels of marital satisfaction. Professors love to say there are four of this and eight of that. It's how they get high.

According to Millie, women were most satisfied when they perceived their marriages as egalitarian. She took great care to say *perceived as*, maintaining her value-free scientific objectivity. But I thought it obvious that in intellectual terms Millie tiptoed around an elephant in the room. I am referring to the fact that there never has been a man on the face of the earth who woke up in the morning thinking, "I can't wait to be egalitarian today." Which in my humble opinion meant, following Millie's logic, that the women who reported the happiest marriages were either the most delusional or married to the best liars.

However, when you teach in the so-called halls of knowledge, you learn PDQ never to be honest. No one questioned Millie's dubious research, nor for obvious reasons did anyone ask where she classified her own marriage on her scale. We all felt sorry for her, though sometimes I found it hard to remember her arrogance hid desperation. The subtext to anything she said was: *Who, me? Married to a sicko pervert? You must be confusing me with someone else.*

Personally, I thought her husband's flashing the least of her worries, since it got Henry away from her. Whenever he licked his lips with his snakelike tongue I shook with pins and needles of disgust.

Gossip though she was, Phyllis was far too self-protective to dwell on Henry. And the mere happenstance of

Millie being both woman and professor made her, in Phyllis's mind, a feminist of the highest order. It was like a sorority that accepted all women. Millie walked on water and could do no wrong. When I had the hubris to suggest that her life stank, seeing as how she stayed married to Henry, Phyllis said, "How mannish of you to assume you understand a woman's lived experience."

You'd think that being dead, these sorts of remarks would no longer drive me crazy, but if anything they seemed more noodle-brained than they did when first uttered. Being a ghost clears out your mental noise and clutter, and you're left with nothing but the truth about your life. Maybe that's why Cecilia acted oblivious to everything. Ghost reality was scary shit.

You'd also think one sex criminal in the department was more than enough. But, like a couple surprised to learn it's expecting twins, we were blessed with a second one.

Doctor Dumont Dungworth was an effete prick that blackmailed female students into giving him blowjobs. That we were the *psychology department* made our criminal insanity all the more hypocritical. Dumont was an anemic looking man with a bad comb over, though I suppose there are no good ones. When he smiled his green teeth glistened.

He specialized in human factors psychology. Contrary to what the name suggests, this sub-area deals with non-human things like machines and computers, and how or why some were, from a cognitive standpoint, more user friendly than others. What rats were to Henry, portable e-devices were to Dumont. The main difference was that Henry was nicer to his rats than Dumont was to his human subjects, whom he acquired from his terrified first-year students in rather the same manner one might say Hitler acquired Poland. To pass Dumont's course, students had to participate in his obtuse experiments. This violated university policy, but nobody wanted Dumont for an enemy.

I saw many an eighteen-year-old reduced to tears after Dumont humiliated her or him for failing to grasp his labyrinth instructions.

"I'm confused," a student might say. "Do you want me to go to the next screen?"

"Well, I might," Dumont would answer. "But I heretofore believed that human intelligence went beyond mere reptilian impulses as contained in the basal ganglia. Maybe you'd do better in a glass tank with a dish of water and some dead flies."

Many students and even some faculty were scared to talk to him.

Dumont always had an attractive female student for a research assistant, and each year he threatened to fire her unless she gave him blowjobs aplenty. (A study that will never get done is why men who preferred oral with women never had a conscience.) One year the assistant filed a sexual harassment claim, and got expelled on a technicality. Dumont also got some fraternity smart asses to text her obscene messages for extra credit.

Through word of mouth—granted, an unfortunate choice of words—the message got passed down over the years that his assistants had best put out or shut up. In return, he wrote each girl a glowing letter of recommendation for grad school. I saw one once and made a copy of the missive, which read in part:

To Whom It May Concern:

It is my pleasure to recommend Jane Doe for your graduate program. As my research assistant this past academic year, Ms. Doe has shown herself to be a true professional. She always was willing to go that extra inch to ensure that our experiments achieved their maximum potential. She worked with me late into the night on countless occasions to make certain I was satisfied with her work. Modest to a fault, she is not one to blow her own horn, but

I am confident she will raise the bar in your
program.

Dumont was one of the few male profs who always wore
a suit and tie, and on his lapel he featured a button that read:
I heart humanity. As if living up to the hype of his button,
Dumont appeared on the local news for the volunteer work
he did to bring computers to poorly funded schools. On TV,
he came across like Gandhi in the Peace Corps.

"Knowledge is the key to power, not war and violence,"
he said. "Every computer given to an underprivileged child
means one less kid who throws away his future."

He neglected to mention that he used the Internet to
watch porn. I caught him doing this in his office on a number
of occasions. He'd smile his green smile and change the
screen as fast as he could, but there'd be a second or two of
naked women before he made the switch. Had I been a
matchmaker, I would've hooked Dumont up with Harvey
and Madge of BDSM fame. I once found Dumont drooling
over a video clip of a woman in bondage being forced to lick
dog food off her master's toes.

Dumont also served on the campus diversity board—a
joke, since pretty much all the profs at my school were so
white they made snowmen look like boys from the hood.
Diversity Day consisted of Swedish Americans trading
meatballs with Norwegian Americans.

You might ask: what were the supposed feminist
professors doing while all this was going on? They kept
themselves busy lecturing about patriarchy, and were not
about to compromise their grave missions to do so. Getting
the university embroiled in scandal equaled a shortcut to the
unemployment line, and people understood which side of the
bread the butter was on. No one knew about Dumont the
same way no one knew about Henry. As an employee, you
had to sign a confidentiality agreement that forbade you from
going public with anything that presented our beloved

institution in an unfavorable light. What malpractice lawsuits were to hospitals, sex crimes were to universities.

"I feel like I whored my way into grad school," complained one of Dumont's assistants to the Director of Student Success—whatever the hell that meant—who was about as trustworthy as the serpent in the Garden of Eden.

"Pulease, let us remembuh owah professional decorum," drawled the director, a former Second Runner-Up to Miss Chattanooga named Dr. Emily Crabb, who left for a meeting whenever the violated girl wanted to talk to her.

"Ahm sure it's not as bayad as all thayat," Emily added, hurrying out of her office.

Our esteemed director sprayed her black hair into a Miss America upsweep and, simulating sweetness, tilted her head when she smiled. I assumed that her platform as a Miss Chattanooga wannabe was ice cream socials, as she believed they were the solution to the world's ills. Or, as her thick Tennessee twang put it, "ass cream socials." If someone said that morale was low after a student got raped, the director replied, "Sounds lack a good tahm for an ass cream social." When her husband wanted sex, I imagined her handing him a banana split. Many of us referred to her as Little Miss Ass Cream, or LMAC for short.

With lawsuits being anathema to colleges, LMAC lived her life inches away from the guillotine, ever mindful that the Board of Directors could replace her at the slightest twitch of bad publicity. So the periodic rape or suicide of a student got treated as nothing a scoop of Rocky Road couldn't fix. Her epitaph should read: "Ahm sure it's not as bayad as all thayat."

For as long as she'd been at Elmer Butthead, LMAC ushered in the fall semester by standing at the podium in the campus theater to say how ever so proud she felt to be welcoming new students, and she hoped they loved to be challenged as much as we did. Too bad she didn't say that the girls would be sexually assaulted and wouldn't be able to do anything about it. As for boys, the men ignored them as irrelevant and the women avoided them because of their genetically predetermined arrogance. And as for the professors, please be informed that the men were egomaniacal sex offenders, and the women spent their careers trying to compensate for the fact that they were too nerdy to be popular in high school.

Small wonder that when people asked if I was into women or men, I replied, "Neither." After working at Elmer Butthead, I found it impossible to believe anyone could be anything but an idiot. When colleagues got murdered I pretended to mourn, but whom was I kidding?

I consider my fateful second day at Elmer Butthead to be the worst day of my life, even worse than when Misty Rose kidnapped me. Or now that I think of it, worse than the day I got murdered.

It started out okay. After my disastrous, loopy first day, I woke feeling refreshed from a much-needed fourteen hours of sleep. However, my good mood did not last. In an extraordinary coincidence, it ended the moment I entered the psych department to teach my 11 a.m. class on Crime and Emotion—or, as it was called with affection, 43489-LXC.

I tried, I truly did. When a couple of students in the back of the room texted each other on their smart phones, I sounded polite when I asked them to stop. I did my best to give a reassuring answer when asked, "Is this class hard?" But I reached a new level of anti-communication when I had to explain what "introspection" meant.

"Introspection," I said. "You know—when you talk to yourself or think to yourself about what you're doing, or how your life is going."

The students wrote down my strange words, in the manner of young people terrified of flunking an exam. One boy raised his hand.

"Only crazy people talk to themselves."

I made sure I remembered to smile.

"Not necessarily. It's perfectly normal to talk to yourself. To reflect on life. How many of you know what I'm talking about?"

Not a single hand got raised.

Following a brief silence that felt like it lasted for an eternity, I asked, "How many of you plan to go to graduate school?"

Pretty much everyone raised a hand. So here they were, our next generation of therapists. No wonder people thought they were better off smoking crack.

"Well, haven't you ever felt like there's two of you?"

A student chimed in. "You mean like schizo?"

"Not at all. There's a part of you that others know, and a part of you that only you know."

One of the students had taken out a pair of earphones, and started listening to something on her smart phone. From the way she bopped around, I figured it was rock or hip-hop.

"Please, no earphones in class."

After I repeated it a third time, she complied.

Thinking I was one of those genius teachers they make movies about, it occurred to me that I could use what just happened to make my point about introspection.

I turned to the girl who'd been wearing earphones. "What made you not want to do as I asked? It was a little voice inside you, wasn't it?"

She picked up her pen, and doodled on her notepad.

"I dunno."

The class ended at that moment. Some students giggled as they hurried out of the room.

I went to my nondescript office, where I stared into space until Wicki, my student from the day before, arrived at twelve on the dot, as requested. I appreciated her punctuality.

Since I had no idea how to answer her hieroglyphic-like questions from the day before about which classes to take, I figured we'd go together to Boris to find out how everything worked. I already learned from being a student that secretaries knew everything, and my instincts told me not to go to Henry. If I came across as not knowing the most trivial of policies, he'd pounce on it to point out my incompetence.

But as it turned out, something unexpected became the main topic of my conversation with Wicki.

No sooner than she took a seat did she start to sob.

"I'm sorry," she said, wiping the tears from her flustered cheeks.

"You have nothing to be sorry about, but why are you crying?" I leaned forward in my swivel chair to express my concern.

"It's Dr. Dungworth," Wickie explained. "He threatened me. He said if I didn't. . . uh, you know, like, please him orally, he'd see that I never got into graduate school." She sniffled a little more. I had a box of Kleenex on my desk, and she helped herself to several.

"Wicki, are you sure you didn't misunderstand what he meant?"

She laughed through her sobs. "If only. 'Give me head, bitch,' doesn't have many meanings, does it?"

I admitted it did not.

Since it was the first I heard of this proclivity on the part of Dumont (whom I could tell didn't like me any more than Henry did), it came as quite a jolt. I felt an animal-like fear in my heart for Wicki, and for some reason myself.

"Let me close the door." As I got up to do so I saw Dumont in the hallway talking to someone, and our eyes met for one panicky instant.

For years I believed that I paid my karmic dues via Misty Rose, and indeed from age six onward my life had been good. But I sensed that a whammy of an epic scale was in store for me at Elmer Butthead. Too bad I didn't follow my gut instinct and start looking for another job. Maybe I'd still be alive.

Once I stood up, I became too antsy to sit down.

"Wicki, I am so sorry this happened. But I'm not the person to talk to. You need to go to the Director of Student Success. If you'd like, I'll walk you over to her office."

She smiled in a sad kind of way.

"That's okay, I know where it is. But I'm not finished telling you what I had to. I told him how I liked your class, and we started talking about phobias. I mentioned my acrophobia, and out of nowhere he said, 'That's good to know. I won't have you blow me from a high tower.' I just sat there, not knowing what to say. Then he grabbed my arm and told me he liked to have it spat on and—"

"Please discuss this with Dr. Crabb. She's a woman, she'll be very understanding." (About as understanding as a computerized telephone voice, but I had no way of knowing this.)

"Thank you, Dr. Gamble. I'll . . . I'll go there right now."

"You're sure you don't want me to walk you over?"

"Really, I'll be fine."

Shortly after Wicki left, there was a knock on my door.

"Department meeting in five minutes."

It was Boris the secretary.

"Thanks," I said, dreading the thought of spending two hours with Henry and Dumont, pretending that everything smelled like Chanel No. 5. Not that Millie or Phyllis promised a barrel of laughs. And the other two members of the department thus far expressed not the faintest interest in getting to know me. This struck me as odd, since when I did the math they must have voted for me along with Phyllis. Clearly the men didn't want me there, and Millie would've voted with her husband.

Boris stood in the doorway, having not been invited in.

"So how do you like us so far?"

"I couldn't be happier. Everyone's been so kind and helpful." After a pause, I added, "Would you like to come in and have a seat?"

"Why, thank you," Boris said, as if no one in his life had extended such lavish courtesy before. He had a way of focusing his attention on you that soothed the soul. When Boris entered a room, you knew everything would be okay.

"I shouldn't stay long. I'm up to my neck with students. You know—the start of another school year. Let's have lunch sometime."

"Sounds good. And thanks again for yesterday."

Boris laughed. "Happens to the best of us. My lips are sealed."

"Gee, thanks."

"Oh, and Ben—don't let Henry or Dumont intimidate you."

Being told not to be intimidated made me feel all the more so, but I tried not to let it show.

"What do you mean?"

He looked both ways before answering. "You have the wrong plumbing between your legs. They'll barely notice your existence."

"Huh. Interesting."

"Everyone can tell you're an amiable sort. That you won't make any trouble."

"Well, I hope not."

"What was it Dumont said? Oh, right—you're like a blurry smile in the background."

I wondered if this was a subtle way of Boris giving me the lowdown on how to handle Henry and Dumont, but I thought it wise not to inquire further for the time being.

"You make me sound like the Cheshire cat."

Boris's laugh seemed disconnected from his deep-voice demeanor. He sounded like a monkey or bird.

"Hey, Dumont said it, not me."

As he left to walk back down the hall, I wondered what he knew about life that I didn't. All day long he worked with these lunatics and never had a stroke or a nervous breakdown.

Ghost 4

I decided to scare some students. When you're a ghost, you realize after awhile that scaring people is one's periodic duty, a necessary function. (Except of course for Cecilia, who wouldn't recognize a higher purpose if it bit her on the ass.) But just as I started walking toward the student center, a blinding brightness appeared before me. At first it looked like high beam headlights. Ever the optimist, I thought maybe it was the light everyone talks about seeing when they're ready to cross over.

"Finally," I said to myself. "Good riddance, Cecilia."

But whoever was in charge of this abracadabra stuff hadn't finished with me. As the light faded, I saw a female form take shape. The figure didn't look like a ghost and she didn't look human. She was translucent, as if a person and a ghost mated. Even the smallest movement of her body made iridescent ripples, like there were rainbows in the air that I never noticed before. I wondered if ghosts could have acid flashbacks, but as the image grew distinct I knew she was real—or at least real like me.

The filmy young woman with the shimmery prisms of color looked about my age. She was black—which to me looked aqua—and sported waist-length dreadlocks. Tall and slender like a runway model, she wore a designer T-shirt atop her designer jeans, with super-cool black stiletto boots.

"Hello, Ben," she said, as if we were old friends.

"Uh, hi." I wiggled my ghostly fingers in a wave for want of knowing what else to do.

"By the way, who are you?"

"I am your spirit guardian."

I snorted. "Yeah, right. Tell me another one. Like I have a guardian spirit."

"*Spirit guardian*," she corrected. "Is it because I'm black that you don't believe me? Do you assume all spirits are white?"

"Not at all. I just haven't lived the kind of life where you think about what your spirit guardian looks like. Though now that you mention it, it's fishy that you don't have wings."

She looked heavenward for her exasperation. "Wings—I can't believe it. They went out with Quiche Lorraine. Bentley, we take pride in what we do, and I must say your flippant attitude is not appreciated."

"Oh great, now I have two of them. 'Bentley, don't do this. Bentley don't say that.' Did Cecilia pay you to hassle me when she goes off duty?"

She looked at me with a shrewd expression. "Pay me with what? Ghost currency? I have nothing to do with Cecilia. I've never met her and I never will. I'm here only for you. Spirit guardians work strictly one on one. Otherwise it gets confusing. You know—conflicts of interest."

"Well, if you're my spirit guardian, where were you on about a million different occasions? Make that two million. When I think of all the shit—I mean, crap that I had to—"

"It was what it was," she interrupted. "You survived."

That made me laugh, but not in a happy way. "In a manner of speaking."

"Look, you think you're the way you are because of unfinished business. Am I right?"

"Well, yeah. What other reason could there be?"

"There are wrongs to be made right, no doubt about it. But there's more to it than that."

She extended her arms; there were dazzling sparks coming out of each finger, like fireworks.

"The truth is, you have too much life force. You died, but even death couldn't finish you off. Some people have surplus left over. Think of it like an eraser on a pencil. The eraser is only so big. Sometimes there's still more scribble. And you're . . . you're a lot of scribble."

"What about Cecilia? She has the life force of a paper towel."

"Let's keep the focus on you, shall we? There's work to be done. Real work, not that mamby-pamby pseudo profiling you did with the cops. 'On the verge of solving the case?' You weren't even close, and you know it. The living are making a mess as usual, and because you have surplus life force you've been called upon to stop it. That means find the killer, with no monkey business. The murders will stop. Boris will get out of jail free. People will learn the truth about Wicki. And your Boy Scout good deed will make up for things you did that were. . . well, less than celestial. It will clean up the remaining scribble, as it were."

All this talk about my scribble pissed me off.

"I never said I was perfect. But I don't think I was *that* bad."

"According to our latest calculations, there have been 47,821 instances in which you could have been kinder and more forgiving. And you've certainly been pulling your share of sophomoric stunts since you died. Essentially, you spent seven years believing that Wicki's death should've given you license to do whatever you wanted to anyone. It doesn't work like that. You saw it for yourself in the park the other day, with Kingsley Shufflebottom and his friend. Something stopped you from causing serious harm—a fundamental force for goodness that hasn't abandoned you, even when you've tried to scare it away."

I crossed my arms in challenge.

"Yeah, but how come other people get to do whatever the hell they want? I got murdered, for crying out loud. Why should I care about anything? If Elmer Butthead can't bring up its enrollment rates, at least it's Number One in homicides."

"Why should you care? Because, dodo head, it means you get to leave here and go on to your next phase. I would have thought that to be self-evident."

The possibility of leaving this dump made me want to run around the block in ecstasy, but things still didn't add up.

"If you know who did it, why can't you just go poof and make it right? Why did the murders happen at all? Who exactly are you, anyway? Where are you from? Who or what is in charge?"

She touched my hand. I had to admit it felt comforting. Neither hot nor cold, yet soothing.

"I'm sorry, but I signed a confidentiality clause."

I thought she had to be kidding, then realized she wasn't.

"But I have . . . people have a right to know what—"

"If we made an exception for you, we'd have to make an exception for everyone. Does that sound fair to you?"

"Fair? You wanna talk fair?"

"I know, it's a terrible blow to one's ego to be a ghost. Classic Adler masculine protest, though one's contemporary sensibilities wish he called it something else. That's why you have to do it yourself, to get back the best part of you. Believe me, Ben, from one client to the next I've heard it all. Sometimes I feel like I work at a returns counter in a department store."

I hated admitting it, but mentioning a trailblazing psychologist caught my interest.

"Did you study Adler?"

In utter seriousness she replied, "Individual Psychology is a required training course for what I do. Fictional final goals, creative power of the self—the whole enchilada."

In spite of myself I began to trust her.

Do you have a name, or are spirit guardians not into things like that?"

She put her fingers to her mouth in embarrassment; she had long, flashy nails.

"Golly, I'm sorry, Ben. Where are my manners? I'm Elaine. And please don't call me Laney. It drives me up the wall."

"My spirit guardian is named *Elaine*?"

She frowned. "What's wrong with that?"

I could tell I hurt her feelings, which did not seem prudent under the circumstances.

"Nothing, I suppose. Do you have a last name?"

"Now you're being ridiculous. Does Beyoncé need a last name? Does Cher or Madonna?"

I started to like her a little. "My, aren't we the diva?"

"You don't know the half of it."

She made a silly face.

"Anyway, have a seat, and I'll tell you what I can." Elaine sat on a bench I hadn't noticed before and patted the spot next to her.

I figured I didn't have much choice. Sort of like when your computer crashes and you have to click a box that says "OK."

"You see, Ben, before anyone is born . . . Let's put it like this. I assume you know how competitive you are. Imagine you're sitting in a room, and someone—let's say his name is Ed— is reaching into a bowl and pulling out slips of paper one at a time. And each time Ed reads what the paper says, someone volunteers to accomplish that task."

"Why does anyone have to accomplish anything? Pardon my redundancy, but what does it accomplish?"

"Because Ed likes to know that aspects of the all-encompassing cosmic miracle are being fulfilled by various entities. The list of possibilities is of course infinite."

"Yes, obviously," I pretended to agree. I wanted her to get to the point.

"So one soul agrees to need help so that humans learn charity. Another agrees to have a bunch of kids to learn patience. Do you see what I mean?"

It sounded far-fetched, but she had no reason to trick me.

"And I agreed to what exactly?"

"You could have chosen something easier, but there you were saying, 'Me, me,' when the option appeared that read: *No one will care about my pain.* The soul before you picked *I will work hard at my job but never get promoted*, and got a huge round of applause. Naturally you didn't want to be outdone by someone else. You agreed to never know love from other people so you could prove love exists anyway."

"What about my mom? She loves me."

Elaine toyed with one of her dreads, wrapping it around her finger. "Yeah okay, your mom loves you. She's cool. But she doesn't know much about you, does she? Admit it—you only let her see the real you in drip-drops, like a leaky faucet. She doesn't super-duper love you, it's just a he's-my-son-and-I-love-him type of love. When you brush aside people who want to know you, it's because you're unconsciously trying to uphold your end of the agreement you made. Sort of like someone on a diet refusing a dish of ice cream."

"Okay, let me see if I get it. My soul made a promise to this Ed person or entity or thingamajig before I was born. But I died without fulfilling it because I never did find love and acceptance?"

Elaine frowned in thought.

"You're not a hundred percent on the money, but you're close enough."

"What does solving murders have to do with love or people knowing my pain?"

"That's for you to find out. What if at a baseball game they sang the National Anthem and then instantly proclaimed it was the bottom half of the ninth inning?"

"So there is a Big Kahuna, and it's this Ed whatchamacallit? And it's not Edwina? Is there more than one Ed? What about all the sickos and the starving children and—"

She made the time-out signal with her hands.

"I've already told you more than I should've. And since when do you care about starving children?"

"I'll have you know I paid each month for a child in Africa to be fed and clothed and go to school. They sent me photos of her and she wrote me letters."

"Yeah, yeah, yeah, I know that. So you think you deserve a medal? Forgive me if I do not swoon in your presence."

"I'm just saying that if every soul makes some gargantuan cosmic promise, I don't see why the world has to be so loused up."

Elaine clasped my invisible shoulder.

"Everything in due time. For now, worry about the case. It's not about fingerprints or DNA. It's about state of mind. Start with your home department when you first came to Elmer—I mean, EBCLA. Make a chart of the main psychological disorder people in your department had at that time. Then go where it takes you. Think of it like testing a hypothesis."

"There's just one problem. Everyone in the department had and still has every psychological disorder that exists. Their biographies could be copies of the DSM."

"Your sarcasm wears thin after awhile. But if you refer to the *Diagnostic and Statistical Manual of Mental Disorders*, go for the gusto. Don't worry about piddling things like fear of cumquats."

"That's it? That's the only clue you're giving me?"

I could tell she experienced a moral dilemma.

"Okay, I shouldn't do this, but I'll make it easy for you. What phobia instantly comes to mind when you think of the people in your department?"

"That's easy. Pantophobia, the fear of everything."

"Very funny. C'mon, you can do better than that."

Generic encouragement had a way of bringing out my negativity. It surprised me that Elaine didn't already know this as my spirit guardian. Maybe she wanted to see how far she could push it before I lost my cool.

"You're asking me to be specific about something that defies specificity. It's like saying there's a difference between the thirty-third and theory-fourth bullet hole in a body that's been shot thirty-five times."

"Again with the sick humor. You should've gotten your Ph.D. in Defense Mechanisms."

"Then what about alethephobia, the fear of hearing the truth?"

"Not quite. But you're getting warmer."

"Okay, I give up. What phobia do you have in mind?"

"Affectphobia. The fear of feeling emotions. Duh."

I thought about it for a moment.

"Yeah, I guess you're on to something there. Kind of strange, if you think about it. Psychologists are always saying to patients, 'What are you feeling?' But they themselves avoid feeling anything at all costs. Or at least in my department."

"Yes," Elaine agreed. "And remember the four main manifestations of this fear of emotions?"

"Um, not offhand. It's weird. I remember everything, but then there are these funny blanks. Not ha-ha funny, but just—"

"It's part of being a ghost. Your existence is at odds with the time-space continuum."

"Oh."

She sighed.

"Anyway, people can be intimidating or bullying to control others, and hence control what emotions get expressed. Next, they may avoid confrontations, by limiting what is addressed, and not permitting other topics. Or sometimes people are overly formal, applying rules when they are not needed to avoid certain discussions. And let's not forget narcissism, the inability to accept anything that contradicts the self or presents it in a bad light. Think about these four strategies for avoiding emotion, think about your department, and see what theory of murder it leads you to. *Voila*, you'll solve the case."

Listening to Elaine rehash my psych department glop made me re-experience little tingles of the pain that became my everyday existence. She more or less described the last seven years of my life.

"It's mind-blowing, isn't it? The way some people will do anything to preserve workplace alienation. When I think of Wicki, and how they wouldn't—"

"I know, I know. It stinks. Yet, it's telling that someone else's death means more to you than your own. Would Adler say you harbor feelings of inferiority, or is this your way of striving to be superior? A thin line indeed."

I hated talking about myself as a case study, and changed the subject. "What about Cecilia?"

"What about her?"

I hated explaining the obvious. "Do I tell her about this?"

"Oh, that. You'll know if it's time to involve her. But not a word about me, or the deal's off. Non-negotiable."

This aspect of the deal sounded easy enough to pull off. I never liked talking to Cecilia anyway.

"Does it matter which murder I start with?

"Start with yourself. It will tell you everything you need to know. Plus it will get Boris out of jail PDQ."

"Really, me? But that's what seems so odd. That the same person who murdered me murdered—"

"Look, you ask me what to do, and when I tell you, you pick it apart. Why should I tell you anything?"

Elaine may have been a spirit guardian, but I could tell I got on her nerves.

"So what exactly happens after I straighten things out? Assuming of course I do."

"That's up to you. Concern yourself not only with finding the bad guy but your conduct and attitude in doing so."

I shook my head in exasperation.

"So I'm supposed to be not only a forensic psychologist ghost, but a *happy* one?"

Ignoring my question, Elaine spoke as if explaining to a child or an exceptionally dense adult—which of course was unnecessary.

"You have three options. Being stuck here is the first one. How do you like it?"

"Gee, not so much. How do you think I like it? Still, if Cecilia would just shut up—"

"Never mind about Cecilia. Your next option is Hell."

For some reason this struck me as funny. "Like I've never been there before."

She spread her fluid arms, and a tableau appeared.

"Behold the eternity you can choose. And remember, it's forever, not just a slow-moving semester."

A vivid flash of red gave way to what appeared to be a hotel meeting room. Some guy stood at a podium, droning on in a barely audible voice about some dull, picayune psychological finding while clicking on a PowerPoint. A lethargic, robotic audience took notes. It was hot enough to be Hell, due to the hot air of the speaker as well as the familiar fact that everyone was too dweeby and scared to draw attention to themselves by turning down the thermostat.

"Why it's . . . could it be an academic conference?"

Elaine nodded with authority.

"And remember, it never ends. It will be nothing but that speaker and everyone taking notes. It will get to where you can't remember anything else."

"But I thought Hell was the same for everyone. When I thought Hell existed, that is. Which, if I'm being honest, was intermittent. Obviously I've told people to go to Hell, but that's a figure of speech."

"Obviously the cosmos is intricate in ways you never realized. Hell can be whatever is the worst possible thing for those who deserve it."

I shuddered for the horror I saw.

"Are the earlier murder victims, like, in Hell?"

"You'd enjoy that, wouldn't you? Sorry, but I cannot comment."

"What if someone tried to make it better? At the conference I could tell a joke to liven things up. Or turn down the friggin heat."

"If even one person tried one time to make it better, it would no longer be Hell. But that never happens because it *is* Hell. That's the point."

"Oh."

"Now, take a look at Heaven." She extended her arms again.

This time there was a beautiful green hill, with blue mountains and lakes all around. The sun beamed at about 75 degrees, and a light breeze caressed the fields. A few hip looking people sat together, taking in the view. Everyone wore a T-shirt and jeans. They listened to *Black Dog*, by Led Zeppelin, and passed around a plate of brownies. When the brownies were gone, more brownies appeared. No one said much of anything. In the center of the field was a marble statue of John Lennon.

I wept out of sheer joy.

"Why, it's . . . perfect."

"I thought you'd like it." The vision disappeared with the wave of her hand. "Now then, do you have any lingering questions?"

"Yeah. Is Zeppelin the only band they play?"

"I can't believe that's your question. No, you can hear other bands."

"Which ones?"

Elaine sighed. "Whichever ones your iddy-biddy heart desires."

"*Exile on Main Street*, by the Stones?" I asked, seeking further assurance.

"*Yes*. And yes to whatever else you want to hear."

I rubbed my hands together in anticipation, then cracked my knuckles, which felt good.

"Okay, I'm sold."

"Finally." Elaine snapped her fingers, and a computer tablet appeared in her hand. If she lost her gig as a spirit guardian, she could become a stage magician.

"You may borrow my tablet, in case you need to make notes," she said, handing it to me. "And don't even think about hacking into my password-protected files."

"Gee, thanks. Do you get internet service?"

"What do you think? Of course."

A honking horn distracted me. I turned to look, and when I faced forward again Elaine had gone. Something of her essence lingered, like perfume.

"Aw, c'mon," I said to no one in particular. "Gimme a break."

Some stupid student walked by without seeing me. There was no reason why he should've seen me, but for some reason it ticked me off. I shoved him and he fell down. Then I smashed his glasses.

If you're alive, the least you can do is pay attention.

Human 4

A new faculty member's first department meeting is a big deal. You wonder if you'll fit in, and will you understand what everyone's talking about? Should you say something to make your presence known, or should you keep quiet in case you say something incorrect? But overall, you're excited by it—or at least you would be if you weren't sitting on information that by all rights should get one of your colleagues fired, not to mention put in jail. I thought about bringing up what Wicki told me, to get it out in the open, but the voice of caution triumphed. I decided to deal with it after the meeting. And anyway, since Wicki went to the Director of Student Success, I felt sure that Dumont would be smelling the coffee even if I did nothing more. I wondered if maybe cops would show up at the meeting and drag him away, like on a TV show.

Henry sat at the far end of a long wooden business table. He shuffled through papers with his reading glasses at the end of his nose, which made him look scarier than usual. Behind his back, Phyllis and her ilk talked about his male ego trip in remaining chair year after year, but year after year he ran unopposed. Phyllis and the others claimed they didn't want to be in conflict with Millie, but after awhile I realized it had more to do with not wanting to let go of complaining about an authority figure.

Millie never sat next to Henry at meetings. She whispered and laughed with Phyllis as if there were no men in the room. Instead, Dumont sat next to Henry, which intimidated me all the more.

"Hello, Bentley," Dumont said. "Or do you prefer 'Ben?'"

He'd already asked me this when I interviewed, and while it's possible he forgot, I thought he said it to signify how little I mattered to him.

"Either is fine." I took a seat next to Phyllis.

"I remember my first semester teaching," said Dumont. "It was love at first slide."

After a moment of silence, he said, "'Love at first slide'—don't you get it?"

I feigned a slight chuckle. Over the next seven years I became very good at pretending to laugh at unfunny remarks. College professors are not famous for their wit.

Dumont continued: "I knew within five minutes I belonged in a classroom and not in private practice, which I'd been conflicted about. The students got every single one of my sardonic asides, and when I raised a provocative issue, boy, were they eager to comment. You see, I employed highly demiurgic strategies. And they've been eating out of my hand ever since, like friendly deer."

"I wished you picked a different simile," Phyllis said.

Dumont looked at me as if we shared a conspiracy as guys.

"Phyllis gets on my case because I like to hunt."

"Here it comes, Bentley," said Phyllis. "'Hunting maintains the balance of nature.' If it's so natural, why doesn't nature make magic bullets that kill off deer? Dumont knows it's really about his power trip as a man."

"Venison is piquant," Dumont said. "And deer overpopulation is bad for the environment. My wife hunts."

Phyllis said, "You mean your ex-wife? Or should I say one of your four ex-wives?"

Dumont ignored her query.

"Bentley, do you hunt, like any good rural American?"

"Uh, no," I said. "My dad used to before. . . before some stuff happened when I was a kid. Now he's into gun control." Misty Rose never shot me, but from time to time she threatened me with a shotgun.

Dumont leaned back in his chair, stroking his chin in thought.

"Interesting projection. I ask about you, Bentley, and you tell me about your father. You may want to look into that."

Before I could think of how to respond, Dr. Sidney Steenrod, another woman prof in our department, entered the room and, as would prove typical of her, began a new conversation unrelated to what people had been saying. Like that tree falling in the woods with no one to hear it, Sidney did not think anyone existed unless they were in her presence. But under the circumstances I found myself grateful for her solipsism. Talking to Dumont made me nervous.

Sidney looked about twelve years old. She stood less than five feet tall and had a squat body, with chaotic dishwater hair that seemed to stay short without ever getting cut. But hers was an intimidating presence. She reminded me of this creature from a sci-fi movie that was nothing but a brain in a glass case. I would not have wanted to play chess with her. Sidney's research was on misogyny in psychotherapeutic techniques. She believed the entire psychotherapeutic model was a patriarchal obsession, which made her an anti-psychology psychologist. Like Phyllis, Sidney was single in an asexual way. Though they did not look related, at times they functioned like a singular entity— Shyllis or Pidney, take your pick.

"God, Millie and Phyl," Sidney began, making a point of addressing the women in the room and not the men. "I just came from the most incogitable session of 30078-LXC I ever taught." As I came to know, this course was Psychology and Feminism.

Millie lit a Sherman's Natural, flicking out the match with an ironic wisdom.

"Let me guess. One of the boy geniuses in the class said he didn't see why he had to take this course." She took care to turn her head from us as she exhaled the smoke.

Sidney said to me, "Would you mind moving down one seat so I can be next to Phyllis?"

I thought the question hurtful, not to mention she never even said hello to me as a new faculty member. But I did as she requested.

"That goes without saying, Millie," Sidney continued. "Of course the Bozo didn't want to take the course. Boys never do. But he actually said, 'I assume this class is about bashing Freud.' I of course replied that bashing anyone was not the point. Everyone deserves basic respect."

"He sounds like a typically narcissistic boy," Millie said. "What did he say next?"

Sidney giggled.

"As you can imagine, he kind of slumped down in his seat like the sub-human he was. But then he said, 'So what's the problem with women and psychology?' Naturally I said that *our* problem stemmed from a culture of male privilege, and how the course enabled women to find a healthy self-image when patriarchal society teaches them they are less than nothing. Freud of course made it much worse for women. He depicted us as hysterics who suffer from psychosomatic complaints, when we are so much more than that."

Phyllis clapped in approval.

"Touché."

"Wait, it gets better. He asked me—that is to say, he had the gall to ask me—if I was raised to think I was less than nothing. I told him that I came from several generations of university professors, and that wasn't the point. No matter how much I achieved academically, society taught me to feel like less than nothing. The kids at school made fun of me because I wasn't obeying all the sexist rules. I told him that from an early age I vowed to fight sexism and racism and ageism and classism and lookism and heterosexism, but as far as the patriarchy was concerned none of this mattered because I didn't look like I existed to please men. Boys made me feel ashamed to be Valedictorian of my high school class. A few young women, too, who'd been brainwashed to believe all the hetero-patriarchal lies. Imagine crying your eyes out in mortification because you're Valedictorian. So if I felt like less than nothing, imagine how it was for other young women.

"Well, let me tell you, there was dead silence in the room. And then this boy, the same one, said, 'Why didn't you just tell them to fuck off?' Some of the class started laughing. So I said, 'That's it. I've had enough today. Class dismissed.' I held it together as they left the room, their mouths hanging open for my desultory words. I hurried to my office, shut the door, and cried. My stomach's been acting up ever since. It must be the yogurt I had. The chemical additives."

Phyllis rubbed Sidney's back, while Millie snubbed out her cigarette, got out of her seat, and hugged Sidney as she would a daughter.

"Boys don't know how to deal with strong young women," Phyllis said.

Millie added, "Score one for the feminists. Well done, Sidney."

Like trying to picture one's parents having sex, over the years I'd hear tell of Sidney crying over one thing or another. But I never saw it with my own eyes and I could never imagine it happening. It was like imagining a brick tied into a knot. Sidney wasn't the nastiest person I knew, but I never saw any expression of genuine human emotion. As far as I could tell, she was nothing but her identity as a feminist.

"The Freudian idea of women is unconscionable," Dumont said. "It never made sense to me. It demeans both genders."

Sidney ignored him.

"Henry, put me on the agenda. The University Student Retention Committee met. We came up with some best practices to ensure every student feels welcome in our classes."

Henry looked up from his papers like Zeus staring down with his thunderbolt.

"Got it, Sidney. So we're waiting for Rayana?"

"Gee, how unusual," Sidney said, with nasty sarcasm.

"She said to start without her," Phyllis shared. "She'll be here, but she had a special FCLC meeting at the last minute. Just another day at Elmer Butthead."

"Are they still squabbling with the president over Student Measure 21?" Dumont asked.

"Are they ever," answered Phyllis. "But the president is using it as a bargaining chip to put through the BOD concretization document, which by the way was approved by the NPGW."

"They really are a sick bunch of bastards." Dumont shook his head in disgust.

Another woman hurried into the room, carrying a mess of books and folders like a hapless restaurant worker balancing a stack of dishes.

"Did I miss anything?" she asked.

"We're just starting, Rayana," Henry said.

Dr. Rayana Gluck scurried to the opposite end of the table to give adequate dumping space for her chaotic assortment of materials. Rayana bolstered the myth of ethnic diversity at Elmer Butthead. She was Hispanic-Jewish (though raised atheist) and had natural kinky hair that she wore in a short halo around her head. Rayana could pass for a light-skinned African American, so she frequently got featured in Elmer Butthead brochures. Despite or maybe because of her gangling presence, she had an electric quality, as if always on amphetamines, though Phyllis claimed this was not the case. Rayana bit pencils and chewed pen tops, and had trouble relaxing. You either found her mesmerizing or bizarre.

Rayana's research concerned the psychology of women who choose to remain single in our patriarchal society, which demographic she boasted as her own. Unlike Phyllis or Sidney, Rayana made reference to having had boyfriends in the past, but she spoke of this phase of her life as would a reformed sinner or sober alcoholic. All of the men she described were lemons: Married men. Gay men. Heavyduty drunks and dopers. Zombie-like men strung out on anti-psychotics. Traveling businessmen who lived in Hong Kong or Honolulu.

But Rayana had a Teflon mind. She believed her bad choices were not her own doing, but rather stemmed from a patriarchal society that taught women to look for contentment outside themselves. She claimed to have found happiness for having grown past this false idea, though I found her so-called happiness about as convincing as that of a flight attendant who had to clean up vomit. If Sidney seemed devoid of emotion, Rayana came across as high voltage, forever teetering on the edge of a psychotic break. She may have been many things, but happy could not have been one of them.

"You look splenetic, Rayana," Millie said.

"Splenetic? I am downright bellicose." Rayana looked through her mounds of files in a frenzy.

"Okay. Department meetings—found it."

"What happened at FCLC?" Millie further inquired.

"Oh, nothing," Rayana answered. "Just that I feel like I've been raped. The BOD teamed up with the NPGW to table our new document on assessment from the ATCP. After all that work."

"Are you serious?" Millie asked rhetorically. "Those fuckers."

"I know. It gave me a sinus attack. I had to take a Tylenol 3."

"Join the club," Phyllis said. "I woke up with a pounding sinus headache. In fact, I've had it since yesterday."

"It's the time of year," said Millie. "Every fall I am one giant walking headache."

"There must be an increase in global warming air toxins," Sidney said.

"It's the heating system," said Phyllis. "My headaches are even worse during winter."

"Mine, too," Millie agreed. "Also my stiff neck and backaches."

"I'm exactly the same," Sidney replied.

"Okay, let's bring the meeting to order," said Henry. "First up is Sidney, who—" His cell phone beeped, and he picked it up.

"I'm sorry, Dr. Crabb just texted me."

No one said much of anything as Henry left the room. I waited in vain for one person to welcome me to my first department meeting, or offer what all the alphabet soup stood for.

Henry re-entered a few minutes later.

"There's bad news," he said. "One of our seniors is dead. Kimberly Ann Kulwicki jumped off the roof of Shuck Library."

"Wicki?" Dumont said. "How sad, she was my new RA. She seemed fine yesterday."

Millie extended her hand across the table to place it on top of Dumont's. "I had her last year in Marriage Counseling. I thought to myself, 'This student has Atychiphobia.' Naturally, my hands were tied, so I couldn't reach out to her. It's not your fault, Dumont. If a psych major doesn't know enough to seek professional help, what can anyone do for her?"

I started to say, "We can still try to—" But Millie started one of her uninterruptible spiels.

"The answer is that no one can do anything for her. Young women must be raised with as much confidence as boys. They need to learn that it's not only okay to have boundaries, but you can't live without them. It's basic mental health. I learned at a young age that no one would look out for me if I didn't. Or actually, I take that back. Henry looks out for me. We look out for each other. But some people never find that."

She took a minuscule pause, so I said, "I don't think it's fair to compare—"

"Frankly, I don't see how anyone can expect to find a truly happy life—not a falsely happy one, I mean real happiness—if gender roles continue to perpetuate patriarchal inequalities. Not just my research, but the research of so many scholars across disciplines have found the same thing. The more egalitarian people perceive themselves to be, the higher they score on happiness measures. Now, you may ask if this also includes androgyny. In a perfect world, it would. But because of all of our sexist biases, more androgynous people—who should have the advantage, if you think about it—often are made to suffer unnecessarily . . ."

And so it went for about half an hour. Everyone else appeared to be attentive, so I wondered if I were the only one hoping to leave the room the moment Millie finished.

The Atychiphobia that Millie claimed Wicki had was a morbid fear of failure. But I knew that Wicki feared Dumont. I also remembered her fear of heights—so I thought it likely that someone pushed her off the roof. Even if she had jumped, wouldn't it take more time to reach this official conclusion? It was only my second day as a professor, but I smelled a rat the size of a brontosaurus. I decided I owed it to Wicki to expose the truth about this dump.

"Bentley, are you crying?" asked Henry with a sneer, when Millie at long last concluded.

"Oh, not at all. My eyes get watery sometimes. I can't control it."

"I'll be extra-careful to keep my smoking away from you," Millie offered.

"Thanks."

"I have the opposite problem," said Phyllis. "I practically live on eye drops."

"I keep telling everyone—it's the pollutants," Sidney said. "The capitalist government wants to kill everyone."

Sometimes instead of saying what's important, you talk about something else.

"That makes no sense," I said. "If everyone died, no one could buy anything."

Sidney smirked with superiority. "Of course it makes no sense. It's capitalism."

"The dean said there would be a formal announcement later," Henry said. "Now, where were we? Oh yes, Sidney, you were going to tell us about student retention best practices."

We continued with the meeting as though nothing happened.

Ghost 5

I thought it Zen of Elaine to disappear, leaving me with nothing but a koan-like riddle to ponder: My department's affectphobia had something key to do with finding the murderer. As Elaine said, this condition often manifested as an intimidating presence that controls what is or is not expressed, limits the scope of what can be addressed, acts overly formal or pompous so that meaningless rules censor what can be expressed, or is narcissistic—the notion that you are superior to other people and all that is discussed must confirm that or be rejected.

Elaine said to start with a chart of the department from seven years ago. I used her computer tab to accomplish said task. But I didn't see what it told me, since everyone in the department did all four things on a regular basis:

	Henry	Millie	Dumont	Phyllis	Rayana	Sidney
Intimidating	X	X	X	X	X	X
Censoring	X	X	X	X	X	X
Rule-crazy	X	X	X	X	X	X
Narcissistic	X	X	X	X	X	X

Everyone in the department was extremely defensive—and to a pathological degree. Anything that appeared to be benign or even collegial happened strictly for show, including alleged alliances. Everything happened to make someone look good or politically correct or to fuck with your mind.

As Elaine instructed me to do, I next considered popular theories about homicide. Two leapt out at me, the first being neutralization theory. This is when a killer feels okay about killing because she or he denies that there is a victim, or that even a crime had been committed. For instance, So-and-So deserved to die, so there is no victim and there is no crime.

However, I found myself favoring the concept of murder by design. This is the idea that murder makes sense to commit, given one's threats and assets at a given moment. This logical self-defense mechanism is in competition with another drive to protect that self by not committing murder. But under certain circumstances, the decision to kill may seem the most viable alternative. And of course, it must be seen as doable.

I thought that given the flattening out of emotion that occurred within the department, murder by design made for a good theory to work from. I next considered who might've wanted to see me dead, still sticking with the original faculty lineup as Elaine said to do.

Henry hated me before we met, and things spiraled out of control from there. Millie hated me because she knew that I had good reason to hate Henry. My existence reminded her of the truth about her husband. If I went away, she could live out her days in blissful denial. As for Phyllis, maybe over time she figured out that I didn't exist to be her personal lump of clay—that I had actual opinions and feelings of my own. It could be that this posed too much of a threat to her delicate balance. Dumont—what needs to be said? As far as I could tell, Sidney was born with an inability to feel emotion, a psychological variation on congenital analgesia, in which people don't feel physical pain. She did what she could to make sure no one learned her secret, claiming episodes of emotion that never happened. So what would stop her from killing? Rayana was just a mess. She lived so enmeshed in panic that it never occurred to her that people were different from inanimate objects . . .

I felt a tap on my shoulder.

"Elaine, what a pleasant surprise. Long time no see."

She shook her head in displeasure. "Always with the snarky remarks."

"Just doing what comes naturally."

She wore a scolding expression. "What you need to do, naturally or otherwise, is solve the case."

"The case? What case?"

"Not amusing. And I'm not your mother, by the way. And the only reason she put up with your tapioca crapioca all these years was because she felt guilty about the Misty Rose thing. But she thinks you have much more in common with your father than you care to admit. Another lost cause that she ministers to as best she can."

"Tell me something I don't already know." Truthfully, it stung to hear this, but I made damn sure Elaine didn't know it. Unless, of course, she knew it anyway.

"Serious matters aren't funny, though for some reason you think they are. Perhaps a holdover from Misty Rose— you had to convince your little boy self that the abuse was just a silly cartoon."

"When I listen to you analyze me, I am more convinced than ever that psychology should be abolished. Oh, and by the way, I still come up blank. I don't see how one person's fear of emotions made them any more my enemy than someone else's."

She gave a rueful laugh.

"Of course you don't. That would require some form of communion with another entity—in this instance, me. So why consider that I may be on to something when instead you can show that I'm not?"

Though a rare occurrence, I found myself unable to think of a snappy comeback.

"Think of Boris in jail," Elaine said. "He's locked up for something he didn't do. You of all people should have empathy. Here, take a look at how brave he is, even though the fear and sorrow ooze out of every pore."

With a wave of her hand, the screen on her tablet showed Boris talking with his wife, Jamie, and their two kids, Something and Something, in the visiting area of the county jail. Boris was a big guy, and he looked like a gigantic carrot in his orange jumpsuit. Jamie hugged him and kissed him on the lips, while the two kids clamored for Daddy's attention like dogs at a dinner table. With a big smile he lifted each one into the air and held them to his chest, his eyes closed in tenderness.

"We miss you so much, Daddy," said either or both of them.

"Show him your drawings," Momma Jamie urged.

The drawings were typical child crayon efforts, but Boris looked at them as if gazing at the Mona Lisa.

"Oh, these are very good. I'm so proud of both of you."

"You can keep them, Daddy."

Boris and Jamie exchanged a meaningful glance. I sensed that these reminders of his kids were more than he could bear.

"Tell you what," Jamie said. "Let's keep them on the refrigerator until Daddy comes home."

"I can't wait," Boris said. "We'll all play fetch with Barky." I assumed that Barky was the revolting name of their dog.

"Tell us again, Daddy, how you saved your unit from getting bombed."

"Okay, I get it," I said to Elaine. "Do I really have to keep watching this?" A little bit of wholesome Americana went a long way with me. I preferred horror movies and stuff like that.

"What's wrong? Do you find their normalcy a waste of time? Ben, you're the worst type of snob because you don't even know you are one. Maybe we should visit the psychology department. Something may jog your memory."

I only just met her, so where did she get off making such personal remarks?

"I've visited the psycho department a number of times, thanks all the same. Remember the dog poop and the magic marker? And let us not forget the skunk."

Cecilia chose that moment to reappear, so Elaine vanished. That I didn't know what she intended to say next made dealing with the tedious Cecilia that much more annoying.

"I've decided to forgive you," Cecilia said, as if it were the greatest moment in history. Frankly, I didn't remember what I said to set her off. It never took much.

"Like I care if you forgive me."

"Obviously nothing changed in my absence. I don't understand how people get so bitter."

First Elaine, now Cecilia. Would it never let up?

"*Life* makes people bitter, as you call it. I prefer to call it honesty. What I don't understand is how you could be a professor at Elmer Butthead for all those years and be the same shmuck you were when you started."

"I loved being a professor. I loved life. Why does that make me a shmuck?"

"You couldn't possibly work at Elmer Butthead and love life. Being a college professor is as low as you can get. It doesn't get any more anti-life, anti-everything. Specs of dust have more fun than college professors. Your heart shrinks to the size of a raisin. You're an egghead. You're an obsessive-compulsive zombie."

Cecilia stared at me, and tsked-tsked.

"I feel sad for you, Bentley. I have no idea what makes you so inimical. I don't think you know, either."

"Inimical—you mean unfriendly? What does it take for one of you lunatics to talk like a human being?"

For once I was the one who ran off in a huff. I scared the night watchman out of the theater building, went to the wire box, and set the stage on fire, just to get the anger off my chest. As I watched the hapless firefighters, I thought about a fall kickoff ass cream social in the blackened cinders. If only I could appear before LMAC and say, "Ahm sure it's not as bad as all thayat."

Human 5

I got through that first department meeting in a fugue state, and soon as it ended I asked Phyllis if I could talk to her. I figured since she thought of me as a confidante I could tell her what Wicki said before she died. Plus as an old timer, Phyllis could explain what the next step should be. This gave her the opportunity to gossip and be feminist at the same time, which I imagined would put her in seventh heaven.

We went to my office, and I locked the door.

"What I'm about to tell you stays between us," I said. "I have to know I can trust you."

I could tell my words excited her.

"Of course, Ben. Come to me with *anything*, and it goes no further." She feigned zipping her mouth shut to punctuate her point.

I told her what Wicki said about Dumont, and also about Wicki's fear of heights.

"Ben, before you go any further, you're not telling me anything I don't already know about Dumont. Every year it's someone else."

The smug way she said this, as if nothing mattered except being one step ahead in the gossip marathon, caught me off guard.

"Surely, then, it's been reported. Why does it persist?"

I couldn't believe it, but Phyllis laughed.

"Welcome to academia."

"I . . . uh . . . what?"

"Ben, this is a dirty little secret of college life. Men mess with women students, and there's nothing to be done about it. Bad publicity, legal battles—it's avoided at all costs."

"The patriarchy," I said, trying to get on her wavelength.

She yawned without covering her mouth. "I suppose you could call it that, though it's not the way I conceptualize it. There are many other factors."

In other words, I could never be right about anything.

"Like what?"

"Oh, things you'll figure out in due time. You must realize, there is idealism, and then there is pragmatism. Reality. It's delusional to think otherwise. Do you have a crucifixion complex?"

"It's not about me. A student died because of her professor. This is a homicide and sex crime. Dumont needs to be reported to the cops. He must've gotten someone to force her up to the library roof."

"Whoa, Ben, slow down. If this went public, you might as well kiss your job good-by. And the publicity you'll get— nobody wants to hire a blabbermouth."

"But—"

"You just got your Ph.D. Do you really want it to come to nothing? Focus on the good you can do, the students you can reach. You don't know for certain what happened. The Law of Parsimony takes one only so far. If she had a fear of heights, that could be why she *chose* the library roof. Suicidal people sometimes get daring."

"The autopsy will prove I'm right. I'm convinced that she didn't jump."

Phyllis patted me on the head.

"That's sweet of you to show such concern. But you see, Elmer Butthead *is* this two-bit town. If we had a scandal like that, there'd be no more Elmer Butthead. And if there were no more Elmer Butthead, the whole town would be up shit creek."

"Are you saying the cops will cover it up, too?" My hands made fists for my anxiety.

"It never ceases to amaze me how quickly professors can add two and two."

"But we can fight back. If we raise a royal stink it would look bad if they fired us."

"No, that must never happen. I could never do such a thing to Millie."

"Millie?! What about her?"

Phyllis proceeded to tell me about Henry's flashing, and how Millie would be destroyed if the cops investigated the department.

"I don't want to talk about this any further," she added. "Millie's like my sister. You see, Ben, women aren't like men. We stick together."

She made me so angry I could barely see, though I tried not to let it show.

"Well, if you stick together, what about female students that get molested? Not to mention murdered."

"You should never say 'male' or 'female.' Those are sexist words. Like 'girl' or 'lady.'"

She used some of these words herself, but that didn't count.

"Okay, then. What about the *young women* students who get molested?"

"Leave faculty out of it. It's an administrative matter. That's why they make those big fancy salaries. If there's foul play, they'll know what to do."

"That's insane. I can't believe you're saying this."

Phyllis gave me a haughty look.

"I don't have to listen to you. As a woman I define my own reality. You're as bad as the boys in my intro class. I will not be bullied."

And thus did I let the matter drop, at least where Phyllis was concerned. I didn't bother talking to anyone else in the department. I headed toward the library, exploring the building from various angles. I determined it quite possible that a push off the roof could've looked like a jump. I thought the building might be closed because of Wicki, but it wasn't. No announcement had been made yet to students, so as I entered the main floor I saw dozens of kids on computers, playing online Poker and such. I rode an elevator to the highest floor, and spied the flight of stairs to the roof. It had been taped off, but I stepped over it.

I noticed something on the staircase. There were muddy footprints of an athletic or jogging shoe. I happened to remember that Wicki wore flip-flops to my office. A couple of voices mumbled from the top of the staircase; they sounded like cops. I took a picture of the shoe prints with my phone, and darted back across the tape.

With firm resolve, I marched to the office of the Director of Student Success, Dr. Emily Crabb, a/k/a LMAC. Older faculty knew to make an appointment with her weeks in advance, but being brand new I assumed I could talk to her then and there, and sure enough I did.

"Bentley, come in, hayve a seat," Emily said, beaming with southern hospitality. "Would you lack some coffay?"

"No thank you." I noticed a framed picture on her desk. She and some dweeby looking guy stood on either side of a younger dweeb who wore a cap and gown.

"That's mah son," she said. "His daddy and Ah are evah so proud. *Summa Cum Laude* from Ole Miss. And mah dawtuh—she's expecting her first chald in Decembuh."

"Congratulations." I noticed a trophy on a shelf behind her desk, and squinted to read the writing.

"Are you admiring mah Miss Chattanooga runnuh-up award? Ah keep it on display. Ah am not ashaymed of mah pageant life past. It taught mey a great deal about poise and confidence."

"Well, you certainly do seem to have plenty of both."

"Whah, thank you, Bentley. Ah do hope your classes ah going well, and thayt Ah see you at our next ass cream social. How can Ah help you today?"

Staring at her relentless toothsome grin, I already hated her. She knew perfectly well a student just fell to her death—she was the one who told Henry about it. Yet the bullshit was so thick she couldn't pretend to be even the slightest bit upset. Everything was fine, fine, fine. Totally under control.

Some primitive survival instinct told me to get up and leave, but I proceeded to tell her about Wicki and Dumont and Wicki's fear of heights. Then I told her about Henry the Flasher. By the time I finished, I had an odd, seasick feeling in my head, a kind of vertigo from life moving faster than I could keep up with it. But I kept on talking. Emily smiled while I spoke; with her cherry red lipstick she reminded me of a scary clown.

"Is thayt everything?" she asked me when I finished.

"Yes." Looking for signs of humanity in her face was like looking for a contact lens in the dark.

"Well now, the thang is, Bentley," she drawled, "Ah already heard tell of these rumahs about your department. And Ah can assure you we are doing everythang possible to see if they merit futhah attention."

"Rumors? From what I've gathered, it's common knowledge."

"Ah am going to have to stop you right theyeh. Doctuh Dungworth and Doctuh Zwieback have civil rahts, too, you know."

"Yeah, but—"

"Yeah but nothing. Let's leave the cause of death to the po-lice. Ah thank you need to get settled in, and stop telling people how to do theyah jobs. If you have issues in yowah department, they raghtfully should go to yowah Chair."

I couldn't believe it.

"I should go to Henry to talk about Henry?"

She shrugged. "I thank you've answered yowah own question. If you aren't willing to confront those whom you accuse, thayat should tell you something. Ah am ever so sorry, but Ah need to get bayack to some pressing business. Pulease close the door on yowah way out."

As I stood up to leave, I noticed a pair of running shoes behind her desk.

"So you're a jogger?" I pointed at her shoes.

"Mah, but you are observaynt. Ye-yes, Ah run evry day-ay. In the mornings."

"Those look like they get good traction. What brand are they?"

"Wah, I don't even remembuh. I hayve so many othuh thangs on mah mind."

"Do you mind if I take a photo of them? I'm looking for a new running shoe."

LMAC rolled her eyes and shook her head. "That's not necessary, but I'll show them to you." She bent down to grab one of the shoes. I saw that it had been made by Run-a-Thon.

"Ays Ah sayd, pulease close the door on yowah way out."

I walked back to my office in a haze of anger way beyond anything I knew before. I wanted more than anything for LMAC's shoe print to match the one on the stairs. I wanted to see her carried out of her office in handcuffs. No, better yet, in the middle of an ass cream social, making a speech. I imagined having psychic powers, and I'd tell Emily her daughter's baby would be born without a head. Then, when my prophecy proved true, I'd go up to Emily and say, "I told you so." That would show her who she was messing with.

But my anger had a way of morphing into fear—if not paranoia. Whenever something scared me, it made me angry, and vice-versa. I did not know on that fateful day that these would be my primary emotional states of being for the rest of my life. I resembled a kid trying to draw a picture with only two crayons. My seven lost years at Elmer Butthead consisted of one ceaseless Misty Attack.

But first I dealt with something else.

Just as I approached my office, Boris spotted me in the hallway.

"Henry wants to see you immediately," he called out.

I feared the worst, and was not disappointed.

No sooner did I sit down than did Henry stick it to me.

"Bentley, I assume you're aware of our sexual harassment policy?"

"Uh, yes." The wall behind him was covered with degrees and plaques of honor. He had a Donald Trump-like massive desk and swivel chair.

"If I were you, I wouldn't answer in the affirmative quite so quickly." He had a habit of licking his thick upper lip, like a gangrenous Mick Jagger.

"I don't know what you mean."

"I mean, read the policy and memorize the damn thing as if your life depended on it. It's only your second day, and I already received a complaint from a student."

He paused, and stared at me. His poker face made me feel like I turned into stone.

"I . . . I haven't connected with any students at all yet. I mean, my lectures went fine, don't get me wrong. But I've barely spoken to students otherwise." I knew better than to add: *except for Wicki.*

"A student begs to differ with you. And before you ask, I am not revealing a name."

"I already figured you wouldn't." In fact, it said as much in the damn policy he claimed I did not know. At this initial phase, the student's identity stayed protected to prevent retaliation. But I also knew Henry made the whole thing up. He wanted to tell me without telling me that I'd better not make a fuss about Wicki.

"I could report you right now, and you'd be out of a job. You realize that, I assume?"

I couldn't look at him anymore.

"Yes, Henry. I do."

"I can have you blackballed from academe. And from the APA. My friends, Harvey and Madge, said they sensed a peculiar vibe from you—something inappropriately sexual. Good lord, all they did was invite you to dinner with their children. Are your urges that hard to control?"

I couldn't decide whom I hated more: Henry or Harvey and Madge.

"You told me they thought I was nice."

Henry sat there, motionless, looking right through me.

"I said, you told me they thought I was nice."

Henry remained immobile except for blinking his eyes.

"I'm very good at what I do, Bentley. I will not let you trick me into changing the subject. You are inappropriate, and it must stop at once if you want to keep your job."

"I understand."

"I am willing to give you another chance. Read the sexual harassment policy backwards and forwards. First thing tomorrow I will quiz you to make sure you know it."

"Yes, Henry."

"It is absolutely unacceptable to sexually harass a student."

"I agree, Henry."

Then I said something I regretted for the rest of my life, something that never stopped making me angry at three in the morning: "I'm sorry if I caused any trouble."

In the moment, all I knew was terror. I saw myself as a little boy in the basement with Misty Rose. Survival at all costs.

"That's good to hear, Bentley. That's a start—owning up to your shortcomings and getting past your defensive ego."

What a prick.

"Thank you, Henry. I appreciate all you're doing for me."

The fucker actually laughed.

"It's all part of my job. *My* job."

"Absolutely."

I lost count years ago of how many times I replayed that scene in my head. Sometimes I pretended I stood up to him with quiet dignity, taking out my phone to call an attorney or the police. Other times I pretended I disarmed him by saying something unexpected like, "I think I know the student you mean. She (or he) made a pass at me." But my favorite times were the ones I pretended I reached across his desk and strangled him. Or shot him in the balls with my imaginary gun. I also imagined finding out if Phyllis ratted on me, or if Emily did or maybe both of them did. Without being suicidal, I thought about shooting myself through the head in front of any or all of them, so that they'd feel punished every day for the rest of their lives.

But while the blackmail took place, I only thought of my Ph.D. going down the drain after two days on the job. I figured I could look for a different position in a year or so. I just had to hang in there for now, and get myself out of the hot seat. Elmer Butthead didn't have a faculty advocate or union, and if I hired an attorney it might make everything worse. Not to mention I couldn't afford one.

Besides, I knew if I gave up and let Elmer Butthead win, I'd be worse off as a person. Misty Rose gave me all the demons I could want. I pretended to be a patient; the advice I gave myself was to keep the job. Henry saw he could control me, so if anything he wanted me to stay around. And maybe at some point in the near future, I'd find a way to zap him back. I'd get even with Henry and Dumont and LMAC and Phyllis and everyone else. I had no more integrity than they did, but someday I would. I'd be more than just another irrelevant egghead masturbating my cerebral cortex.

I went back to my office and did a web search for LMAC's running shoes. They did not match the shoe print on the stairs. I imagined LMAC making fun of me, and popped a Xanax. Then I popped another one. My nerves subdued to a dull roar, I kept looking on the Internet at track shoe sole patterns. After about a half hour, I found a match—a regional athletic footwear manufacturer called Great Lakes Runners.

On impulse, I drove to a variety store a couple of towns over and bought a disposable cell phone with cash. Disguising my voice, I called the local police, and told them Wicki had a fear of heights. Then I threw the cell phone down the sewer.

Ghost 6

"I know what you're thinking, and forget it."

The intrusive voice of Elaine broke my concentration.

"When you relive the past, all you want to do is get revenge, which to you means punishing people way beyond their crime. Your anger is stupid anger. The only thing you accomplish by scaring people is making them scared. They'll be harder to reach, not easier. You think you're more logical than you are. And when A doesn't lead to B like you assumed it would, you blame everyone else."

"Well, Miss Smarty Pants, I guess you know everything."

"Badmouth being a ghost all you want, but you should be grateful for a second chance. Some people, when they die, it's like the fat lady has sung, capital-T-capital-E The End."

"All my life I've been told to be grateful. When Misty Rose kidnapped and raped but didn't kill me, I was supposed to be grateful. I get murdered and turned into a ghost but I should be grateful. Who do I thank for these wondrous opportunities? You? Ed?"

"You'll figure out."

"You know I hate it when you say that."

Elaine shrugged, and her shoulders made ripples of color.

"So sue me."

"I would if I could."

She ignored my bratty remark.

"You get bent out of shape over nonsense. The things people say—so what? You're the critical one. No one forced you to be a college professor."

I sighed; when ghosts sigh, they look like deflating balloons.

"Fine—I deserved to die. They all hated me. I'll bet it had nothing to do with the other murders."

"Stop projecting your own feelings onto others. Don't say, "They hated me.' Say, "I hated them.' Own it."

"Okay, I hated them. Is that better? All you do is criticize."

She held her head high, like royalty.

"I never criticize. I guide."

"Oh, sorry. I misunderstood."

Elaine took a moment to regroup. She closed her eyes, and with her fingers made all these sparkling swirls around her body, sort of like a deep sleep tornado.

I caused my spirit guardian to lose her cool. How many people could say that?

"I thought we had an understanding, but I guess not," Elaine said after a minute. "It's as if you don't remember how to think of something nice—to be in a good mood. Some terrible way of being is taking control over you."

"Life's funny that way. Apparently, so is death. You're not human, Elaine. You don't know how it feels when positive thinking and positive action and positive this and that get you nowhere but screwed."

"Sounds like PTSD."

"I'm a ghost with PTSD?"

"I admit it's an outlier on the bell curve. But it does happen. Indeed, there's been talk that it's more common than we realize. When spirits turn demonic, it may be that some inner howl becomes all they are."

"Well, isn't that too wonderful for words? Being dead gets better and better."

Elaine shook her head in sorrow.

"This is not something that will go away through flippancy. You need to chill."

"Please at least tell me Wicki is okay. I mean, in an afterlife-ish way. Is she in a good place?"

Elaine shook her head with displeasure.

"Wicki is where she is. When will you realize that your obsession with her is merely a projection of your helplessness over your own childhood?"

"Or maybe it pisses me off that she got murdered because she got raped. Is it possible for some things just to be rotten?"

"You pick all the wrong times to get angry."

And with that, she was gone.

Seldom one to follow the advice of others, my mind went wild with revenge scenarios against the department, each more diabolical than the one before. But just as I started enjoying myself, Cecilia popped back.

"A penny for your thoughts?" she said. "You seem happy for once."

"Did you really just say, 'A penny for your thoughts?'"

"I hate it when you make fun of me. What have I ever done to you?"

"Nothing, I guess."

There we were, stuck together at Elmer Butthead, and she found my grumpiness to be the problem. But why try explaining anything to her? I'd have better luck teaching a clam how to throw a Frisbee.

Yet for once Cecilia was right—it made me happy to even the score with people who did me wrong. It's been said that forgiving people sets you free, but nothing compares to fucking over someone who fucked you over.

I hated admitting it, but I began understanding why I became a ghost.

Seldom had I felt more exuberant then when I set the Student Success building on fire. The thought of all its smarmy and meaningless projects being reduced to ash gave me a sense of fulfillment I seldom knew in my abbreviated lifetime.

I ran into Cecilia, who cried ghostly diamonds as she watched the greedy, dancing flames.

"What am I doing here? I'm a good person. I deserve happiness. Why is there all this destruction? The sky is green—I mean, red, from all the flames. It's like I'm in Hell."

If she was too dense to realize I started all the fires and things, I was not about to disillusion her.

"At least it's not boring."

The local news reported on the continued destruction of the Elmer Butthead campus, which President Shuffle-Ass kept saying was nothing to worry about, he had everything under control. Police Sergeant Candy MacDougal said it was too soon to say if the arson and vandalism bore connection to the murders, though she remained confident that Boris killed me, and all the other nonsense people expected her to say. She still had no explanation for my posthumous penmanship samples. According to a local poll, a majority of people supported the notion that living hands caused the destruction, though seven percent had the wisdom to know that these were acts of the supernatural.

But even these people did not suspect me. Four percent believed Satan caused the damage, while three percent said God did it.

I had to admit it felt wonderful to do whatever I wanted, after so many years of never doing what I wanted, thanks to Elmer Butthead. If my actions displeased Elaine, she'd get over it.

For the first time, I noticed an additional skill I possessed as a ghost. I could make the flames higher and more widespread by controlling them with my mind

Human 6

Wide-eyed youth that I was, I thought sex would make me feel better. Looking back, I can only think: how dumb.

I drove a couple of towns over to a singles bar. Like millions of other lonely people, I sought salvation from a total stranger. I didn't find it, but my depression led to more to be depressed about. That is to say, I couldn't perform. Not even close. I'd picked up a nice enough girl, and she gave me the standard spiel about how other things were more important. But I felt like an overcooked piece of elbow macaroni. I drove around for a short while because I couldn't think what else to do, and when I happened to drive by the singles bar I saw the same girl going back inside, presumably to get something less important than the supine thing I gave her.

That night I had a dream about Misty Rose. This happened on occasion. In times of stress I often experienced fleeting dream images of being a kidnapped little boy. But this time I met her as a grown man, and we talked like old friends. We even hugged and—I think—French kissed. Before waking up, I heard her say, "You finally know what it's like." Being a psychologist, I knew this meant a shift occurred inside me, though I didn't know if it would be for the better or for the worse.

Checking my email on the morning of my third day as a professor, I learned that LMAC would be hosting a special ass cream social that afternoon. We also got a message from our undistinguished university president, Dr. Bailey Blankenship, notifying us that the matter of Wicki's suicide would be kept private at her family's request. After a few token words about this being a difficult time for us all, he added a friendly reminder about the clause that forbade us to go to the media with anything that presented Elmer Butthead in an unfavorable light.

The dispatch came with a heading: "From the desk of President Blankenship." There was a thumbnail-sized photo of him smiling from his desk, pen in hand, as though taking a fleeting instant to smile for the camera while never ceasing his all-important work. He looked like a sleazy game show host. I'd already heard that behind his back he was known as "Blankenshit."

I dreaded going back to the department for my third day. Just knowing that I might run into Henry or Dumont in the hallway filled me with stomach-churning dread. In a rational sense I knew they couldn't harm me, as I knew they wouldn't stab me or shoot me or throw a bucket of boiling oil at me. But I feared them anyway, as if the cruelty in their eyes could zap me with a death ray. Seldom is fear rational, but it trumps logic every time. I thought about calling in sick, but since it was only my first week I hadn't accumulated any sick leave and also I worried that Henry would use it as another nail in my coffin.

I drove to campus in a panicky state, clutching the steering wheel so tight it left imprints in my palms. I kept playing a movie in my mind of entering the door to Lab Hall, riding the elevator alone to the psych department, walking down the hall, turning the key to my office door, shutting it behind me, and feeling safe and alone behind its lock. I thought or hoped my imagination could be so powerful that it dictated reality.

Stepping off the elevator, I saw Henry and Dumont talking to each other at the end of the hall. My office was about halfway down; maybe they'd be so absorbed in their conversation they wouldn't notice me. By necessity, people walked in the hallway all the time. Surely everyone didn't speak to everyone every single time.

I took a deep breath, and began the short journey that felt like it took eternity. I reached my office door, and got out my keys.

I dropped the keychain on the floor.

Cursing my clumsiness, I reached down for my keys as Henry said, "Ben, come here, we were just talking about you."

I felt my guts turn inside out as I stood up and walked the short distance to where they were standing.

"Hi," I said with a smile.

Henry and Dumont acted jovial, as if by nature generous in sharing their friendliness. It seemed all but impossible that they could be any other way.

"Dumont just told me a zinger," Henry said. "Tell it to Ben, Dumont."

Dumont looked this way and that.

"Just wanted to make sure the women weren't around. You know how they can be. The three musketeers—Sidney, Rayana and Phyllis."

"Except they're more butch than the originals," Henry added. "Millie can't stand them, but if you tell anyone I told you I'll deny it."

"They can't even stand each other," Dumont said. "Rayana and Sidney have this ongoing catfight. King Kong versus Godzilla."

"They seem like friends," I said.

"Obviously you need a crash course in Women 101," said Henry.

"They act like the bosomiest of buddies, but they're more like bosom bitches," Dumont said. "If you're smart, you'll keep a safe distance."

"Uh, thanks for the tip."

"So tell Ben the joke, Dumont," Henry said. "Just like you told it to me."

"Well, this guy picks up a woman in a bar, and after he fucks her he hands her a hundred dollar bill. Feeling insulted, she slaps his face and says, 'What do you think I am?' And he says, 'Well, you told me you were buy sexual.' Get it? B-u-y sexual as in b-i sexual?"

Dumont and Henry found this to be a real knee-slapper, and they doubled up with laughter upon the retelling. I wasn't quite sure what to do, so I smiled a bit and buried my face in my hands to suggest feeling overwhelmed by humor.

It appeared that they forgot that I, too, studied psychology. I knew that this back and forth mind fuck between scaring me and soothing me was intended to cause uncertainty and insecurity, whereby I'd become dependent on their moods to determine my own. They wanted me to be their emotional toy, denied my right to free will. One of the best ways to obtain power over another person is to keep that person confused.

Sometimes people lose their temper and sometimes people don't understand the needs of others. But I realized that what Henry and Dumont did to me was intentional. They must have had conversations about planning their strategy. And their goal had nothing to do with pointing out an intellectual flaw in my thinking but to bully me—to frighten me into submission. They found pleasure in watching me squirm, and saw it as a signal of victory. A reason to celebrate.

"We're hearing great things about you, Ben," said Henry—the same person who the day before accused me of sexual harassment.

"I . . . uh, I read the policy like you asked me to." Though in truth I didn't have to because I already knew it.

Henry gave me a friendly nudge with his elbow.

"Then you're all set. I just wanted to make sure you understood certain things."

"Don't you worry, Henry," Dumont said. "Ben is going to work out fine. I have a feeling we'll be seeing him for a long, long time."

"Gee, thanks, guys. All I can do is my best."

For once, having an 8 a.m. class came in handy. I managed to excuse myself and swallow a Xanax before hurrying to my students. I expected the same debauched burnouts from the previous day, but Wicki's death had a sobering effect. Though only about half the class showed up, those present sought explanation and assurance.

Before I could say anything, a girl raised her hand.

"Can we talk about Wicki?"

"Is that what everyone would like to do?" I asked.

Not all, but a few of them nodded in the affirmative, so I took that as a yes. I simply let students say what they had to say, and used my psychologist body language to validate them. When someone finished speaking, I summarized what she or he said to show I listened and took their words seriously. If a student cried in the midst of speaking—which happened several times—I let her or him take a moment before continuing.

Of course, I wanted to tell them that they needed not ponder why Wicki killed herself, because she didn't. I felt guilty for not blurting out that someone murdered her.

"Wicki and I started college together. She helped me pass my math classes. She was such a good person."

"Why would she do this? She was always so happy. She wanted to work with developmentally disabled kids."

"I can't believe she's gone. I never told her how I felt about her, and now I never can."

"Once when I got really depressed, she sat up all night with me until I felt better. She let me cry in her lap."

One student cut right to the core of the matter:

"Why doesn't this school care about students? There's no memorial, no nothing. Shouldn't they at least offer grief counseling?"

The class could not have been more unlike the meeting from the other day. Did someone have to get pushed off a roof to bring students and faculty together?

Walking back to my office after class, I felt a knot building in my chest. I started crying before I made it to the safety of my office, where I wailed like a baby. I realized my own denial over the death of this girl, who deserved so much better than she got. My problem wasn't sex or taking Xanax. Doubtless more students would come to me for help, and I felt trapped—impotent, if you will, unable to do anything. This was about much more than my usual Misty Attacks. I realized after only a few days that there was no room for caring about others at Elmer Butthead.

However, I had yet to become totally jaded, and my low mood led to an epiphany. I believed with all my heart that I found a way to make sure this never happened again.

To hell with all the paranoid legal bullshit. I'd start with Phyllis, since so far I knew her better than anyone else. I'd explain to her why we as faculty needed to get past the dysfunctional lies and cover-ups and make our school a place that protected students. I knew Phyllis's first response would be to point out flaws in my reasoning—she regarded this as a sacred duty—but I intuited that flattery would go a long way with her. My experience with Misty Rose taught me how to humor people. And if as a child I could manipulate a psycho kidnapper-child molester, surely I could get a fellow Ph.D. professor to see the logic of my ways.

We needed to go to the police, and if we stuck together we'd win.

I felt something akin to heroic as I walked to Phyllis's office.

I saw her typing away on her computer pad, her office door slightly opened. In Faculty Land this meant: *If it's really important you can talk to me.* Perhaps you'd have to be part of a college culture to understand the elation experienced when a professor you wanted to talk to was available.

I made a point of seeming meek as I knocked on Phyllis' door. She thought men who didn't come across as domineering were cute, like stuffed animals she could mother.

"I'm sure you're busy, but can you spare a minute?" I illustrated the smallness of my request with my extended thumb and forefinger separated by about one inch.

She smiled.

"Sure, Ben. Have a seat."

"Thank you so much. I'm really stumped, and I need your wisdom to tell me what to do."

"I'll certainly try."

As I sat down, I could tell I captured her attention. Her face lit up like the Christmas tree at Rockefeller Center. Besides her framed Ph.D., the most noticeable objects in her bland office were two huge posters. In big, humorless black letters, one poster read: *What part of NO do you not understand?* The other poster stated: *I live for myself, not for a man.* The dust jacket of her book, *Love Yourself First*, was framed beneath this declaration.

"It's about Wicki, the student who—"

"Ben, didn't we already go through this?"

"No, wait, there's more. I promise."

She looked at her computer tab and then at me. "Okay, go ahead. But make it fast."

"Of course, thank you. In my class this morning, we talked about Wicki and how the university needs to start—"

"Oh my God, please tell me I heard wrong. You did what?"

"The students talked about Wicki. They're upset. She was their friend." My confidence evaporated. What did I do wrong now?

"Do you have any idea how many policies you violated? You are not qualified to function as a grief counselor. This type of thing goes beyond the faculty job description and sets a dangerous precedent. I'm guessing you permitted students to badmouth the university without correcting them. If your class upset even one student, we could be sued for every last dime. Maybe you don't care about having a job, but I sure as hell do. Please at least tell me you didn't bring up your ridiculous theory about murder."

"No, I didn't. But how should I have handled it?" I asked, not wanting to know.

"Any number of ways. Change the subject. Remind them that legally they are gathered only to discuss course materials. If I were you, I'd email the class—no, I take that back. Email leaves a paper trail. It's better just to drop it. Next time the class meets, have a lot of other material to go over, and if anyone tries to talk about her anymore, don't recognize the comment. At the department meeting yesterday, Sidney presented what are called best classroom practices. I'm sure she'd be happy to share these with you. In fact, I'm pretty sure Sidney's in her office."

"I don't want to trouble her, please don't—"

Phyllis ignored me and dialed an extension on her phone. "Hi, Sid? Could you please come to my office to talk to Ben? Great, thanks. Oh, and bring a copy of the best practices from yesterday."

I of course attended the very meeting in question, and already had a copy of the best practices, but Phyllis seemed to have an odd memory—like, no memory at all. She also appeared to have a listening deficiency, not a good thing for a psychologist.

"Thanks, Phyllis, but I was at the meeting, remember? I already have a copy of the best practices."

Sidney opened the door and stepped right in to the office, without knocking.

"Hi Phyl," she said, ignoring me, as she launched into one of her out-of-nowhere monologues. "I read this blog about how women shouldn't go out drinking alone, because they were asking to get raped. Or not asking, exactly. It was written by a woman, after all. But it said that they were putting themselves in harm's way by getting drunk in a roomful of drunks looking for someone to have sex with. Women need to keep their wits about them, and all the usual sexist, blame-the-victim garbage. Once again, a woman cannot live her life. Just because she's drinking alone in a pick-up bar doesn't mean she's looking to get picked up. Only a man would think such a thing."

"If a boy student approaches me in that way, I *freeze*," Phyllis said, placing her hands in a pantomime of leaning against a blackboard. "I tell the young women in my class to do the same."

"I do the same thing," said Sidney.

There were a number of remarks I wanted to make in response to Sidney's spiel. But so doing would've distracted us from why I was there, so I let it slide.

"Hello, Sidney," I said.

"Ben, I didn't even notice you. I hear you need a copy of the best practices." Sidney handed me the same list as the day before.

"I talked about these at the meeting yesterday. Next time pay more attention. Paper comes from trees, you know—we shouldn't be wasteful."

"I have my copy from yesterday."

"Have a seat, Sid," Phyllis said. "I've been explaining to Ben about how to handle a class when students talk about something inappropriate."

Sidney sat down next to me. "Did someone say something sexist or racist?"

Phyllis jumped in to answer on my behalf.

"He told me they talked about the student from yesterday. You know, the one who . . ."

"Say no more," said Sidney. "I hope they didn't upset you, Ben. College-level teaching is an emergent skill. You'll find that over time you know how to handle these things. Just yesterday I had a student get on my case about Freud." She proceeded to repeat the anecdote from the day before—almost word for word, as if from memorization. Phyllis reacted as though she hadn't heard it before, and giggled and sighed at all the right spots.

"Men are so condescending," Sidney concluded. "Not you, Ben, but most men."

"They talk down to you," Phyllis agreed. "They act like you don't know anything, and pay no attention to anything you say."

"How unfortunate."

Sidney said, "Remember to have a firm hand in the classroom. Don't let the asshole jocks bully you." Of course I said nothing about jocks, asshole or otherwise, but I didn't point this out.

"If you'd like," Phyllis said, "I'd be happy to observe one of your classes, and afterwards tell you what you need to improve."

"I can do that as well," said Sidney. "Phyl and I are the ones to talk to. Stay away from the men with their male bullshit. Oh, and Rayana. She's . . . let's just say she's on her own page."

"You handled that well," Phyllis teased. "It isn't easy for Sid to say neutral things about Rayana."

"She gives new meaning to 'sociopath.' Thank God Phyl is here for me to unload."

"I'll let you know if I need help," I said, seeking to change the subject.

"Anytime," Phyllis said, aggravating me though I tried not to let it show.

"Anytime," Sidney added, aggravating me more, so I tried harder not to let it show.

Fate had not finished with me yet. No sooner did I step into the hallway than did I see Rayana. She stood there gripping her smart phone as if it were the pivotal point of the world.

I smiled and said, "Hi," and hoped I could just keep walking.

"Please, come into my office for a minute."

"Um . . . yeah, okay."

Rayana's office featured the same "No means no" poster that Phyllis's did. She also had a large framed poster of Gloria Steinem with the quote: "The best way for us to cultivate fearlessness in our daughters and other young women is by example." There were some wall hangings of what I took to be some form of tribal folk art.

As she gestured for me to sit down, Rayana said, "I saw Sidney go into Phyl's office. I hope Phyl was able to keep Sidney under control. She's someone you want to avoid at all costs."

"I guess so. I mean, nothing bad happened."

"I can tell you're being polite." She said this with a look on her face that suggested my true crime was something far worse.

"I try to be polite."

"Well, don't. Honesty is everything in academe. Or in life." It appeared that there existed the university world and something separate from it called life, but I didn't ask her to elaborate. After only a couple of days, I saw what she meant.

"Anything but the truth is unacceptable," Rayana added. "Whatever it is, just let it out. Tell the truth, and you'll always be safe."

I deserved the Dunce Award for what I did next. I took Rayana at her word, and shared with her the same old story about Wicki and her fear of heights and Dumont.

When I finished, Rayana leaned forward with a sneer. "Why did you tell me this? Just to upset me? You know, I hope, that there's nothing that can be done about it? It's depressing—I feel helpless. Thanks a lot, Bentley, you've managed to spoil my entire day. I find that unacceptable."

"I don't feel so hot myself." I hoped she'd take the hint that her emotional state of the moment did not eradicate the rest of the universe.

"So you saw me, and figured I could be your emotional garbage can. Well, I have news for you, Dr. Bentley Gamble. I do not exist to be used by men. Men think women are there only to make them happy. My mother was my father's slave. He thought I should be, too. But I stood up to him. When he told me to get him a beer, I told him to get it himself. Even when he yelled at me, I never blinked. I wanted him to know that nothing he said or did hurt me in the slightest."

Rayana repeated this story many times over the years—whenever someone hurt her in the slightest and then some, which proved all too easy to do. If only she *had* been someone who never blinked.

"I'll bet Sidney told you to tell me this, just to freak me out. God, poor Phyl, having to put up with her. But that's

Sidney in action. If Phyl wasn't here I don't know what I'd do."

"But I—"

"I'm not comfortable continuing this conversation, Ben."

Fortunately, my smart phone beeped, which meant I had a text message, and therefore a way out of this mini-mess. Too bad the text message came from the office of the president:

> Please report to President Blankenship's office immediately.
>
> Melinda Joshua, Administrative Assistant.

I decided it best not to tell Rayana or anyone else about this misbegotten invitation. My apology to her deserved a mini-Oscar.

"It's a bit late for that," she said, as I hurried on my way.

Ghost 7

"Boo!" Cecilia tapped my shoulder from behind.

"How original. You must've stayed up all night planning that one."

"Oh, don't be such a sourpuss." More cheerful than usual, she did a little dance to signify her good mood. I managed not to appear impressed.

"If I didn't know better, Cecilia, I'd think you got laid."

"You say these things to offend me, but I don't care anymore. Because I know something you don't know."

"That's been self-evident for as long as you've been here."

Putdowns aside, I assumed that she, too, met up with her spirit guardian. Whoever it was, I did not envy him or her.

"Aren't you going to ask me what it is?"

"What what is?"

"You're so mendacious. Perseverate all you wish. I'll bet you're dying to know what I know. But I'm not going to tell you. Not after all the mean things you did. Maybe next time you'll think twice before you vandalize and deface campus property."

I knew Cecilia was a moron, but even I had trouble comprehending what she said. Obviously, her spirit guardian swore her to secrecy just like me. She saw in this secret an opportunity to teach me a lesson, as if I were not only a little boy, but *her* little boy. Only someone as delusional as Cecilia would find my harmless pranks more offensive than what happened to me—or to her, for that matter.

"How about making sense? I was murdered, in case you hadn't noticed. So what if I messed up a few lousy offices of a few campus louses?" (She still didn't know I set the fires.)

"Because it's vulgar and cruel. Because they did nothing to deserve it."

"I beg to differ. They did everything to deserve much worse."

"They didn't kill anyone."

"How the hell do you know? Did you call the psychic hotline?"

She put her hands to her ears, which always drove me up the wall.

"It's not my fault you feel guilty."

I will say this for college profs: I am not aware of another group of people so good at pissing each other off.

"What in the goddamn motherfucking world would I feel guilty about?"

"If you hadn't vandalized your department, the police wouldn't have taped it off. And I wouldn't have tripped. I'd still be alive."

Ouch, that stung.

"Well . . . what the hell were you doing in the psychology department in the first place? Did you come to gawk? To feel superior?"

"I was just walking by. Stop trying to change the subject. You blame yourself for my death. And I'm telling you to cut it out. You know it's ridiculous to feel that way."

"Yes, you're right. It's ridiculous. Which is why I don't feel that way."

"Deny it all you want. But I don't blame you Not even the teensiest bit."

"Your words certainly come as a relief, since none of this occurred to me until you brought it up just now."

Cecilia looked at me as if her patience merited sainthood.

"It's okay, Bentley. Really. I know that your guilt stems from. . . from other feelings you have toward me."

"Say what?"

"You know what I mean. I didn't think so myself, but I—well, let's just say something happened that made me see the truth. When you act juvenile, it's because you like me. You know, like, like-like me. It makes perfect sense."

"Perfect sense in Opposite Land."

"Bentley, for once can we be serious? You need to understand that I don't feel the same way. And when you take your frustration out on me I must draw a line in the sand. I am not interested in being your girlfriend. You must respect my boundaries, and stop treating me like it's my fault we aren't dating."

If it weren't for not having a body, I'd have sworn I had wax in my ears.

"Girlfriend? Dating? Golly, let me give you my high school ring and take you to the malt shop. What century do you live in? Not to mention we're ghosts. Not to mention I'm about as hot for you as I am for a paramecium. In fact, make that a dead paramecium."

Cecilia patted me on my ghostly head with her ghostly hand.

"'Me thinks thou dost protest too much.' All you're doing is convincing me that I'm right."

"And how did you arrive at this profound realization? Did a little bird tell you?"

"That I cannot share. But let's just say I know it must be true."

So her spirit guardian had a sense of humor. Or maybe she/he thought it would make Cecilia feel better, and *no harm no foul*, as they say. In concrete terms it made no difference. I planned on getting away from Elmer Butthead as soon as possible, and if ghosts could, as Cecilia put it, date, it was news to me. I harbored some curiosity as to Cecilia's cosmic task, but I had enough on my plate already.

"I'm too busy for this crazy talk," I said.

"You don't look it." This much was true, the only busyness going on was in my mind.

"I'm . . . I'm thinking about my research."

"Are you sure that's what you're thinking about?"

"Cut the crap, okay? I want to fuck you as much as you want to fuck me. In other words, zero. Zilch. Nada."

She removed her hair tie, and shook out her ponytail. Since she wore her hair tied back for as long as I'd known her, this marked the first time I saw it loose. It had a gossamer quality.

"I've been told I have sexy hair."

Say what? Cecilia coming on to me was the last thing in the world I expected ever to occur. Yet, how typical of her to project her desires on to the other person. To contort her own fucked up-ness into my problem.

"Yeah, you hair's okay."

She twisted a few strands with her fingers.

"Do you really think so?"

"Yeah, I do. And I also think this conversation couldn't end soon enough. In fact, let's pretend it ended sooner than now."

With her invisible elastic band, Cecilia pulled her hair back into its usual ponytail.

"It may interest you to know that I found out how ghosts can. . . well, you know."

"No, I don't know. Nor do I want to know."

I assumed her spirit guide told her how ghosts you-knowed their way to sexual paradise. True, my ever-inquisitive nature urged me to learn more, but not from Cecilia.

"I find it hard to believe that you of all people wouldn't at least be curious. I thought you were a critical thinker."

"Like I care what you believe."

She bent her arm so that her hand touched her shoulder. With her free hand, she pointed to her elbow. "Do you see this?"

"Your elbow. So what?"

"It's also where the funny bone is. If we bang our funny bones together. . . well, do I have to draw you a picture?"

I hated it when I bumped my funny bone into something. But surely Cecilia was making this up. Or her spirit guardian played a trick on her.

"You mean when my ulnar nerve bumps against my humerus bone?" For some reason talking about this made me uncomfortable, almost embarrassed.

"Now who's the egghead?"

"Fine. Have it your way. You'll see how absurd you are."

I maneuvered my elbow near hers, and pulled it back slightly to thrust into her elbow but good.

What happened next is hard to describe.

Imagine your entire being shimmering with orgasmic splendor. Every nerve of my anti-matter overflowed. I was at one with all desire. I'd call it an out-of-body experience if so doing were not redundant.

I saw Cecilia struggling to catch her breath, and that it did for her what it did for me. Intuitively we next tried what I guess you could call a form of mutual masturbation. I poked her funny bone with my fingers, while she did the same to mine. Our ghost bodies vibrated as I let out a great moan. Cecilia wailed a moment later.

"You sure do know your way around a funny bone," she said.

"You're not so bad yourself."

"I must asseverate that this was a highly pulchritudinous experience."

"Yeah, not too shabby."

For a while we both stared into space. I wondered what living relationships would be like if all you had to do was touch elbows. Surely things would be much less complicated. The current means for human copulation made all kinds of messes. But maybe it wouldn't change anything. Henry would've offended women by flashing them his elbow, and Dumont would've forced his assistants to . . . I dunno, maybe lick his elbow or bite it? And it would have the same emotional weight, which in these instances would be devastating.

Cecilia said, "So what does this mean?"

"What do you mean, 'So what does this mean?'"

She turned away from me in a huff.

"You just answered my question. Typical man. Ten seconds after it's over, you completely lose interest."

"Interest in what? We barely speak to each other."

Cecilia laughed with sarcasm.

"Let's do it one better and not speak to each other at all."

"It was your idea in the first place."

"Oh, like I had to twist your arm. Let's forget it ever happened. I am far too evolved a soul to need your melodrama."

"Cecilia—"

"I'm not speaking to you."

I didn't experience my usual relief when Cecilia stormed off. Was I so desperate for companionship that I craved Cecilia Puff, Ph.D., scholar of patriarchal Hanover House rhetoric?

No, I couldn't permit myself to think that way for even a moment. I hurried to the English Department, and entered Cecilia's former office. It had been emptied out. Even the desk was gone, as if she died of something contagious. And in a way she did, by virtue of the fact that everyone dies. Still, it struck me as very Elmer Butthead, to erase all suggestion of someone having existed, once they ceased to exist.

I didn't want my visit to prove a waste of time, so for want of knowing what else to do I emptied out the English Department's file cabinets, and threw all the files down the sewer.

I felt a little better, but not much.

Human 7

The president's office was on the ground floor of the ritzy, mock-Tudor house he got to live in rent-free for cutting the occasional ribbon. Walking across the campus green in the calm September sun, I made a point of standing in the pine grove I liked so well, with a conviction that it would be the last time I got to do so. I was certain the prick planned to fire me—for reporting Henry and Dumont's sex crimes, my accusation of murder, and/or having a heartfelt discussion with my students. Take your pick.

I might as well have been walking to my beheading. Yet the president's administrative assistant, Melinda Joshua, was the first person at Elmer Butthead who welcomed me the way I thought any newcomer should be welcomed. It was amazing how in just a few days, basic courtesy seemed like some dim, remembered Christmas from childhood. While Melinda's clothes and makeup said *I work for the president*, her casual manner and trendy black haircut said *I'm cool*—or at least by Elmer Butthead standards.

"So nice to meet you, Bentley." She shook my hand. "I hope we haven't struck you as too uncivilized so far."

I laughed, as did the three other people seated in the spacious waiting area, who likewise gave off a friendly vibe. I couldn't believe it—maybe there were okay people who worked at Elmer Butthead.

"So you're the notorious Bentley Gamble. I'm Leanne Moses. Film Studies." A woman prof extended her hand. I guessed her to be in her fifties. She wore her graying hair in a loose knot on top of her head, and her jeans and bulky sweater gave her a pleasant no-frills appearance. She reminded me of a middle-aged Katharine Hepburn.

The two other people introduced themselves: Janelle Waverly from Chemistry, and Horace Tweed from Folklore. Janelle had great red hair, a thick, wavy mane around her head. She wore a long, colorful dress. Horace was that rarity among the faculty, an actual African American. In his black leather jacket, he looked like a hip guy.

Unlike the psych faculty, they didn't hit you over the head with their research agendas. But as I learned over time, Leanne studied film noir murder mysteries, Horace studied the transition of true-life murder stories into folk legends, and forensic chemist Janelle wrote about fatal toxins that were difficult to trace. This gave us a common thread across disciplines, and in the ensuing years we'd talk about how one of these days we'd do a joint project on homicide.

"Blankenshit loves to keep you waiting," Janelle said.

I looked at Melinda, who added, "Don't worry, Bentley. You're among kindred spirits. Anyone who can make Blankenshit scream bloody murder after only a couple of days is okay in my book. Whatever you did, I hope you keep doing it."

So it was just as I feared. But given the irreverence of my present company, I tried to appear relaxed.

"We're hear to meet with him, too," said Horace. "Same old same old."

"We're the executive committee from Faculty Governance," Leanne explained. "Since I'm the biggest masochist of all, I get to be president. Every month we meet with His Royal Highness Blankenshit, and every month he keeps us waiting as long as possible."

"When we ask him afterwards to comment on our recommendations," Janelle said, "he says he can't remember meeting with us."

Melinda raised her right hand in mock oath. "I am witness to this. He's utterly incompetent, so naturally the Board of Directors worships the ground he walks on."

"What are some of your ideas?" I asked.

"Nothing much," Horace replied. "Just things like not laying off employees while he gives himself another raise."

"And running his own illegal publishing racket on the side," said Leanne. "But you look like such a nice boy. We shouldn't corrupt you."

"We have tenure, so try though he may to get rid of us, he's stuck." Janelle winked at me.

"Fear of lawsuits," said Horace. "We can't go public with anything, but we do what we can to make his life miserable in private."

"It must be nice to have tenure," I said. "I feel so vulnerable."

"If push comes to shove, threaten to sue," said Janelle. "You should be fine."

I felt a little less heavy inside.

"Thanks for the advice, guys."

"So how do you like the psychology department?" Leanne asked, in a manner that communicated she already knew the answer.

"It's . . . truly a unique experience."

They all laughed.

"That's good, keep your sanity and watch your back," said Horace. "When they fuck with you, stay cool. Dumont and Henry have this never-ending pissing contest, and the others—let's just say they're damaged goods. Must've had unhappy childhoods. Though I guess you'd know more about that as a psychologist."

"Not all faculty are like them," Melinda said. "Some are halfway human."

"It's worse than you may know," I said, and proceeded to share about Wicki and Dumont, and Dumont in general, and Henry with his flasher proclivities.

When I finished, everyone remained quiet for a minute.

Finally Janelle said, "I've heard rumors before. The way they've got it rigged around here, no one can do anything. But murder . . . That poor girl. Can you afford a lawyer?"

"No way."

"Maybe there's someone else who knew about her fear of heights," Melinda offered.

"Thank you for thinking of that," I said. "But they're psychologists. They can pull all kinds of rabbits out of their hats. And I'm guessing even the autopsy will be rigged."

"You've guessed right," said Horace. "The stories you hear about students—there was one a few years ago about a girl who supposedly disappeared."

"Well, Ben, at least you're a faster learner," Leanne said. "It took me a semester or two to catch on. I kept wondering what was wrong with me until I realized nothing was. This damn school drives you bat shit crazy."

Melinda's phone rang, but it wasn't the usual ring tone.

"It's His Majesty's special buzzer," she told me. "That means he's ready for you, Ben."

"Good luck, Bentley," said Horace. "Say as little as possible."

"Remember—lawsuit, lawsuit, lawsuit," added Janelle.

"Keep the faith," Leanne said.

With head held high, I strode into the president's suite. Besides the spacious main office with top of the line furnishings, there was a conference room and a tiny kitchenette. Quite a setup, considering he had his head sewn up his ass.

The photo of President Blankenshit on his emails proved misleading. He looked more gangster-like in person, with twitchy, nervous eyes and a sidelong way of talking, as if whispering to his mob lawyer. The prez and I shook hands and exchanged a couple of formal pleasantries before he led me to the conference room. He carried a crisp manila folder, which I assumed contained my death sentence. Maybe he didn't think I merited the honor of meeting in his main office. He claimed the seat at the head of the table, where the chair had armrests. I sat myself to his left in a humble, armless chair.

On the wall that faced me was a large framed photograph of the modest president himself. He wore runner's garb, and stood smiling at a finish line in a crowded public place.

"I see you're a runner," I said.

He laughed.

"Since high school, and I still make the time. Marathons. My personal best is twenty-six miles in four hours, twenty-seven minutes. Not bad for an old guy, wouldn't you say?"

"Not bad at all."

"Do you run?"

"Not lately. I used to play a lot of sports, but in grad school I got away from it."

He patted my arm, like we were old buddies.

"You can't let that happen. You need to stay in shape."

I cringed from his touch.

"I'll try to make the time."

He cleared his throat a few times, like a virtuoso at firing people doing his preparatory vocal exercises.

"Now then, Dr. Gamble, let us get right to the heart of the matter. It is obvious that you and the Elmer Butte College of the Liberal Arts are not the right fit. We are dismissing you effective immediately. We will pay you for half a semester of employment. It's nothing personal. It doesn't mean you are a bad person or a bad anthropologist. It's just that you are not the right anthropologist for us."

I could tell he had training in how to conduct what the genteel called an exit interview, as one might say "premature ejaculation." He even paused to let me absorb his words. I knew he'd fire me. But the reality of it happening on my third day because other people were criminals and/or cowards felt a hell of a lot worse than the mere theoretical possibility. Freudian cliché though it may be, it brought me right back to the unfairness of having to stay chained in the basement because Misty Rose said so. Once again my panic and rage—life's most unproductive emotional duo—felt like the only things that existed.

I said, "I'm a psychologist, not an anthropologist."

He did not acknowledge his error.

"The final nail in your coffin was how you conducted your class in direct violation of your terms of employment. From what I've gathered, students cried."

Where to start?

"They cried because they thought their friend committed suicide. I comforted them as best I could."

"Obviously, you did not succeed. Policies exist for a reason, Dr. Gamble. People far wiser than you put them into place. And your disaster of a class happened right on top of your threatening meeting with Student Success Director Crabb. You barged into her office without making an appointment, and proceeded to bully her."

"That's ridiculous. What did she say?" I wanted to add that if God can be contacted without an appointment, so can Emily Crabb, but my mind raced in too many directions at once.

"Director Crabb informed me that you threatened to go to the media in direct violation of university policy, unless we fired Dr. Dungworth. That's called blackmail, in case you didn't know."

"I never said that."

The jerk chuckled.

"Who should I believe—my trusted colleague of long standing, or you? Emily is savvy. She's dealt with much worse."

"I have a one-year renewable contract."

"You should've read the fine print. I can fire you any time I feel like it. I can do whatever I want." He leaned back in the chair with satisfaction, as if he ate an entire roast pig with an apple in its mouth.

I forced myself to remain calm.

"If I'm fired what's to stop me from going public?"

"Oh, I'd say a number of things. I'll ruin you, for starters. You'll be unemployable. We'll sue you from here to kingdom come. We'll say you're the one who behaved. . . questionably with a student. We'll say you're criminally insane from getting kidnapped as a child."

He looked down at his file to make sure he hadn't confused me with someone else.

"And I'll sue you right back."

"You'll be ruined just the same. And this is one case I'll make sure we win."

"And I'll ruin you right back. We both know Kimberly Ann Kulwicki was murdered. Just as we both know this meeting is about shutting me up."

I caught a flicker of panic in his eyes.

"Murdered? I hope you didn't share your lurid fantasy with your class."

"No, but I wanted to."

"Now I know more than ever it is best we let you go. You are mentally unbalanced. Paranoid. Please visit our psychology department before you leave campus, to get a referral for a good therapist."

"I'm *in* the psychology department."

"Oh, right. Funny I can't remember that for some reason. You know, I started here in the psychology department. I must have a mental block about it."

He faked a chuckle, but I could see his hands were shaking, and he started to sweat. He dabbed his forehead with a Kleenex.

"Dr. Gamble, it may not seem this way, but I am sympathetic. I'm guessing there was a suicide or tragic death in your past that you can't come to terms with. So now you have to twist our horrible suicide into a homicide. Am I right?'

"No, not at all."

"Then keep your paranoid fantasies to yourself. Or expect a major lawsuit."

"How uncanny that this conversation keeps coming back to lawsuits. Let's make it into a game. Every time one of us says, 'lawsuit,' the other one gets to. . . I dunno, maybe spray the other with seltzer? Punch him in the face?"

"Dr. Gamble, please let us remember we are in a professional setting."

"Tell that to Henry and Dumont. Henry exposes his dick to girls, while Dumont blackmails them to suck on his, and if they don't swallow the cum he makes them do it again. Is that what you'd call professional?"

Blankenshit pounded his fist on the table. His face turned red and then purple. You could see the veins in his forehead and temples as he foamed at the mouth.

"Do you realize you're talking about my golf buddies? I cannot let you slander good colleagues. Do you have any idea how much grant money they've brought in?"

"No, but none of that should matter."

He grabbed me by the T-shirt.

"I'm the one who decides what matters, not you. I thought there was something off kilter when you interviewed. You're not quite a real man, are you? You're a mama's boy, am I right?"

"I . . . I don't know what you mean."

As he let go of his grip, he laughed.

"You know exactly what I mean. It's people like you that need to be stopped. You make a mockery of everything important. You thought you could come here with your newfangled ways and upend the lives of highly respected senior faculty. Well, you can't, because I won't let you. I say what happens. I say what matters. Not some hippie drug addict pervert. This is my kingdom and you're nothing. You'll end up begging to eat dog shit by the time I'm done with you."

I spat in his face.

"You murdered her, didn't you? What kind of running shoes do you wear? Are they Great Lakes Runners? I'll bet they match the shoe prints in my photos. On the library steps. You know, the ones leading to the roof?"

As he wiped the spit off his face, he started panting, as if he just ran a marathon. His eyes were red with tiny blood vessels.

"You are not going to ruin me with your . . . your . . ."

"You mean the truth?"

"She was nothing. Nothing. I am. . . I'm important, damn it. I say what happens, not some. . . not some traumatized. . . little fuck like you. Or her."

"You're insane. I wish you'd drop dead!"

You know what they say: If wishes were horses, beggars would ride. Once in awhile life seems predestined, and this was one such occasion.

All at once, he gasped for air as he stood up. Something about him seemed ready to explode in the literal sense.

"I . . . I can't see very well. My head hurts."

I slipped into instant Boy Scout mode. I hated this SOB, but I didn't want anyone accusing me of depraved indifference. Besides, I didn't think it my place to decide when someone died. That's what separated me from people like Blankenshit himself.

"I'll call 911."

"Yes, please . . . do it right away. I feel so strange."

I reached in my pocket for my cell phone, only it wasn't there. "Shit, I must've left my phone in Rayana's office. I'll run and—"

He collapsed, falling backwards in his chair, landing with a hard thud. His face went from purple to pale blue as he struggled to breathe.

I ran to the main office, and said in a loud voice, "Call 911. He collapsed. I think he's having a heart attack."

Melinda was munching a pear. "Oh, so that's what we heard go plop."

She and the three faculty quickly exchanged glances; Melinda tossed the pear core in a wastebasket and rubbed a bit of antibacterial in her hands.

"I'll check on him," she said. "He has super-high blood pressure."

"I'll go with you," Horace and Janelle said at the same time,. The three walked to the conference room, but I thought it odd that they did not run.

"Relax, Bentley," Leanne said. "We have it covered."

"Are you going to call?"

"Eventually, I suppose."

I lunged for the phone on Melinda's desk, but Leanne grabbed it first.

"Relax, Bentley."

"You mean this has happened before? You mean—?"

Melinda, Janelle and Horace came out of the conference room sporting magnificent grins.

"He's dead," Horace said. "You should've seen him. He couldn't talk but he gestured with his hand for us to help him."

Janelle burst out laughing.

"He was such a pig. He cornered me and felt me up when I first came here. I know he saw me as he took his last breath. He knew we were glad. The son of a bitch. The motherfucker."

Overcome with joy, Leanne ran to hug them all.

"Why, this is wonderful," she said. Then she looked at me. "C'mon, Bentley. Group hug."

"Uh, sure." We hugged for a few seconds.

"You must be our lucky charm," Melinda said, as we broke away. "We've dreamt of this moment for years."

"Yeah, but he died. How can you be so happy?"

"Such a babe in arms," said Leanne. "The fuck was going to fire you and ruin your life. And you're telling me you miss him? That you're sorry he's gone?"

"I wouldn't go that far, but still, someone just died."

Leanne made a dismissive gesture with her hand. "You know the old saying. Ya live, ya screw people over, ya die."

"I know of at least one faculty member he drove to suicide," Horace said.

"C'mon, be honest, Bentley," Janelle said. "Fate handed you a break on a silver platter."

"I have access to his email and computer calendar," Melinda interjected. "I'll destroy any paper trail about canning you."

I thought for a few crucial seconds. No one in psych knew I'd been called to the president's office . . .

"Well, I have to admit, it's nice to have a job. Even if it is this one."

They all laughed some more.

"I have a feeling we're going to get along fine," Horace said. "Obviously, not a word to anyone."

"Uh, yeah. Obviously." The struggle inside myself when truth and falsehood vied for my allegiance was normal, but this was a no-brainer. As for Wicki's murderer . . . for now I'd keep it to myself. I'd save it for another time when it could do the most good. Which in terms of Elmer Butthead meant when it could do the most harm. Wicki's killer confessed and died. I hoped that wherever she was, she felt a bit of peace. As for me, I learned on that auspicious afternoon that in addition to an impressive record of publications and strong teaching evaluations, it never hurt to have something you can blackmail your university with when you go up for tenure.

"So there were a few seconds or so in which you could've called for help?"

Horace started to say something, but Leanne—who never went into the conference room—spoke first.

"It wouldn't have mattered."

"What about CPR?"

"Could you really live with yourself if you saved him?" Horace asked. "He ruined so many people's lives."

Melinda twirled around the room.

"I can't believe I'll never have to look at him again or hear his whiny voice or jab him with my elbow when he tries to touch me or type his King Shit letters or send out his stupid emails for him. I can't describe how free I feel."

I had to admit their glee was contagious. It didn't say much for Elmer Butthead if the most virtuous act I'd witnessed thus far was letting some asshole homicidal president die. But Elmer Butthead housed a never-ending war of sorts, and like any war it changed how you thought about life.

"We should vamoose," said Leanne. "Through the side door where no one will see."

"I'll call the police and the Board in minute or two," Melinda told us.

Ghost 8

While Cecilia was off doing what she did best—hating my guts—and Elaine for whatever reason chose not to appear, I made half-baked efforts to solve the case. I found it more and more difficult to concentrate on the murders. Becoming a ghost resembled becoming a vampire, in that some new molecular strain took over the essence of your being. With each second, I could feel my post-life urge to destroy grow in intensity.

But my detached, egghead nature continued to enjoy aha moments, and this kept me thinking at least a little about who took my life. I needed to get beyond the mental mush of conceptualizing that each department member was equally capable of homicide. Full profiles of each individual were needed, and to do this I needed their fat personnel files. I'd been curious about these files for years, anyway—including my own. Best of all, acquiring them meant doing something subversive.

The files were locked in a metal cabinet in the main office, but since I could walk through walls I could also stick my hand into locked drawers. Though uncommon for anyone to be hanging around the psych department in the summer, I decided to go there late at living entities' night, just in case. I didn't want anyone seeing drawers opening and files being removed without also seeing a human body.

I walked through the police tape and the sawhorse barriers, and the door of the main pysch office. But as my silent, invisible self entered, I saw that I had company.

Boris's wife Jamie, dressed in rather clichéd black pants, turtleneck and gloves, opened the file cabinet from a ring of keys that I assumed her husband gave her. Leave it to the local cops to be too dumb or polite to confiscate Boris's key ring. Finding the file she wanted, she padded to the door and locked it behind herself. I watched as she maneuvered her way through the police tape and saw horses.

Alone in the office, I looked inside the cabinet and experienced little surprise upon noticing that Boris's file had been taken. Elaine herself said Boris didn't kill me, so I assumed the file contained something that suggested he *did* kill me. He remained accused of my murder alone, and I remained certain he didn't kill anyone else. But what if the cops, in their stupidity, thought otherwise?

While on the subject of stupidity, it occurred to me that I shouldn't let Jamie la-de-da walk away with the file. I needed to learn why she stole it.

Though I couldn't fly, I could jump pretty far, so I took off after her. I had to catch up before she got too far away from Elmer Butthead, given my ghostly confinement. I didn't see Jamie at either end of the hallway, so I figured she'd be outside—and if smart, crouching like a cat to her car in the so-called secret alleyway behind Lab Hall.

I guessed right. I saw Jamie, folder in hand, sneaking in the dark alley toward a hatchback draped in shadows. I knew it would frighten her to have an invisible force take the file but I didn't know how else to get it.

I leapt forward as far as I could.

At that same moment, Jamie climbed into her car with the folder. I slipped into her backseat, unnoticed. As she turned on the ignition and backed out, I knew I had only a few seconds before I'd get dumped to the ground by cosmic forces. It reminded me of wearing an ankle monitor.

I lunged for the folder that lay on the passenger side of the front seat. I had it.

Then I fell out of the car and onto the blacktop.

The folder remained with Jamie.

Shit and oh well, I'd have to work without it. Maybe someone else's folder contained something about Boris.

As I made my way back to the main office, I decided to read my own file first. Anyone who claims they're more interested in others than the self is a liar. What I read did not bode well where my own affectphobia tendencies were concerned. Though I started out as "shy and considerate," over time the department found me "intimidating, uncooperative, condescending and short-tempered." But I chose not to linger in Self Flagellation Land. I had bigger fish to fry.

I worked alphabetically on the remaining files. Though I didn't expect any surprises from Dumont Dungworth's file, I gave it a glance.

The file proved worth the effort. I learned that, contrary to what lowly people such as myself had been taught to believe, Dumont had been charged with rape as an undergrad, and again as a grad student. In the first instance, charges were dropped because the victim backed down. The second time he claimed the sex was consensual, and the case petered out for lack of evidence. The kicker was that the Elmer Butthead bigwigs knew about Dumont's past but hired him anyway. From what I could piece together between the lines, Dumont threatened to sue if Elmer Butthead didn't hire him, because he never had been convicted of a crime.

It occurred to me that one of the biggest clumps of dirt Elmer Butthead feared from Wicki was Dumont's story coming out in the wash. The public would know that the school let itself be bullied into hiring a sex offender. Thus, it had all the more reason to silence her. And as long as her death got called a suicide, no one need poke around any further. Dumont knew I harbored animosity about Wicki's death, and since my behavior became less controllable over time, he may have preferred me dead.

Rayana Gluck's file revealed one oddity. The bossy, sexist father to whom she stood up died after a long illness when she was all of five years old. Maybe she never forgave him for dying. Or on a gut level she didn't distinguish him from substitute father figures; she'd had at least two stepfathers. If Rayana were more fucked up than assumed, she confused many people with her mythical father. Certainly she never stopped being frightened of me. Something in my nature made it harder for her to live her lies.

I knew little of Millie Sauerbraten-Zwieback's past. She kept herself far too busy lecturing us on wombats to bother with her life before she married Henry the Flasher. I will say I thought it weird when women hyphenated their last names when a) their husbands didn't and b) they took on not only their father's last name but also their husband's, and c) thought this double-patrilineal end product had something to do with feminism. But then, I never understood how someone sharp as Millie lived with so much denial over Henry.

Her file contained a curious element, or rather a conspicuous absence. Many years ago, Elmer Butthead conducted a routine request for her grad school transcripts, and they never manifested. Over the years, lack of proof of her credentials got lost amidst countless other forms and files. Since Henry's father gave big bucks to Elmer Butthead, maybe this husband-wife team got hired at the same time with few questions asked. And Millie herself felt kind of blackmailed once she learned the truth about her husband. Bye-bye Henry, bye-bye career. She did an endless tap dance of sorts to distract people away from the truth about not only her husband but also herself. Any disgust she felt about her marriage or career had to stay buried.

Moving on to your friend and mine, Dr. Sidney Steenrod, I learned that her famous tale of being the hated valedictorian could not have been true. Her high school transcript revealed that she got a D- in, of all things, psychology. (Her other grades were good but not exceptional.) I wondered if even in high school she got into arguments with the teacher over what she found to be the innate sexism in the discipline. But a D- is still a D-, and she'd pontificated this valedictorian fabrication for so long maybe she forgot it never happened. Her parents' status as academics may have helped her get into graduate school.

Yet all this paled when compared with what else I discovered.

Sidney had been in treatment centers numerous times over the years for bulimia. She tended to wear loose-fitting, asexual clothing, but not as a political statement. She didn't want any of us to see that at four feet eleven inches she weighed seventy pounds on a decadent day. Taking her own rhetoric literally, she herself struggled with society's expectations for women, as opposed to being the valiant, take-no-prisoners crusader against all things sexist. And since she had cause versus effect bungled up in her mind, who could say if she had any conscience at all? Perhaps murder by design made sense to her, given how she tried to extricate herself from her own feelings of inadequacy.

As much as Phyllis Willis loved to gossip, she either didn't know or chose not to tell me about Sidney's issues. Or maybe Phyllis realized she had enough to think about just keeping herself in check. For all the time she spent discussing her brutish truck-driving father, she neglected to mention said father murdered her mother. Ten-year-old Phyllis had to watch as he banged his wife's head against the wall until she stopped breathing. You don't need a fancy college degree to realize how traumatizing that must have been. So much so, in fact, that in all the years she went on about how lousy men were, she could not go near her own pain. When people subvert these experiences, the mishmash manifests in destructive ways.

But then you already knew that from watching TV.

Primal fear, extreme resentment—a veritable Crayola box of fucked-up emotions could have spurred her on to do all sorts of fun things, including murder.

I did not expect anything new from Henry Zwieback's file, and with one exception my hunch proved correct: his father, Henry Sr., had been protecting Henry Jr. for much longer and much more extensively than I realized. The first time he got arrested for indecent exposure occurred at age eighteen, and the girl he targeted had all of nine years of life experience. Later there had been what a local police detective called a "suspicious" cash gift of 50 grand that Henry Sr. made to none other than our late great President Blankenshit. The matter got dropped in a hurry, since Henry Sr. unofficially owned the town, but certainly his son knew about it. Golf buddies make strange bedfellows . . .

As I made each discovery I experienced the ghost equivalent to elation, which resembled what the living called sadism. Not the kinky bedroom stuff of Harvey and Madge, but a cool and smooth sensation of deriving joy from harming the living.

Human 8

A few hours after I almost got fired, the entire campus received an email from the President of the Board of Directors telling us that Blankenshit croaked. The phony baloney all but made it sound like Jesus got nailed to the cross:

Dear Elmer Butte family,

It is with the heaviest of hearts that I inform you of the sudden passing of our beloved President Dr. Hoover Blankenship. He died of heart failure today shortly after 12 noon. I am sure our thoughts will be with his last ex-wife Hortense at this difficult time. For nearly fifteen years, my good friend Hoover led our community judiciously and collegially, always living up to the EBLCA motto, "Students First." He also was a great golf partner who had one heck of a ¾ swing. Further information will be forthcoming as to an EBLCA memorial tribute, as well as the appointment of an acting president.

So the fuckhead did die of a heart attack—or so it appeared at the time. As I replayed those crucial seconds in my mind, I convinced myself that even if someone called 911 it would've been too late.

However, the fact that I spat in Blankenshit's face troubled me. I never let my emotions get so out of control before. Also, in the event that they did an autopsy at some point in the future, traces of my DNA could show up, and I'd have to account for it. Losing my cool led to nothing good, and I determined to make sure it never happened again.

As for his last ex-wife Hortense, I later heard she divorced him for the same reason her five predecessors had: She tired of his having affairs with students, staff and faculty.

(Though I supposed, per the Elmer Butthead motto, he put
students first.) It didn't take a genius to conclude that all
these women engaged in such antics because they had no
choice, since no reasonable standards qualified Blankenshit as
eye candy. I also ran across an underground tale of a student
found murdered. Nothing could be proven, but. . .

The psych department lowlifes saw Blankenshit's death
as an obligation to appear gallant with grief, as if life were
play-acting and here was a golden opportunity to perform the
fake, pompous, one-dimensional behavior they lived for.
Henry began a putrid email thread thusly:

Dear Psychology colleagues,

I cannot express my shock at the sudden
passing of my esteemed friend and golf partner
Hoover Blankenship. I am calling an emergency
meeting in one hour to discuss how we might best
honor Hoover's legacy. Perhaps we could establish a
research event or student prize in his honor. As you
know, he began his distinguished career as a
psychology professor here at EBCLA.

Sincerely yours,
Henry Zwieback, Chair

I thought there should be a horror movie called *It Came
From the Psychology Department*. Henry's missive received a
quick follow-up from Sidney, which read in part:

We should start with sending flowers to
Hortense. Boris can take care of this. The card
should be signed, "With love from the psychology
department."

No sooner had this email been sent than did Rayana
reply to it:

A message of sympathy should not be signed
with love, especially given that Hortense has long
been divorced. I know her well, and she would be

unhappy unless the card read: "With sympathy from the psychology department."

This inspired Sidney to write:

I know Hortense at least as well if not better than you. She is a kind, loving person, and would very much appreciate us sending our shared sentiment of love. "Sympathy" is old fashioned. I love Hortense and we all do and that's what we should tell her.

Rayana answered back:

Yes we all love Hortense, and that is why we should not make her feel awkward. It is obvious, Sidney, that as always you are singling me out for unnecessary criticism, but I shall not stoop to your level. It is not my fault that you project your glaring inadequacies onto me.

Sidney stated:

Rayana, you are in serious need of professional help. I feel sorry for you. It must be difficult being such a horrible person. The department will share its deep and abiding love for Hortense, and that's all there is to it.

Some naiveté lingered in my soul after three days at Elmer Butthead, so I thought I found an easy, King Solomon-like fix to the problem:

Hi everybody,

It sounds like there are some strong opinions here, which is a good thing because it shows how much people care. Let's sign the card with love *and* sympathy, and then everyone will be happy.

Ben

I received the following reply from Sidney:

Bentley, you do not see what is at stake here. People with nothing but love in their hearts are being told that they cannot express it. Love should not and will not be compromised.

Then Rayana weighed in:

I deeply resent the implication that I feel anything but love in this instance. Such accusations are uncalled for and are highly unprofessional. Yes, there is a principle at stake, and that principle is to act with love toward Hortense by sending her our sympathy.

To keep things humming along, Henry sent an email solely to me:

Bentley,

As Department Chair I must say that you are overstepping your boundaries through your feeble effort to resolve a situation that rightfully should be resolved by me. It is pathetically obvious that your true intention is to self-promote, as if you are above it all, and let me tell you, that is far from the case. If you do this again I will report you to the administration for insubordination.

Henry

A few seconds later, he sent a message to the department:

Esteemed Colleagues,

I think there's a good way to solve this minor difference of opinion. And that is to sign the card with love *and* sympathy. Then everyone is happy. Boris, please proceed accordingly, using the department E-Z charge account #723242-62215, and not -62248.

Boris replied:

No problem, Henry. I'll get right on it. As always I am impressed by your wisdom in solving differences of opinion. I already miss President Blankenship.

I thought this suck-up message to be Boris' way of winking at me. But I felt all the more nervous about Henry.

At the time, I thought it inexcusable that people would send such hateful emails over such small matters, especially people who claimed to be intelligent. I vowed never to get involved in these matters again. If you told me that one day I'd be sending equally bad emails and worse, I would've thought you were nuts. Hadn't I survived Misty Rose at age six? I was sure I could rise above petty college politics.

But then again, maybe not.

As the cherry on top of the sundae of shit, LMAC emailed the entire Elmer Butthead community. I found myself reading the properly typed words with her distinctive drawl:

Dear Students, Staff and Faculty,

I cannot bring myself to believe that Hoover Blankenship is gone. The Office of Student Success was but one of many of his achievements, for which all of us shall always be grateful. He was hands down one of the finest men I ever had the privilege to know. Let us channel our grief into doing what our late President would have wanted: putting our students first.

Sincerely,
Dr. Emily Crabb, Director
Office of Student Success

Everyone wore long faces to the emergency department meeting, as if their best friend died. Like teenagers in the school cafeteria, we all took our same seats from the day before. I tried to blend in with the pervasive pseudo-grief.

As soon as Henry called the meeting to order, Dumont raised his hand. "I move that we start an annual tradition of the Hoover Blankenship Psychology Major Research Award, or HBPMRA. The student that has the best research project will receive a one thousand dollar prize."

"I second the motion," Millie said. "Our department, under Henry's leadership, always must lead the way at EBCLA."

After the motion passed without opposition, Phyllis asked, "Who should be on the committee?" I could tell she said this because she wanted to be on it. She had a childish fear of being left out of anything.

Dumont replied, "Well, three people make a committee, so I make a motion that the members be our junior-most faculty—Rayana, Sidney, and Bentley. Since everyone else is busy with other work, I nominate Bentley to be the chair."

There was a brief yet profound exchange of eye contact between Dumont, Henry and myself. I saw this as a scheme to get even with me, their way of saying, *If you think you're so great at conflict resolution, here you are.* I started to say something, but Millie cut me off.

"I second the motion," she said.

I abstained, but the motion got five aye votes and passed. At the time, I determined to show Henry that I indeed could keep conflict to a minimum. How bad could it be to work with Rayana and Sidney? Or, as I later would've said, how bad could it be to be thrown into a crater of volcanic lava?

Phyllis said, "It must be hard for you, Ben, to face such sad news on only your third day. You're still feeling your way around. So if chairing the committee gets to be too much, my door is always open for advice. In fact, if it really gets to be too much for you, I'll gladly take over."

As the brief meeting broke up, I told Sidney and Rayana I would email them to set a convenient time to meet.

Rayana said, "You mean we will email each other."

"Yes," agreed Sidney. "We are all equal, chair or no chair. This is not about seizing power, Bentley."

"Keep your patriarchal power trip to yourself," said Rayana. "Sidney and I are good friends, and we look out for each other."

"Sorry," I forced myself to say. "We'll email each other."

"Men are so condescending," said Sidney. "We'll do this, we'll do that."

"But you just said—" Something told me not to continue. "Never mind."

"Don't worry, Bentley," Phyllis, having listened, said. "You'll learn."

The memorial service was held the following morning in the campus theater. I spied Leanne, Janelle, and Horace seated together in the back. Horace gave me the peace sign, and I returned the gesture. Neither Hortense nor any of Blankenshit's ex-wives were there, nor were any of the (legitimate) children he fathered. The board president told us they were all "grieving in a private way." After he droned on for an eternity, we listened to LMAC, and then Henry—who managed to keep his dick inside his pants. Next came the usual moment of silence, followed by a vocal from a girl who sang about as well as a hippopotamus could ride a surfboard.

Then came the lollapalooza. The board president said that in an emergency session the board of directors—or should I say the BOD?—voted to appoint Dr. Enoch LePutois, VP of Curricular Advancement, the new Acting President of our college. The last name was pronounced "Lay-poo-toys," I assumed to avoid association with the original French "Lay-poo-twah," which meant "the skunk." As I quickly learned, he already got called "Stinky" behind his back, which nickname would become evermore used, since he indeed stank as a president, not to mention as a human being.

When the board president announced the new appointment, someone in the theater—Leanne, I think—cried out, "Oh my God, not Stinky, anyone but Stinky." It was not proper etiquette for a memorial service, but people can take only so much BS. Stinky looked like the aging, snooty Ivy Leaguer he was, as if he were his biggest fan. Students made mincemeat of trying to pronounce his name, but he had so little contact with them it didn't matter.

Following the honest outburst of incredulity, Cecelia Puff, the English professor I met on my first day, stood up and said, "Colleagues, let us conduct ourselves in a dignified manner as academics, especially in the presence of our board president. Let us remember that everything happens for a reason, and embrace this new gift."

In that moment, I knew I hated Cecilia.

The board president harrumphed and went on to explain: "Dr. LePutois has an outstanding record of accomplishment as Vice President of Curricular Advancement, so the board is honored to appoint him." Leanne, Janelle and Horace all stood up and chanted, "What accomplishments?" But they were not recognized. I wondered what the Vice-President of Curricular Advancement did. I guessed he did nothing, but what did I know?

Stinky took the podium, and you'd think that at least in his first remarks as our new prez he'd say something conciliatory. But he had his own agenda, and managed to make a lot of new enemies in only a couple of minutes:

"We have lost President Blankenship, but there is nothing to be gained by dwelling in the past. For my first act as your new president, I will be making serious budget cuts. It is what the late President Blankenship would've wanted. I expect faculty in particular to do the jobs they are paid to do and not behave as if they are administrators. I run a tight ship, and tolerate no shenanigans. That being said, I hope we work together to preserve EBCLA's impeccable reputation and traditions while increasing revenue through higher enrollment rates and raising tuition by twenty-five percent."

United as the three musketeers, my trio of new friends left the room in a huff.

As I learned in the ensuing days and weeks, the three of them, plus a few other faculty, formed the nucleus of righteous rebellion at Elmer Butthead. They spoke up at meetings and refused to produce pointless reports. Unlike lucky me, their home departments were not peopled with the criminally insane, so they took on many a battle without burning themselves out.

At the other end of the spectrum were neurotic professors like Cecilia Puff who remained oblivious to what was happening, because everything in life had to be pleasant all the time. In their delusional state, they saw Elmer Butthead as a kind of miniature world peace. Some people don't get that a *miniature* world peace is an oxymoron that ignores the realities that makes world peace impossible. It's pretty easy to think world peace is just around the corner when no one is dropping a bomb on your house.

These do-gooders often were women, though people like Janelle and Leanne thought they were idiots. But some token male faculty trafficked within this crowd, presumably to get laid. These alleged sensitive New Age men were about as convincing in their feminist sensibilities as Henry or Dumont, but no one noticed or cared. I must say that for supposed brilliant women, it didn't take much to pull the wool over their eyes. I'd watch men treat them like shit, but then the men would say something like, "The U.S. is more oppressive to women than any country in history," or "The sight of a street person makes me cry," and Cecilia and her ilk fell for it every time. (If there were any non-straight faculty, it would've been news to me. Anyone who deviated from the straight and narrow would've stayed in the closet—if not the bomb shelter.)

The psych faculty took one side and then the other, depending on the matter at hand. But they spent most of their time together, as if they could never get their fill of psychodrama and dysfunction.

In an effort to concentrate on something positive, I decided to create a new course. To do so required departmental approval, but I assumed, that for all our department got wrong, it would not stop a colleague from pursuing a topic of interest. Starting with Misty Rose—when I sometimes saw or thought I saw strange things in the dark—I adopted some superstitious beliefs over the years. Like many people, I checked my daily horoscope, and I thought that reports of ghost sightings or other such matters could be true. Psychology was a science, and like all sciences it had its roots in religion and metaphysics. Putting it all together, I thought a course called "Psychology and Metaphysics" would prove interesting. It would explore the paradoxes of science and belief.

After I presented the proposal, you'd have thought I suggested a course called, "Let's Chop Off People's Heads in Real Life." What is interesting in hindsight is how the criticisms of the proposal were much more about me than the course material.

As I believe I reported earlier, Dumont thought I intended this proposal to be a hostile gesture, rebellion for the sake of stirring the pot. Henry seconded this sentiment, and added, "Ben, where does your intellect go sometimes? This is nearly as silly as when you thought that Kimberly Ann Kulwicki got murdered."

Henry's boldness startled me. Just when I thought he couldn't sink any lower, he zapped me every time.

"Is that true, Ben?" Phyllis said. "You thought Wicki got murdered? That's the first I've heard of it."

"Same here," said Sidney, doubling—or should a I say tripling?—the lie.

"Really, Ben. Murder?" Millie added. "You need to get your head shrunk as soon as possible. Remind me to invite you to my classes when we discuss paranoia."

"If there had been a murder, don't you think the police would've done something about it?" asked Rayana. "Or for that matter, our administration? In addition to talk therapy, you might consider medication. Anything that will help with your negativity."

Ghost 9

I figured I might as well sneak a look at the files of
Leanne Moses, Janelle Watson and Horace Tweed, since they
knew at least something and possibly quite a lot. This
required my slipping unnoticed into the film studies,
chemistry and folklore departments, respectively. Doing so
made for quite a trek across campus in the middle of the
human night, but it satisfied my ghostly nature to make my
anti-presence felt amidst so much silence. I thought flowers
and trees were prettier at night anyway, since to my ghost
eyes they appeared lit up.

Those departments were not taped off, and I felt clean
and free of chaos upon entering each one. I must confess to
experiencing a touch of envy. I used to wonder what it would
be like to work in a normal atmosphere, like a starving child
staring into a bakery. Death did little to alter this sensation. I
suppose Henry would've called it a conditioned response.

All three files were thick with tales of near-lawsuits and
termination threats. But, as I expected, I found no dirty
laundry. None of them had anything to hide. They wore their
troublemaker labels as badges of honor.

Leanne, as I already knew, was a grandmother who spent
summers with her extended family in Paris. She wanted to
bring students with her to study French cinema. The big
shots wouldn't allow it. Leanne fought this decision and lost,
which led to some scathing emails, but she got over it.

Other than her typical run-ins with the administration,
Janelle's main issue with Elmer Butthead had been its refusal
to pay for new laboratory equipment, though in the end the
purchase got straightened out in her favor. Horace had a wife
and a daughter, and though there had been a mix-up at one
point with his health insurance covering his daughter but not
his wife, the confusion had been short-lived.

No one ever suspected the president's administrative assistant, Melinda Joshua, of any wrongdoing, but I figured I should check her file, too.

Walking from the main campus to the President's house reminded me of walking from the gardens at Versailles to the palace. I knew I had to be extra-silent—if there is such a thing—because the current president Kingsley "Asshole" Shufflebottom would be asleep. He lived there with his dull wife, Ann (I think), and toy poodle, Valentine. She wore a little pink bow in her curly white forehead—I'm talking about Valentine, not Ann—and snarled at most people, but liked me. I got the impression that this bothered Ann for some unfathomable reason. Maybe since her putrid husband provided the only other companionship in her life, she felt threatened when a rival for her dog's affection appeared.

As I stood before the grim front door in the dark (or for me, whiteness like a blank sheet of paper), I thought about the first time I came to this house to meet with Blankenshit. Over the past seven years, so much had changed—though in a different way, everything stayed the same. Elmer Butthead trudged onward, immune to positive development. Even my being a ghost was the same old same old, depending on how you looked at it.

I stepped inside, and made my way to Melinda's office, where her personnel file would've been kept. (For years I thought it odd that secretaries had access to their files although faculty didn't. But since when did anything make sense at Elmer Butthead?)

As I entered the room, to my surprise the lights were turned on, and Melinda was at her desk. Stacks of files surrounded her. No doubt Shuffle-Ass gave her extra work so that she'd have a shitty summer. Valentine lay curled on the floor next to her, watching everything Melinda did as though it would culminate in getting a doggie treat.

The dog spotted me, and wore a big smile as she barked. I made a shushing gesture with my finger to my mouth and reached down to pet her. I loved being with dogs, even ones with cloying pink bows, plus I didn't want to create any weirdness where Melinda was concerned. Valentine rolled on her back to let me tickle her tummy. She licked my fingers in the trade-off.

Melinda looked up from her computer tab. I stopped petting Valentine, which made her bark, so I petted her some more.

"Oh my God, Bentley Gamble!"

Melinda wore a huge smile, like she won a trip around the world on a game show.

"Um, uh . . . yeah, it's me. More or less."

She leapt over to me. Her hug had such enthusiasm I could almost feel it. I did my best to hug her back.

"You're not scared?" I asked, as she sat back down at her desk.

Melinda gazed at me in wonderment.

"All my life I've seen ghosts—I hope it's okay to use that word—and I know you'd never harm me. So why be scared?"

I suffered disappointment.

"You're not even a little scared?"

She wore a shrewd expression.

"Okay, maybe a little. I will say you're the first ghost I've talked to or touched. Usually I just wave at them. Sometimes they wave back."

"You've never mentioned this before." Valentine scratched my leg. I scooped her up in my arms, and she gazed at me like a baby.

"Of course I haven't. Everyone would think I'm nuts."

"Have any of them been. . . you know, like, from Elmer Butthead?"

Melinda laughed.

"No, you're the first one from this dump. And no, I haven't the faintest idea why. But you're in good company. I can tell the ghosts I see are benevolent. It's a gut level thing."

"The life beyond would be a better place if more people thought like you. How often do you see ghosts?"

Valentine wore a pleading expression that indicated she didn't like sharing my attention with someone else.

Melinda tapped her chin in thought.

"On average, I'd say about once a month. Sometimes it's hard to tell if I'm seeing the same one again—they can be a little fuzzy—but yeah, give or take, about every four weeks I see something. Or should I say someone?"

I couldn't help being intrigued.

"How old were you when this started?"

She laughed. "Are you going to psychoanalyze me?"

"Do I look like a shrink?"

"No, can't say that you do. To answer your question, since my fourth birthday. I remember it so clearly. As I blew out the candles, I saw a ghost standing behind my father."

"What was it doing?"

The dog closed her eyes in ecstasy as I scratched her under the chin.

"The ghost was a she. She clapped and smiled like everyone else. I remember she had buckteeth. Then she vanished. I told my folks about it that evening, and since I wasn't at all scared, they thought I was being cute. They said it would be our secret, and not to tell anyone else."

"Then what happened?"

"Nothing much. I mentioned it a few more times, until finally they said it wasn't funny anymore, and to stop talking about it. So I kept it to myself. Except for a boyfriend who turned out to be a shit, but I'd rather not go there."

In a gregarious mood, I said, "Then this is a momentous occasion for you, too." Valentine wiggled as if to say she wanted me to put her down, and nothing appealed to her less than my holding her.

"Yeah, I guess it is." Melinda walked back to her desk as Valentine scampered out of the room.

"So what brings you to this neck of the woods?"

I thought for a moment.

"I suppose there's no harm in telling you. But not a word to anyone. Not even the three musketeers."

"Of course."

I told her I wanted to finish the job I started and find the murderer. I didn't mention Elaine because if I did the deal would be off the table, and I didn't mention Cecilia because I had better things to do. Melinda never liked the bitch anyway. It's strange how even in death I had to be selective in what I said. I wondered if in Heaven you finally got to tell the truth, though given the usual nature of the truth maybe it cropped up more in Hell.

When I finished, Melinda asked, "So you're here to look at my file?

"Not to to insult you, but ever since Blankenshit—"

"Say no more, I get it." She walked to the cabinet and took out her file.

"Live it up. By the way, can I get you anything? Coffee, an English muffin?"

"Thanks for asking, but we ghosts don't eat or drink. It's bad for our health."

"I've always wondered about that. Do you . . . That is to say, can you. . .?"

"Do you mean go to the bathroom?"

"No. That wouldn't make sense since you don't eat or drink."

"Do you mean sleep?"

"No, but you're getting warm."

"Oh, you mean sex. Trust me, the less said the better."

Melinda's file had little to offer. She graduated high school and finished a two-year program at a local business college to become an administrative assistant. She'd worked at Elmer Butthead for fifteen years, and planned to retire in fifteen more. Her emergency contact person was her older brother, who did some freelance landscaping for Elmer Butthead every spring. Melinda lived in one of the nicer apartment complexes in town; it had a view of a lake. In the seven years I knew her, she had three successive relationships, none of which resulted in cohabitation. But she had a fatalistic outlook about such things.

Even as a ghost, I couldn't understand how someone could be happy with so little. There were people she didn't like—witness Blankenshit—yet they never seemed to spoil her mood. Like Boris, she knew something about life I didn't. Or maybe I used to know it but forgot it after working at Elmer Butthead, and even my ghostly mind failed to retrieve it. I couldn't tell anymore.

"You're clean," I said. "Except for . . . Well, you know what I mean. And that doesn't count."

"I'm disappointed. You mean you've never suspected me of poisoning—"

"Face it, Melinda, you're one of those pitable souls destined to be a good person."

In a playful gesture, she ran her fingers through her Louise Brooks bangs.

"Ugh. And here I thought myself a creature of danger and mystery."

She told me about a useless, tedious summer project the esteemed president dumped on her—just as I suspected. I answered more questions about how I spent my time as a ghost, and she showed me an asinine memo the board of directors sent out concerning our college's "excessive communication." Just looking at the document made me glad that I no longer had to deal with such bullshit.

"You're looking well, Ben," Melinda said. "I know it must sound bizarre, but you seem more relaxed. More. . . I dunno, more yourself. I can't explain it."

I wondered if I agreed with her assessment. Frankly, since I died I hadn't engaged in much self-reflection.

"I suppose I should say thanks for the compliment." I added, "You look well, too." I didn't mention her blue skin and white hair.

"You're saying that to be polite. I've been working on this garbage for ten hours straight. I can't look anything but fucked, and I don't mean in a good way."

That amused me, so I chuckled a little. When ghosts laugh, it sounds like someone screaming after falling off a cliff.

"It's funny how things work out. Just when you think there couldn't possibly be a worse president than the current one, the next one finds a way to make the last one seem not so bad."

Melinda sighed.

"Maybe we're cursed. We do have more than our fair share of. . . you know, people not living so long."

"Hmm, cursed. You could be on to something. I'll see what I can find out."

"Yes, please do. And drop by again. Make it soon."

For the first time in I-don't-know-how-long I felt validated by a human being. I got an extra jolt of jazziness when I jumped people in the park.

I couldn't care less what happened to Kingsley Shufflebottom. But I did care about Valentine and Melinda and had nothing against Ann (if that was her name), so I waited for a Sunday when no one was around to set the President's house on fire. Next, I went into the custodial building and got a container of toxic waste, which I emptied into the swimming pool. Then I destroyed the president's so-called extra car—a BMW—with a baseball bat.

Human 9

Ah yes, the Hoover Blankenship Psychology Major Research Award Committee, or HBPMRAC. Rayana and Sidney—who acted like best buddies fighting in the trenches of World War II— stood in the hallway with me and insisted we convene our committee as soon as possible because, as they put it, I didn't know what I was doing.

"We're in trouble," Sidney said, before the committee ever met and with me right next to her. "Our chair has no experience."

I began equating the department hallway with a medieval torture chamber. Whenever I stepped into it, something fucked happened.

"We better get started right away," Rayana concurred. "June will be here before we know it, and we have to teach the chair how to run a committee and how to select a student for the prize."

Turning to me, Sidney said, "There'll be no good old boys network in this committee."

"Leave your patriarchy outside the door," added Rayana.

"I've, uh. . . I've been on a lot of committees," I said in a weak voice. The conversation caught me off guard, and I struggled to speak at all.

"You don't sound sure of yourself," Rayana said.

"I thought you were going to say that he didn't sound enthusiastic," said Sidney. "As you can see, Bentley, contrary to stereotypes women think for themselves. And we were not born biologically driven to be nice any more than men were."

I worked hard to remind myself that given the precedent set by Dumont and Henry and what had to be the women's suppressed anger and the depression thereof, they found me a safe target for projecting their poison darts. Of course letting them do this angered and depressed me, but I thought

I could take it. Or in any case I had no choice. I didn't have tenure.

I even tried to convince myself that I should take their attitude toward me as a compliment. Unlike Henry or Dumont, I came across as non-threatening. They could assert themselves without worrying I'd retaliate. Good little me, taking the high road. No doubt others would notice. Or so I tried to convince myself.

"When can we all meet?" I asked, hoping to redirect the conversation.

They both took out their smart phones, I assumed to check their calendars.

"I can do Wednesday, any time after one," Sidney said.

"Wednesdays are impossible," said Rayana. "What about a Thursday morning?"

"Are you insane?" Sidney asked. "Thursday is the worst day for me."

"Then what about Tuesdays?" Rayana asked.

"That won't work unless I mutate into two physical entities," said Sidney. "I have my NPGW sub-committee meeting."

"Can't you miss one meeting?" Rayana asked.

"Not if you want the concretization document to survive. We were told Stinky hates it."

"What about Monday or Friday?" I said.

At pretty much the same time, Sidney and Rayana said, "Those are my research days."

"Well, you yourselves said that we need to convene right away."

"I don't care for your tone." Sidney made a cross face.

"It's unacceptable," Rayana concurred. "I'm not comfortable continuing this conversation."

"It's obvious you were a jock," said Sidney. "Or I suppose you still are one. You have all the usual bullying male traits. It threatens your manhood to be nice."

"Yes, keep your bullying to yourself," Rayana said. "Things need to be done democratically. Sidney and I will come up with criteria and a selection process, and you'll follow the procedures."

We managed to meet a couple of weeks later. Before we got to the agenda, Rayana zipped up her coat and said, "My God, it's freezing in here."

Dressed in a sweatshirt, Sidney said, "You're kidding, right? I'm so hot I feel like I'm going to melt."

"I can't believe you're saying that," said Rayana. "I'm frostbitten. I'm a Popsicle."

"I feel like I'm stranded in the Sahara Desert." Sidney opened her plastic water bottle, and took a long, dramatic swallow.

"I need hydration before I parch to death."

About twenty minutes later we agreed that the thermostat should be set at an even seventy degrees. Both Rayana and Sidney kept saying how cold or hot they were, but at least we moved on to the agenda.

As for creating committee bylaws, Sidney talked non-stop about how everything I suggested sucked, and showed herself to be as difficult to interrupt as Millie. Rayana gave me a look that signaled she realized how rude Sidney behaved, but did nothing to stop it. I got the impression that these two communicated through a form of osmosis as to whether they'd be united or divided at a particular moment. Having withstood united, I now would be treated to divided.

We went through a list of our senior majors, and what each one planned to do for their capstone research project. Blame it on my forensic bias, but I thought a project by a student named Chesterfield Charleston on determining sociopathology in convicted rapists sounded like it had both social and intellectual value. Much more so than a student working with Henry on the same old behaviorist rat-a-tat-tat, or Millie's student who studied wombat parenting

"Bentley, you can't be serious," said Sidney. "This is so typical it's stereotypical. A boy wants to advance his capitalist career by further exploiting women who already have been exploited as rape victims."

"But if we learn more about rapists, maybe we can stop—"

"Rape will stop when men stop raping. And they'll stop raping when we stop living in a rape culture. When we eliminate hetero-patriarchy. It's that simple."

Sidney shook her head for the cosmic disbelief she experienced from my suggestion.

"But what about—"

"Psychology," interrupted Sidney, "will be no good to anyone until it stops looking at problems through obsessively linear male logic. This prize in Hoover's honor is not being given to glorify male hegemony."

Before I could stop myself, I said, "I'm brand new, and even I know that Hoover fucked—no, raped, dozens of women right here at Elmer Butthead."

"I'm uncomfortable," Rayana said. "I sense a hostility bordering on sexual harassment."

Sidney looked as if no one in history had to carry so heavy a burden before.

"Rayana, would it be possible for someone to let me finish speaking? You all get to talk. For once can it be my turn?"

Neither Rayana nor I said a word.

"As I've been trying to say," Sidney continued, "shame on you, Ben, for believing unsubstantiated stories. Hoover was instrumental in getting my research funded on several occasions, and all of it concerned radical feminist issues. Does that sound like a serial rapist? I know some of the women he allegedly seduced, and they're homely as cows. They exploit the very real problem of rape with their lies."

I did not have a difficult time noticing Sidney's narcissism in action. If you validated her, you were good. If you didn't, you were bad. *The Universe Explained*, by Dr. Sidney Steenrod. All her rhetoric boiled down to this. Self-righteous about her own homeliness, she broke the expected politically correct rules as needed for her convoluted logic of the moment.

"If we're going to give a prize," Sidney continued, "It should be for what is prize worthy. What is cutting edge, liberating our discipline from the shackles of Freudian misogyny? I say first of all the prize therefore should go to a young woman instead of a boy. Such as my student, Federina Feldspar, whose senior thesis concerns the irreparable harm done to all women's self ideal from watching the unavoidable sexism on television."

"What are some examples?" I asked in an interested tone of voice.

"God, hold your horses, Bentley. It's only the third week of the semester. I haven't watched TV in twenty years. But I know what it's like. All the women are dumb and helpless, all the men are smart and powerful. Oh, and everyone of course is straight."

I experienced a sense of relief when Rayana entered the conversation, albeit that my relief did not last.

"You can't say that about all TV," said Rayana. "PBS and BBC have a few non-sexist programs. I watch them sometimes."

"Oh, because you watch them they must be okay."

Rayana held her head high.

"Yes, as a matter of fact. I wouldn't watch them if they weren't. Science programs. Literary classics. News."

"Like science isn't sexist. Or literature—arcane novels dripping with gender inequality. And the news doesn't favor men? Oh no, not in the slightest."

"I think we're getting off topic," I said. "Let's get back to the research prize and—"

"Stop telling me what to do," Sidney said, in a forceful manner.

I wanted to say, *and you stop telling me what to do*, but my non-tenured gentility got in the way.

"Ben, apparently you don't listen," Rayana said. "I told you the other day that honesty comes first. This is an important conversation we're having. And as for the research prize, I nominate my student, Luanna Lercy, for her advancing study on single womanhood and healthy self-image."

"There's no such thing as single womanhood and healthy self-image," Sidney said. "Not in our society. Any woman who isn't married with a ton of non-freely chosen children to prevent her from achieving her life goals is treated as an untouchable."

"I'm single," said Rayana. "I have no kids. And I am a contended, powerful woman."

"Goody for you," Sidney said. "I have come to expect that you think of no one but yourself. I'm talking as a scholar. I'm talking about millions of women who wake up every morning with no idea who they are."

"Yeah, but it is possible to change, that's all I'm saying. It's like Phyllis's book. You can learn to love yourself first."

"Don't you dare drag Phyl into your twisted reasoning."

I noticed it was time to end the meeting.

"This has been fascinating," I said. "But we're out of time."

Sidney glanced at the clock with regret, as if she were just getting started.

"I must say, Bentley, you didn't do much of a job chairing the meeting. We have an agenda for a reason."

"Yes," Rayana agreed. "If you'd like, you can sit in on my FCLC sub-committee meeting and see how I chair it."

"Or study Henry," said Sidney. "He's on an incredible male ego trip about remaining chair, but he does do a good job of running meetings."

"He sticks to the agenda," Rayana said.

I smiled and said, "Thanks, you've given me a lot to think about."

As I left the meeting room, I heard the two continue their debate on whether or not single women could be happy in our society. I understood that from their respective points of view, much was at stake. Sidney constructed her identity upon sexism and various other isms, hiding her bulimia from the world (though I didn't know about it yet). Rayana avoided facing her chronic depression by attempting to convince herself and everyone else of her happiness. And as I'd learn years later, her issues with men involved abandonment as well as politics.

Nonetheless, as I walked into my office for refuge, I felt terrified by what they could do to my career, and brimming over with hatred as strong as espresso. I didn't like the fact that every day at Elmer Butthead thus far inspired me to take a Xanax—or maybe a couple—and I decided I had to get through the day without any, no matter what. Drugs had never been more than a recreational pursuit, and in recent years not even that. I didn't relish the prospect that getting settled in my career would cause me to become an addict.

I got a call on my office phone. Henry wanted to see me at once. I could all but hear the bottle of Xanax saying, *Now you have a good reason to use me. Anyone in your position would feel the same.*

But I kept my resolve and walked over to Henry's office drug-free. Or rather, drug-free for about the past eighteen hours.

I can't say it surprised me when I saw Dumont sitting next to Henry, though it scared the hell out of me. I felt like I'd acquired an anti-Aladdin's lamp. Instead of wishes coming true, all my worst-case scenarios did.

Henry and Dumont smiled as they welcomed me and I took my seat.

"This is your lucky day," Henry said.

"Definitely," concurred Dumont.

"You see," Henry continued, "I walked past the meeting you claimed to be chairing. Don't take this the wrong way. I'm asseverating when I say that your style of chairing leaves much to be desired. But fortunately I have considerable perspicacity."

"This is true," said Dumont.

"Sidney and Rayana in the same room are like a couple of bees fighting to be queen. But I don't believe people should make excuses for themselves."

It depressed me that I lacked the confidence to point out that Henry of all people shouldn't be lecturing on self-responsibility, not to mention that if he knew about Sidney and Rayana, why did he stick me with them?

"I agree. I'll do better next time."

"Indeed you will," Henry said. "I've made sure of that."

I found myself daring to hope. Maybe he planned to change the committee membership. Thinking fast, I decided to tell him I'd be willing to keep chairing the committee if someone replaced Sidney or Rayana. So far, Sidney had been worse, but I wouldn't quibble either way.

"Dumont will be your mentor," Henry said. "Anytime you're uncertain, bring it to him. Show him your syllabi and lesson plans. Invite him to observe your teaching. And lest we forget, he'll observe how you chair the new HBCMRC."

"I'll only be observing," said Dumont. "I'll make notes on what you can do better, but how you handle Sidney and Rayana is up to you."

"We're like a family," Henry said. "We see you as our little brother."

"Yes," Dumont agreed. "In fact, there's something you can get started on, as a return favor to me. I have to select a new research assistant for the academic year, since Wicki. . . you know. There are three girls interested, and I can't decide between them. So I'll give you my files, and you can decide for me."

I'd never before met two people who took such pleasure in cruelty. They were not accustomed to people trying to halt their careers as sex criminals, and worried over what I'd do if they didn't destroy my free will. They had to take the wild out of my wild card nature.

A few minutes later, with the three student files under my arm, I trudged back to my office. Just as I unlocked the door to enter, Phyllis tapped my shoulder.

"I get the impression a lot's going on," she said. "What did Sidney and Rayana say? What did Henry and Dumont say?"

"Sidney, Rayana and I narrowed the research prize down to three students. Henry and Dumont are helping me."

"Oh." I could tell she didn't believe me, and it frustrated her to act as if she did.

Once inside my office, I popped a couple of Xanax, promising myself that I'd not take any the next day.

In this manner my first year at Elmer Butthead unfolded. I felt more nervous and pissed off at myself every time I talked to Dumont about something I didn't want him to know about—which meant every time I talked to him. I hated having to pick his research assistant. When the deadline for student appointments came, I called in sick for a couple of days. So Dumont chose his own assistant—as it happened, the student who complained to Little Miss Ass Cream, who told her it's not as bad as all that.

For not a single instant of any HBCMRAC meetings did Rayana or Sidney let up on each other and/or me. In the end, I withdrew my nominee, and flipped a coin in Sidney's favor. So our first recipient of the Hoover Blankenshit Psychology Research Award happened to be Federina Feldspar, for her study entitled, *A Dystopian Feminist Psychoanalytic Praxeological Polemic on Heterosexism in Television.* As you can imagine, Federina was a barrel of laughs.

Dumont watched it all with a sick, green-toothed grin, and never failed to tell me afterwards about all I'd done wrong. He had plenty to say about my teaching, too. Henry got busted for exposing himself for the umpteenth time, but we pretended not to know. Millie kept smoking and babbling. Phyllis winked and whispered. I kept taking Xanax as not directed by my physician.

Elmer Butthead as a whole appeared to be in competition with my department for overall fuckedness. Stinky cut budgets as though being the president consisted of no other task. Actually, I take that back—he gave himself a raise, and new furniture for the President's house. He said "we" had to make the best possible impression on potential investors.

Stinky also created several new administrative positions, including Vice-President to the President, to give himself less to do. He appointed Little Miss Ass Cream our new VPP. The female psych faculty pretended to be enthused about having a woman as near-president of the college, but other women faculty such as Leanne and Janelle took it as an insult—Stinky's way of sticking it to the faculty. Horace and the other activist male faculty concurred. Whenever Stinky addressed the school, he blamed all problems on the faculty—specifically, what he called a "certain contingent" of the faculty.

Toward the end of the school year, I ran into Leanne, Janelle and Horace in the faculty dining room, and sat at their table. I listened to them share their miseries. At the end of a sad tale by Horace about having to lay off all part-time faculty in his department so that our esteemed president could install a rock garden, I said, "Why can't Stinky have a heart attack like Blankenshit?"

Leanne, Janelle and Horace exchanged glances.

"Lightning never strikes twice," Horace said after a pause.

"So who needs lightning?" Janelle said.

All three of them laughed, though I didn't get the joke.

Ghost 10

Elaine hadn't reappeared, and it crossed my mind that she asked for a new assignment. Maybe, like so many before her, she couldn't handle me once I revealed my true self. But abandonment issues had become so much pop psychology twaddle. Cecilia continued not to speak to me, and I kept myself amused by throwing rocks at the windshields of passing cars.

When that got boring I thought more about Boris's mysterious employment file. It had to contain something incriminating. Why else would his wife steal it? I knew all the dirt on everyone else, and didn't see how I could go any further without knowing Boris's dirt as well.

I figured the file had to be in one of three places: his home, his lawyer's office, or hidden in his prison cell. All three locales were beyond my radius. I supposed I could ask Elaine for special cosmic permission to leave the Elmer Butthead campus area. But my pride wouldn't let me. And I didn't want to ask Melinda Joshua to steal. She had enough burdens in life just by being the asshole president's administrative assistant.

I was about to give up on finding the file when the obvious occurred to me.

I was a ghost. I could haunt people. Duh. I could take possession of someone's soul, and tell them what to do. It would only be for a short time, and for a worthy cause. What could be the harm? Plus it sounded like fun, a commodity ever in short supply at Elmer Butthead.

The only question was who to select for the task. Tempting though it was to take possession of a psych professor's soul, I wouldn't trust any of them. Besides, none of them came to campus over the summer. I figured it should be someone swift and agile—someone who could run fast and sneak about as needed.

A student athlete would be ideal, preferably one whose mind was easy to control. Lucky for me, one of Elmer Butthead's supposed ways of giving back to the community—a phrase I found irritating for some reason— was to host a summer athletic program for the local community college. So in the pitch darkness of the living's broad daylight I watched the summer track team practice.

A kid who looked about eighteen stood out from the other local yokels who thought it a good idea to waste their summers at Elmer Butthead. The coach kept singling out the kid for praise, telling the other young jocks to do push-ups or pole vault like this one teen. Here was a youth who lived to be told what to do. Obeying instructions rewarded him every time. (If you'll pardon the behaviorism.) His name was Timothy Something-That-Sounded-Like-Glokenspiel. My hearing started getting a bit garbled at times. No matter, I waited in the purple sunshine for his practice to finish. I found the darkness of daylight lethargic and depressing.

After practice, he emerged from the locker room, combing his crew cut dry with his fingers. His freckles looked like white dots against his blue skin. As Timothy put on his earphones to listen to hard rock music, I entered into him. It just sort of happened; I knew how to do it without thinking, like a mama dog knows how to whelp her puppies. For me, entering a living human soul felt like curling up inside a featherbed in winter. I understood why spirits took possession of the living. It made one feel so snug and comfy. And let us not forget the benefits of having a body.

I don't think Timothy shared my enthusiasm. His heart all but stopped as he broke into an epic sweat. He cried so hard he almost choked, even though I could hear that the song in his earphones was upbeat. As he leaned against a street lamp and shook, one of the other community college kids walked over to him and said, "Are you okay, Timmy?"

I meant to have Timmy reply something like *Yes I'm fine,* but instead he said, "Go swallow your dick, fuck face."

The other young jock punched Timmy in the nose. Timmy grabbed him by the throat, but I got him to stop before he killed him. This was not a humanitarian gesture on my part so much as common sense. Timmy couldn't be of much help to me if he got arrested.

As the other athlete ran off and told Timmy to swallow his own dick, I realized some fine-tuning was needed for our partnership to accomplish its intended purpose. I directed Timmy like a robot, and though he fell to the ground at one point in a fetal seizure, by the time we got to his car he seemed fine. By "fine" I mean a blank slate, a glorified amoeba that I could control however I saw fit.

As a boy, I wanted to be an astronaut, and in a way I felt like Timmy's body was my space capsule and his brain my control panel. I experienced no elation when we successfully drove away from Elmer Butthead. Guiding Timmy took all my concentration.

I figured that the folder would most likely be at Boris and Jamie's house. I doubted that their lawyer advised Jamie to commit a felony offense by stealing it, and I supposed it would be difficult for Boris to keep it hidden in his jail cell. I also knew his wife would be at work and their kids in daycare. Jamie couldn't feed her kids as a stay-at-home mom with her hubby in jail, awaiting trial for murder one.

To be on the safe side, I had Timmy buy a black ski mask. Oh, I almost forgot—he also purchased a teeny-tiny handgun. I figured small was better because it would be easier to conceal. Thank goodness for his daddy's credit card. Say what you want about gun control, but in this circumstance it pleased me that Timmy could buy a gun with no questions asked.

The salesman asked, "You want ammo, too, son?"

I only wanted Timmy to have a gun to wave around as a Plan B, in case someone tried to stop him from acquiring the file. Upon reconsideration, though, I thought we might as well load it with bullets, in the case of Plan C—someone waving a gun at *us*. I of course had nothing to lose, but it would be bad karma to let Timmy die.

"Yes, sir," said Timmy in a monotone voice. "What's a gun without bullets?"

The salesman laughed. "Sort of like breakfast without two eggs sunny side up."

"My mom is a good cook," Timmy said in the same robotic tone.

The gun bought and loaded, we drove to the quaint suburban home of Boris and Jamie Lang. I had Timmy put on his ski mask. As I predicted, no one answered the door. I'd become quite skillful at the mechanics of ghosthood, and I managed to extend my hand through the door to unlock it, while remaining inside Timmy's body. Too bad we weren't a circus act.

Barky, their beagle, looked confused. I'm sure he didn't know what to make of Timmy/me. Living up to his name, he barked a couple of times. Then he ran off to hide.

I figured the file would be hidden in the grown-ups' bedroom, possibly under the mattress. But as usual, nothing proved to be easy; the file wasn't there. Timmy opened every drawer and looked inside every box in the closet. He also checked each article of clothing. Our search of the kids' bedroom proved no more fruitful. Nor did the kitchen, bathroom, or small living room have what we were looking for. After poking around the basement and the front and backyards, I had us give up. The file was not to be found at the Lang home.

Boris's attorney had a small office downtown that employed a secretary-receptionist. While they both took their lunch hour, I had us slither into the office and check the file cabinets. They had a file on Boris, but it contained nothing but post-arrest information.

This meant that we had to visit Boris in jail. Jamie must have slipped him the file when the incompetent local guards turned their backs. Or maybe they got bribed or didn't give a rat's ass. Back when I was a little thing called alive, I worked on the Elmer Butthead case with the cops, and a major obstacle had been the peanut butter-thick denial even from law enforcement that anything so not nice as serial murder transpired in their apple pie of a town.

I got so absorbed in trying to figure out how to get inside the jailhouse with the gun that I almost forgot to have Timmy take off his ski mask. The best I could come up with was have him stick the gun inside the front of his underwear, and keep my metaphorical fingers crossed that a) the guards would not frisk Timmy's crotch, and b) the gun would not go off by accident.

Upon entering the musty jailhouse, Timmy said to the deputy at the front desk, "We're here to see Boris Lang."

The deputy frowned.

"Maybe I have wax in my ears, young fellow, but it sounded like you said, 'we.' Maybe I need to get my peepers examined, but I only see one of you."

I directed Timmy to say *Golly, did I say we? I meant to say I'm here to see Boris.* But he said, "My soul is possessed by a demon. Please, will you pray with me?"

He all but had the words, "help me," appear on his belly, like in *The Exorcist.* How typical of my luck to get ratted out the first lousy time I took possession of a living human. And I must protest the character assassination in being called a demon. I found this to be extreme xenophobia on Timmy's part—which means a fear of anything different.

Fortunately, the deputy had a sense of humor. It was good to know at least one person in this dump of a town did.

"Ha-ha, you almost had me there," said the deputy, while I squeezed with all my might on Timmy's vital essence. "Sure, I can take you to see Boris."

"Thank you, sir," Timmy said with a wooden quality, like a kindergartener reciting a line in a play.

"First, though, let me pat you down," said the deputy. "I have to make sure you don't have a gun on your person. You know—just a formality." The deputy said all this with a grin, as if saying between the lines that of course a clean-cut

(white) young man such as Timmy was too busy going to
Bible study meetings to be hiding a gun. Ours was a law-
abiding and God-fearing hamlet.

If ghosts could have heart attacks I would've had one as
the guard felt along Timmy's arms and legs.

The deputy made a quizzical face.

"What do we have here?" He stuck his hand further
inside Timmy's pocket.

"Oh looky, a ski mask," the deputy said with a chortle.
"What are you trying to do, rob a bank?"

"No, sir. That would be against the law."

I sighed with relief for Timmy being back under my
control. This made Timmy cough for some reason.

"Have a summer cold?" asked the deputy.

"Yes, sir. A little."

"Those can be the worst. My wife makes me ginger root
tea with honey and cinnamon."

"I'll have to remember that."

The deputy gave him one last pat.

"You're clean. No surprise there. I have to say, son, I'll
bet you have no trouble pleasing the ladies."

The deputy winked. He must have meant the large bulge
in Timmy's crotch, thanks to the gun.

"I do okay," Timmy said.

"I'll take you to Boris. Such a nice guy in such a jam.
How do you know him?"

"Um . . . I don't. I want to meet him. I want to tell him
that I, uh . . ."

"That you're praying for him?"

"Yeah, that's it. I'm praying for him. Yeah, that's what I
do, all right. I pray for him."

"Well, aren't you a fine young man."

"Thank you, sir. I hope to be a police officer someday."

"Something tells me that's just the career for you. Have
you graduated high school?"

"Yes, sir."

The deputy laughed.

"You know something? I don't remember one gosh darn thing from high school."

Obedient under my control, Timmy laughed, too.

The deputy led us along an L-shaped hallway, where the cells were located. Most of them were empty, but I guessed they kept Boris somewhat hidden, for his own sake as well as that of the local police, who would not want to be reminded about the unpleasant fact of murder.

"Someone to see you, Mr. Lang," said the deputy.

Boris got up from the foam-covered concrete slab he called his bed, and grimaced at the unfamiliar sight of Timmy. Being a gentleman, the deputy walked back to his desk, giving Boris and Timmy privacy.

Now, you will admit that this situation posed confusion for all concerned. They don't teach you how a spirit who's taken over someone's soul should converse with an innocent person charged with murder—and to make matters worse, the murder of the spirit's human form.

"Er. . . um. . . Hi," said Timmy. "I . . . I'm writing about your case for my college newspaper. Do you by any chance have a folder about yourself that I could borrow?"

I couldn't believe the wimpy cover story that came out of Timmy's mouth, thanks to me. I'll never improvise a conversation again.

Boris's eyes got as big as an owl's, or one of those paintings they used to have of starving kids with big eyes.

"Who are you? Who sent you?"

"Uh, like I said, I'm a student, and I—"

Boris lunged his arms through the bars and grabbed Timmy by the collar, slapping his face hard, one side and then the other.

"Cut the crap. Did the cops send you? Did Elmer Butthead?"

"I'm just a student."

Boris's slaps turned into punches. "Quit lying. I can't take anymore bullshit."

I saw no choice but to tell the truth and hope he'd believe me.

"Boris, it's me, Bentley. Ben Gamble. I'm a ghost. I had to take over someone's body because . . . well, it's complicated. But I'm here to help you."

He pulled on Timmy's shirt collar so that his head hit the prison bars. "A ghost? Very funny, asshole. I'm fighting for my life. For my wife and kids. Whoever put you up to this, I'm not laughing."

"I'm not joking. I'm Ben. I know I don't sound like myself. But I needed a body."

He punched Timmy in the nose, just like the kid on the athletic field did. If I didn't know better, I'd have thought it was National Punch Timmy in the Nose Day.

Boris looked puzzled by his bruised and bloodied target's lack of response. I had full control of Timmy by this time.

He cuffed Timmy's jaw. Again, no reaction. He banged Timmy's head against the bars some more. Still nothing. Timmy remained as blank-faced as if he'd just sat through one of Henry's lectures.

Timmy's voice said, "Remember how I turned in my schedule late every semester and you'd send me about a million reminders?"

Still skeptical, Boris said, "What about it?" But I could tell he began to take me seriously.

"And remember when Dumont had you make a thousand photocopies of a journal article he ended up not using?"

Boris wore a weary smile, as if starting to hope.

"Ben—if you are Ben—what night class did I ask you to help me with about five years ago?"

"Calculus."

"What did I have for lunch every Friday?"

"Tuna on a Kaiser roll. With a dill pickle."

"And what are the names of my kids?"

Shit, he would have to ask that. I tried to conjure up some conversation about his kids, but my dead anti-brain couldn't come up with anything.

"Uh . . . I can't remember. Sorry."

Boris turned away from me/Timmy in disgust. Then he turned back around and gave Timmy another blow to the head.

"Any numbskull would know my kids' names. I talked about them every day."

"I'm bad with names."

"I know a setup when I see one. Get the hell out of here before I smash your head in."

Human 10

At the end of my first spring semester, I planned to spend the summer doing personality inventories of convicted murderers. But day-by-day, I found myself wanting to do nothing but stay in bed, like I had done most weekends during the school year. Despite my resolve to tough it out at Elmer Butthead, I occasionally checked out the job market online. But I lacked the oomph to get it together to apply anywhere. My confidence had been run over by too many eighteen-wheelers over the school year. Inertia became my sole companion.

An image formed in my mind of someone sinking in quicksand while someone else offers a hand to get them out. But the person in quicksand chooses to pull the other person down into the muck, rather than be saved. That's how I felt about Elmer Butthead. At the time, I thought I was light years away from ever doing the same thing myself. I ignored the basic psychology of anger as a substitute reward.

Around mid-July I got it together to do some prison interviews. I listened to twenty different convicted murderers tell me about their lives, from as far back as they could remember up to the present moment. Some were men and some were women; their ethnicities varied, as did their station in life before conviction. Some claimed to be innocent, while others claimed to be sorry for what they had done. Some found religion while others did not.

But what they all had in common was an amazing composure—and most of them were not on meds. I said to each of them, "You seem calm," which caused some to shrug or disagree. Yet half of them said it was because they had nothing left to worry about. As one woman put it, "What else can they do to me? I'm serving life without parole. I've already done the worst thing imaginable. If I die young, what difference does it make?"

No way did I want to end up in prison, and killing people was not on my bucket list. Yet I found myself envying such peace of mind. I wondered what it would feel like to no longer worry that something bad would happen. Or, given life at Elmer Butthead, to not know for a fact that something bad would happen because all that ever happened was bad.

You know you don't like your job when you'd trade places with a convicted murderer. I experienced a twinge of jealousy when a faculty member had to resign for having a painful incurable disease. Yet I'd tell myself it wasn't so bad, enough of the self-pity party, think wonderful thoughts and you can fly to Never Land, and all sorts of positive affirmation garbage that a cognitive therapist would recommend. Supposedly emotion followed thought, so if your thoughts were nice you'd feel nice.

Supposedly.

I dreaded the new academic year starting in September much more than I dreaded it back when I'd been a student at whatever level. My apprehensions intensified when Stinky convened a mysterious, mandatory meeting for all faculty one week before classes started. It was held in the campus theater, and I avoided sitting next to or making eye contact with anyone from my department. Just seeing them from a distance made me jittery. My insides felt like they did when, as a stupid kid, I once feasted on fresh pineapple with a chocolate milk shake. I had to fight back the urge to lose my breakfast.

Phyllis sat next to Sidney; the next seat had a barricade of coats, and on the other side of it sat Rayana. Some things never changed. Stinking of cigarettes, Millie brushed by me without saying anything, taking a seat as close to the other psych women as she could. I didn't want to talk to Millie any more than she wanted to talk to me, but I took it as a bad omen just the same. Dumont appeared to be hitting on a new woman faculty member. Henry stood near the podium talking to Little Miss Ass Cream, who would soon introduce Stinky. Cecilia Puff from English smiled as she gave a prolonged,

New Age hug to another woman, as if life consisted of floating on a pink cloud.

I took solace in finding Leanne, Janelle and Horace, and grabbed a seat next to them. It gave me a sense of empowerment, like sitting with the badass kids in the school cafeteria.

"Does anyone know what this meeting is about?" I asked, sensing not to bother with asking how their summers went, or other small talk.

"Why should you care?" asked Horace with sarcasm. "You're only a professor. You're nobody."

Janelle said, "Stinky better not go near the salary equity resolution, though I've heard that's what's up his sleeve."

"I'd like to be a tarantula climbing up his sleeve," said Leanne.

"Can he stop the resolution?" I wanted to know. "I heard it was a no-brainer to get the board to sign off on it."

Though we didn't belong to a union, the Elmer Butthead bylaws included language to the effect that salaries would be equitable. But for years women profs of equal rank, experience and achievement to men profs had lower salaries. On the other hand, Boris, the sole male secretary on campus, made more money than the dozens of female ones.

After many thwarted efforts, faculty governance passed a legally robust resolution to eliminate this inequality. In practical terms, it meant raising the salaries of numerous women profs and staff. I thought that the psych women profs would be ecstatic to hear this, but they said they'd believe it when they saw it. I chalked this sentiment up to mandatory departmental negativity, but now I wondered if I judged them in haste.

"Stinky thinks he can do whatever the hell he wants," said Janelle. "Just wait—he'll have some convoluted rationale for opposing it."

"But what about the board?"

"What about it?" Horace said. "The board will fall down and worship him. He'll save money."

I don't want to make myself sound like a moral crusader, because that would be untrue. My own salary would stay the same either way, and like many, if not most people, I tolerated any number of inequalities that did not affect me. But something about hidden agendas, thinking that people were easy to fool and going out of your way to do the wrong thing drove me crazy. Misty Rose was a microcosm of the psych department, which was a microcosm of Elmer Butthead. Stinky hadn't said a word yet, but the hatred exploded inside me like a war movie.

"How do you stand it?"

"I hope tomorrow will be better," Leanne said "I try not to—"

The lilting voice of LMAC cut off the chatter.

"Weylcome bayck, faculty," she said with her Miss America enthusiasm. "And an extra wahm EBCLA weylcome to the new fayculty."

She paused for applause, but little manifested.

"It is mah distinct honuh and pleasha," continued LMAC, "to intrahduce to you this monin owa distiynguished preysident, Dr. Enoch LePutois."

Stinky walked to the podium with the confidence of a shark about to snack on a foot. There was a dismal clapping of a few hands.

"Thank you, Dr. Crabb," he said, as LMAC stepped behind him like a politician's devoted wife. "You are an outstanding Vice President to the President."

Leanne muttered, "I wonder if she sucks his dick."

"He sucks hers," Janelle interjected.

Stinky harrumphed a few times as the mic squeaked. "Friends, this is a glorious new day for EBCLA. For today we embrace the individual. We embrace true equity. We celebrate our triumph over the shackles of thou-shalt rhetoric, and restore freedom. I have been in close communication with the BOD, and I anticipate it is but a matter of days until it agrees with me and disapproves Faculty Governance Resolution FGR-5694."

Numerous hands got raised, but Leanne stood up and spoke without being called on.

"For the benefit of new faculty, would you kindly explain what this resolution concerns?"

"A resolution that states compensation should be based on gender," Stinky said.

"No, it states the opposite," Leanne said. "Compensation should *not* be based on gender, as it is now."

Stinky chuckled with superiority.

"Our legal counsel begs to differ. All employees agree in writing to the offer that is made, and promotion and raises are determined from that point forward based on individual achievement. Period."

"No, not period, but question mark. I am the only woman in Film Studies. I've been here longer than any of the men, and I have more publications. You tell me why I make less money than—"

"Dr. Moses, surely this is a private matter between you and the personnel office. We cannot and should not mandate how well you bargain for a raise."

LMAC nodded her head in cheerful agreement.

"That motherfucker," Janelle murmured.

"We all know what's going on here," Horace called out. "Saving money so you can give yourself more raises and hire more administrators to do your job, which as best as we can tell is to do nothing."

"Dr. Tweed, I resent—no, let me say I deeply resent the implication that I put anything before our guiding principle of students first."

"I defy you to name a single student," Janelle shouted. "If any money is saved, it sure as hell isn't going to students. It's going straight into your pocket, and you know it."

"Dr. Waverly, my salary is determined by the BOD. You are free to take this matter up with them."

"You hate women," said Janelle. "A powerful woman scares you to death."

Stinky said, "I see no need to dignify that with—"

He collapsed on the stage.

"Oh mah word," said LMAC. "Puhlease, someone cawl 911."

"I'm doing it," Cecelia Puff called out. "Oh please, God, bring help right away."

"I know CPR," Dumont said, hurrying to the stage.

"This is just dreydful," LMAC said, as Dumont compressed his hands on Stinky's chest.

"If you fayculty ownly knew how hahd yow Preysident hays been working to improve ower student success rayte. His whole laff is students."

"He's not breathing," Dumont said, with a look of sorrow so insincere it should have run for public office.

Melinda Joshua, the president's administrative assistant, stood up from her seat in the front row, and turned to look at Leanne, Janelle and Horace, who gazed back at Melinda. None of them wore sadness on their faces, nor did most people in the theater. But unlike most everyone else they didn't look shocked or surprised.

Sure enough, Stinky was pronounced dead by the medics a few minutes later. Like Blankenshit, he appeared to die of a heart attack.

At this point, it still got labeled coincidence. Since the only people who claimed to like either president were phonies, Elmer Butthead lacked a collective sense of outrage that might've motivated the cops to start sniffing around.

A memorial was held for Stinky two days later. Like many faculty, I did not attend it, though morbid curiosity compelled me to watch the video. LMAC had to be either psychotic or the greatest actress of all time, because she cried a Great Lake's worth of tears while delivering the tribute speech. Cecilia Puff ran up to the stage to let LMAC cry on her shoulder.

LMAC overcame her anguish soon enough. A couple of days later, she got appointed the new Acting President. Or, as some folks put it, "The Acting Acting President," since

Stinky had been Acting President. She sent out the following email to the Elmer Butthead community:

My dear friends,

As we still mourn the loss of our beloved President [*sic*] Dr. Enoch LePutois, I do not find it appropriate to call for an assembly. Let us continue to mourn in private. However, please know that despite my heavy heart I will do my best as Acting President, and that, as ever, my door is open to you all.

Warmly yours,

Dr. Emily Crabb, Acting President

Leanne Moses hit "reply all" with the following missive:

Dear Acting President Crabb,

With your heavy heart and open door, could you tell us the status of Faculty Governance Resolution FGR-5694?

To which LMAC replied:

Dear Dr. Moses,

I do not know what the BOD plans to do with this recommendation, as its dismissal legally would require us to have a permanent, and not an acting, president.

I expect the same light bulb went off above many people's heads upon reading this. An integral aspect of Stinky's diabolical plan was to get appointed permanent president PDQ in order to commence with fucking people over. This would have killed two birds with one boulder. Technically, the board needed to do a national job search for a permanent president, but they could've engaged in a half-baked effort and chosen Stinky.

In a transparent move to stall for time, Faculty Governance convened later that day to announce that a special subcommittee would be formed to articulate what qualities the next Elmer Butthead president should possess.

One could hazard a guess that a desirable candidate favored eliminating the salary gap between women and men.

LMAC knew she had to honor this request, or else she would look bad. I suppose if she'd been a man, she could've refused Faculty Governance and come across as a ballsy leader—or at least in some people's minds. But it was not an instance of sexism that mattered much to faculty, since anyone with half a brain assumed that LMAC held secret meetings with the BOD to let them know she shared Stinky's opinion of the resolution. To her mind, the special faculty subcommittee amounted to a minor complication; it might take her an extra semester or so to become permanent president.

With the special subcommittee in place, a call went out for each department to elect a representative. This would make for a large, unwieldy committee, but the longer it took to complete its charge, the better.

Henry emailed the department:

Dear Colleagues,

I think this special sub-committee would benefit from the fresh input of junior faculty, so I nominate Ben to represent us.

In other words, the sub-committee would lock horns with the Board, and since I didn't have tenure I made the best sacrificial goldfish. Need I bother to mention that the department concurred with Henry?

Speaking of the department, over the summer Millie and Henry had what they called a second honeymoon in Rome, description of which trek, I supposed, they intended to sound romantic. But it struck me as something a couple did when their marriage was on the rocks. Henry in particular kept talking about the U.S. Embassy and a photo exhibit held there. It seemed fishy to me that he and Millie—neither of whom harbored patriotic leanings—would go all the way to Rome so that they could hang out at the U.S. Embassy. I suspected there'd been a speck or two of trouble regarding

Henry and the zipper on his pants, though I did not bring my suspicion to anyone's attention. When Millie enthused that she felt ten years younger for having made the trip, I took it as confirmation of my worst hunch.

My one accomplishment of the past year was learning to understand Elmer Butthead-ese. I suppose you could also count my not getting fired.

Phyllis claimed she spent the summer writing a second edition of *Love Yourself First*, though I had no idea what she intended to accomplish by so doing, other than *something*— since the first edition accomplished nothing. She said she was looking for a feminist press to publish the updated version, since the sexist mainstream press that published the first version destroyed the entire point she sought to make, which prevented the book from revolutionizing the lives of young women everywhere.

Sidney spent her summer reading Freud in the original German to compare the sexism of his original writings with the sexism in the translations. Rayana, in a moment of weakness, had another affair with a married man, which resulted in not her first abortion, though Phyllis told me not to breathe a word of this to a living soul. In the meantime, Rayana drafted a book proposal called *Happiness is Being Single*.

Dumont told me he looked forward to another year of mentoring me.

"Ben, the call is out for this year's research assistant. This time I expect you to be a seasoned enough junior professor to select my assistant for me. No copping out like last year. You have to learn that as academics we make judgment calls all the time, and if we judged wrong we go on to the next situation and never look back."

"Thank you for being so patient with me, Dumont."

He flashed his sour smile.

"Hopefully this year we can do better than Wacky."

"I think you mean Wicki."

"Oh, right. Wicki. Well, just know that I'm always here for you."

"Thanks, Dumont."

"No thanks needed," he said, putting his slimy hand on my shoulder. "We're a family here in psychology. After my last marriage ended I thought I'd lose it, but just seeing my colleagues and going to department meetings, I felt like I had a home."

"How touching."

"Never feel I'm too busy for you. *Au contraire*, you're my pet project."

I hated it when people said things like "*au contraire*," or, "I beg to differ."

"Sounds like you picked up some French over the summer."

Dumont roared with laughter.

"I enjoy your humor. You're a happy, funny guy."

Both Rayana and Sidney told me, albeit individually, that they couldn't wait to work on the HBPMRAC, our student research prize committee. Phyllis reminded me that if an extra pair of hands were needed, not to hesitate to let her know.

Boris kept saying that one of these days we needed to go to lunch and have a talk. But I wasn't sure if he could be trusted, and day-by-day he remained too overworked to take much of a break. His goal to finish college through night classes and become a high school history teacher dragged out longer than he planned, because our faculty kept him too busy with mindless tasks.

Yeah, I was back for my second year.

Serving on the special subcommittee became the one bright note in my life. Leanne, Janelle, Horace and the others had a psyche-saving irreverence toward Elmer Butthead, and fostered an atmosphere of honesty and mutual respect during meetings. They said and did whatever they had to in order for the presidential job search to be postponed. In the meantime, the subcommittee brainstormed all sorts of ways Elmer Butthead could cut back on administrative fluff, and give the surplus money back to students through lowered tuition, a new scholarship fund, and more competitive, up to date classroom resources. And yes, equal pay for equal work.

I asked Leanne how long we could get away with delaying the inevitable confrontation with Little Miss Ass Cream, and her repeated inquiries about what we were up to.

"Be patient, Ben," Leanne said. I didn't know what she meant, but I trusted her.

The same could not be said for LMAC, who called me up and asked to meet with me, which meant she informed me that we'd be meeting whether I liked it or not.

I decided not to tell anyone about this meeting. At least not yet. Misty Rose taught me to be cautious.

I arrived for our appointment on time and filled with trepidation.

After some fake pleasantries and declining her offer of coffee, LMAC got to the point. With her demure tilted-head smile, she said, "Wayll now, Bentley, suppose you tell lil ol me all about what your subcommittee hay-es been saying about me."

Ghost 11

Moving Timmy's body—or what was left of it— out of Boris's reach, I said in Timmy's whining voice, "I saw Jamie steal your file."

The color drained from Boris's face, which for me meant it became a deeper blue.

"What the hell are you talking about?"

"From the psych department office. She was dressed all in white—or rather, black."

"Never happened. Stop lying."

I hated it when people told me I lied when I hadn't, but in the moment I had bigger bananas to peel.

"Since I'm lying, then there's no harm in my going to the cops to tell them what she did."

Boris grabbed the prison bars with urgency, as if holding them gave him strength.

"If you or anyone else does anything at all to harm Jamie, if anyone even threatens to harm her, I'll—"

"At ease, soldier. No one wants to hurt your wife."

"Is it about money? I don't have any, so you're shit out of luck. Go blackmail Kingsley Shufflebottom. He's loaded. I don't know how you saw. . . what you think you saw. I'm not aware of any hidden cameras. You're making the whole thing up."

"I don't want to blackmail anyone. I just want your file."

Boris scowled. "Why, so you can use it against me?"

"I keep telling you, I'm on your side. I need to know what they have on you so I can get you out of here, and find the real killer." (This sounded so wimpy when Timmy said it.)

"Let's just say—as a hypothetical—Jamie stole the folder. What makes you think she didn't destroy it?"

"Because . . . That is to say . . . Er, well, she wouldn't."

Truth be told, it never occurred to me that such might be the case. Though now that Boris said it, I realized she took the folder to trash it. This ghost BS had impaired my fine sense of logic. If I thought things through, I might've developed a different strategy and spared myself the nuisance of meeting Timothy Something-That-Sounded-Like-Glockenspiel. As things stood, I'd make him drive us back to campus, where I'd leave his body, and be stuck at Elmer Butthead. Unless I wanted to forget about the deal with Elaine, and live on through Timmy's body. After all, he was in tip-top shape, or at least he used to be before Boris got hold of him . . .

"You're not as smart as you think you are." Boris pointed to his noggin. "The folder—assuming there ever was a folder—is no more."

"Oh."

"Now, will you please leave me alone? And next time try card tricks or something."

"Nice try, but I still have the upper hand, and you know it. You tell me what was in the folder that needed to be destroyed. Otherwise I tell the cops what Jamie did."

"You work for the prosecution, don't you?"

"No. I keep telling you I'm Bentley Gamble."

Boris paced about his cell like a tiger in a cage.

"Okay, fine. You're Bentley Gamble, and I'm Florence Nightingale."

"Where's your lamp?" I never could resist a wisecrack.

"Look, do you want to know about the file or not?"

"Okay, okay. Sorry. And I'm also sorry I said I was Bentley. That was. . . It was a cruel joke that the guys at work dared me to do. You see, I'm really. . . I'm a private detective. I've been hired by a local news source to scope out the case. I can't name my client. And yes, we have hidden cameras."

Boris sat down on his bed.

"Finally you're making sense. Sorry about punching you in face and stuff. I'm walking a fine line these days. I don't need some wise ass calling me stupid."

"I'm sorry if that's how you took it." (But not really.)

"Well, here's what you came here to know, nitwit. There was evidence that pointed to my dislike of Bentley Gamble. To be perfectly honest, I detested him. He was okay at first, but he turned angry and nervous and scary. He went nuts. I also think he had a drug problem."

Gee, thanks, Boris. If he hated my guts, did he like the other psych faculty more? I would not win a popularity contest at Elmer Butthead, but I had to have been easier to take than Henry and Company. If nothing else, I made an effort not to overwork him.

"What did you think of the other people in the department?"

"They were nicer to me. They didn't think I was too incompetent to handle a lot of work. They didn't keep postponing taking me to lunch. They were polite and professional."

Each word hurt more than the one before it. I had to resist the urge to seep out of Timmy's body and—speaking of scary—treat Boris to a display of spectral effects he would never forget. Anger-as-substitute-reward déjà vu. Take that, Misty Rose.

If I could eliminate one thing in the world it would be politeness. All it did was shit on the truth. And speaking of polite, if Boris thought there was as little as a one-in-a-million chance that I was Bentley Gamble, how hypocritical to accuse me of being the impolite one.

"But you worked with me—uh, him for seven years. What did the file say?"

Boris emitted a caustic laugh. "You're impatient enough to be Bentley Gamble, I'll say that much. It had to do with a student that died. Kimberly Ann Kulwicki. Wicki."

I could feel my pulseless anti-blood pressure rise.

"What about her?"

"After we found out she died, Henry Zwieback and Dumont Dungworth had a private meeting with me. They said—That is, Dumont said that he saw Wicki in Bentley's office shortly before she died. Then they saw her say something to me. He wondered, and Henry wondered, if Bentley or I said something to make her upset enough to. . . you know, jump from the library roof. I told them that I knew nothing about what Bentley said to her, but she poked her head into the main office just long enough to say that she wanted to talk to me sometime soon about her schedule. Henry told me that he and Dumont figured I didn't say or do anything harmful, so it must've been Bentley. He went on to say that they had an affidavit for me to sign, and which would be sealed in an envelope in my personnel file. It stated that I saw Wicki leave Bentley's office in a state of extreme agitation minutes before she killed herself. I told them I couldn't tell if she was agitated or not. Dumont said that it had to be true, that as a psychologist he knew how these things worked. Henry agreed with Dumont's hypothesis, and told me that signing the affidavit would ensure no one thought that Wicki's suicide was my fault. I asked if signing it would get Bentley in trouble. Henry said that it would be bad publicity if Bentley was implicated in her death, but we should save the affidavit for a rainy day. You know—in case there would be some reason to use it against Bentley.

"I still didn't want to sign it. Something didn't feel right. But Henry and Dumont never steered me wrong. Over the years, I pretty much forgot about the sealed document. But it did give me more reason to hate Bentley. Imagine being that out of touch with the effect he had on other people. And he was a psychologist. Or supposedly anyway."

I managed to keep my ghostly cool, but it wasn't easy.

"So then, when you were charged with Bentley's murder, you thought the affidavit would bite you in the ass."

"You learn fast, whoever you are. Even from the grave Bentley is fucking me over. I thought about removing just the affidavit, but then I figured, screw it, destroy the whole file. Better safe than sorry."

"No wonder you don't like Bentley Gamble."

"As far as I'm concerned, his death made for one less SOB in the world."

I tried to stop Timmy's body from trembling.

"I have one more question for you. Who planted the potassium chloride in your drawer?"

I resisted the urge to point out it must have been one of those polite and professional psych profs he liked so well.

"I sure would like to have an answer for you. I know no one in the psych department could've done it. Who knows— maybe Bentley really is a ghost, and he planted it himself before destroying the department."

Having learned what I came to find out, I saw no reason to linger in Boris's company. I know when I'm not wanted. For maybe thirty seconds I made small talk to make it look good, but even on the best of days I had a short attention span for *how's the weather, how's the wife,* and all that other waste of molecular space.

I thought some more about running away in Timmy's body, but realized that if he went missing the cops would look for him, which sounded like more tedium to deal with. I had Timmy drive us back to Elmer Butthead, and I plunked his inconsequential self on the athletic field as I seeped out of him. Timmy sat up with a groan, holding his head in pain. Probably he concluded he drank too many beers and blacked out. After the fact, I remembered he still had the gun in his crotch, but as Cecilia's grandmother put it, no use crying over spilled milk.

I had a lot of nervous energy to burn off, so I broke into a house close to Elmer Butthead, and threw the sofa through the front window. The millions of glass shards looked like little ghosts. I heard someone scream so I ran away as fast as I could, hoping that no one could see me.

Human 11

Sitting across from Little Miss Ass Cream, I tried but failed to transcend time and space and be someplace, anyplace else. She wanted me to rat on the special subcommittee, and tell her what they said about her. Certainly many words got spent about LMAC, often of the four-letter variety. I had but seconds to decide if I should rat out the faculty and win favor with the Acting Acting President, which could come in handy down the road. My department made me feel like a voodoo doll that existed to get stuck with pins. So getting the Big Cheese on my side could prove prudent.

On the other hand, people like Leanne, Janelle and Horace brought balm to my soul, and if I betrayed them and played both sides of the fence I'd be a basket case. Not to mention a shit.

For not the first time, the BS survival skills I acquired from Misty Rose came in handy. I could humor LMAC by saying just enough.

"Obviously your name has come up," I said, leaving out the fact that during such occasions people called her LMAC. "How could it not?"

"And wheyn mah name comes up, just whut is sayed?" She leaned forward, with her red fingernails folded under her chin.

I faked a laugh, a kind of rat-tat-tat machine gun sound.

"Oh, you know. . . We're faculty, and you're an administrator."

"No, Bentley, Ahm afraid ah don't know. Surely mah position awahds mey some respeyect."

"Obviously. I think it's more that faculty aren't sure where you stand on pay equity. That's the biggie. They worry that you oppose it just like Sti—just like President LePotois."

"Ah see. Weyll, maybe Ah should clarify mah position awn this issue. Theyn maybe we cayn all be on the sayme payge."

"Are you saying you support the resolution?"

"Well, whah on God's greeyn earth wouldn't ah? Does the fayculty really think ah support ayny foam of discrimination?"

I left the meeting feeling better than I had since my AEB life began. I thought it cinematic of life that the next subcommittee meeting would be the same day. I couldn't wait to speak up—in part to give my fine colleagues a sense of security, but also, I must admit, to be seen as someone privy to the innermost circles of information. If you wanted the straight dope on Elmer Butthead, just come to me.

The moment after Leanne convened the meeting, I raised my hand to speak.

" . . . So if LMAC is made permanent president, she will support us. I asked her several different ways, and she said each time that she opposed discrimination, so she supported our resolution."

"Assuming we can trust LMAC, that's good to know," Leanne said. "Thank you, Bentley, for sharing this. But my question, and I'm sure the question of many people, is what were you doing in her office in the first place?"

The question caught me off guard, and disappointed me. Nothing at Elmer Butthead ever got taken at face value, not even amongst the good guys. It reminded me of the mafia, except people didn't get killed—though before long I'd detract the disclaimer.

"She, uh. . . She said she wanted to meet with me. So I did."

Leanne addressed the entire body. "I'm sure Bentley meant well. But in the future, we must maintain strong symbolic boundaries between the administration and ourselves. Nothing— I repeat, nothing—said in these meetings is to be shared with anyone from the administration. Or even the support staff."

"But the president asked to meet with me. What was I supposed to do?"

"Refer her to me," Leanne replied. "If she gives you a hard time about it, keep repeating that she must bring it up with me."

"Remember, she's only the Acting Acting President," Janelle said.

"This circuitous communication style should be your first clue," Horace added. "Why won't she tell Faculty Governance her position? Why only you?"

For about a day or so, I felt stung by my so-called friends. I could scarcely believe it, but LMAC struck me as the kinder person.

Well, like I said, this erroneous notion lasted a day or so. As Acting Acting President, Little Miss Ass Cream proved to be the kind of woman leader who felt she had to out-men the men. In other words, if we thought Stinky or Blankenshit were pricks, just wait till we saw what she could do. I suppose you could say she told me the truth. . . in a manner of speaking. But she had other vibrators to fuck us over with.

A couple of cloying weeks after she met with me, LMAC sent faculty the following email:

Dear faculty,

As you know, we at EBCLA are dedicated to our five Student Success Initiatives: retention, fourth-year graduation, career placement, user-friendly curriculum, and positive experience as reflected in course evaluations. Given these student-first imperatives, the BOD agrees with me that the payment equity resolution is not germane to discussions of faculty value and the compensation thereof one way or the other. Instead, starting next academic year, all faculty will need to turn in an annual file documenting how he or she has contributed to each of our five Student Success Initiatives. If you cannot demonstrate how your teaching has enabled student success over the past academic year, you will be given one year to find a position elsewhere. Tenure will no longer exist. The BOD will declare exigent circumstances, whereby it has the authority to suspend tenure. We believe this is fair, and in the best interests of students.

Sincerely yours,

Dr. Emily Crabb, Acting President

PS: Don't miss our ice cream social on Friday afternoon in front of the pine grove!

For once, the psych faculty responded with recognizable human behavior—sort of. Henry called an emergency meeting, and as we took our usual seats I heard him say under his breath to Dumont, "She doesn't tell me when I can play golf."

"It's like Nazi Germany, only worse," Dumont whispered back.

The security of tenure had long been a major reason why people sought out a career in academia, and I could envision problems on many levels if it were taken away. I worried about my own future as well, especially given the fickle nature of Elmer Butthead politics. But hearing a pair of sex offenders go on about getting their precious bubbles burst gave me a sense of vindication, as if it would be worth it to lose my job just to see these degenerates get booted out the door and preferably into prison cells where they belonged. My hatred of them had grown so powerful it vied for domination with my self-preservation instincts.

"Why is she doing this? I can't believe this is happening," Phyllis kept saying. It did not compute that a woman—as in, not a man but a woman—could take such an anti-labor, un-PC stance. Phyllis might as well have been in Wonderland, or taken too much acid. Often the first to volunteer, she'd prove useless in this latest crisis.

Sidney managed to walk a tightrope of sorts. She said how such a move went against our philosophy of students first, because an unstable faculty pool could not possibly be in students' best interests. I could see the pride she took in articulating such an erudite profundity, but she bypassed the fact that a woman was the bad guy here. Yes, the policy was misinformed, inadequate, but she could not bring herself to say anything against LMAC.

Rayana decided that LMAC must have been going through a rough time—she was, after all, married to a man—and that she needed our sympathy and understanding. Rayana would support efforts to counter the plan, provided that they never digressed into what she termed personal attacks on a woman.

Millie sat there and smoked, looking satisfied, as if she relished this long overdue opportunity to be an old-fashioned radical. I thought she'd treat us to one of her long speeches, but it appeared she did this only when unhappy—or should I say exceptionally unhappy, given her marriage to Henry.

After the meeting, Rayana and Sidney had one of their epic email debates over whether the department should compose its own letter of protest or sign the newly minted campus-wide faculty letter of protest. Sidney stated that the department must unite with other faculty, while Rayana insisted that the smaller, personalized voice of a sole department would be more persuasive. Sidney accused Rayana of having a psychotic fear of uniting with others, and Rayana determined that Sidney had a psychotic fear of intimacy. This took twelve emails to get said. I wanted to offer that the two ideas were not mutually exclusive, but feared Henry's wrath if I expressed an opinion. In the end, though, we engaged in both forms of protest once Henry suggested it. I couldn't decide which possibility I despised more: that it took forever for this obvious solution to occur to Henry, or that his sadism compelled him to prolong the agony inflicted on the rest of us.

On behalf of Faculty Governance, Leanne demanded an open forum for all faculty with LMAC. At said meeting a few days later, LMAC addressed a standing room audience in the campus theater. No ice cream got served.

LMAC began by reading a speech that functioned as a filibuster. I'm sure she hoped it would force us to lose our momentum, not to mention run out of time. Long and tedious, the speech highlighted a bunch of bullshit that Elmer Butthead accomplished over the years, or at least according to LMAC. Without ever once mentioning the tenure issue, she concluded her fifty-minute opus by saying:

"The tahm has come to live in today, not yestuhday. Change is naht always easy, but its alternative is stagnaytion. Do we want to be a stagnant, mosquito-ridden swawmp, or a flowing, vahtal rivah? Do we wont to begin each day listlessly upon the same boring treaydmill, or treat each new day as a fresh challenge, putting our best foot fowward to put owah students first? Ahm shore you will joyn with mey in the lattuh. In fayct, Ah aym laying mah futuh on the lahn for this bettah tomorrow to come true. Thaynk you."

A few people applauded, but most of us sat there in silence.

There were only ten minutes left for comments—or more like eight-and-half, given the necessary gathering of one's paraphernalia at the end of a meeting.

To present herself as open-minded, LMAC called on Leanne first.

"Madame President, No disrespect intended, but I submit that my intelligence has been insulted by your speech, as I'm sure everyone in the audience has had her or his intelligence insulted. People with advanced degrees are not stupid. We all know this is about money and self-promotion. It has nothing to do with putting students first."

Her words were met with considerable applause, though I heard an undercurrent of boos.

"Dr. Moses, puh-leaze let us remembuh our professional daycorum. Yay-es, you ah raht, money is an issue, and thayt is a fayct of laff. It is mah hope that evry fayculty membuh rahses to the challenge Ah have put before you. But if there ah fewer fayculty on the payroll, I cahn create more administraytive positions to bettuh serve our students."

Horace fought to keep his composure.

"It's faculty who serve students, not paper pushers. We're in the classroom with them, and they come to our offices for help, not yours."

Quite a few faculty applauded, including me. Others—such as the rest of the psych department except for Sidney—sank down in their seats, as if to turn invisible and not get fired that very moment.

Cecilia Puff from English stood up and said, "President Crabb should be respected just as we would respect a male president. I am not afraid to lose tenure, because I know my teaching embodies the five Student Success Initiatives. I expect to be teaching here at EBCLA until I am an old woman."

Amidst the mild boos, LMAC said, "Whah, thaynk you, Dr. Puff. In today's world, thayt is whut we neeyd to see more of. Fayculty must stop believing the myth that they ah indispeynsible to the college experience."

Janelle put her hand on Horace's shoulder as she called out, "What about administrators who make two or three times what faculty make and do nothing?"

This remark, too, generated some applause.

A couple of minutes remained, but LMAC looked at her watch and said, "Ahm sorry, but we ah out of tahm."

I found myself standing up. "You may be out of time, but we're just getting started."

It felt exhilarating to say this, but about one second later I panicked, though I tried not to let it show. Had I just blabber-mouthed my way out of a job?

My remark received a fair amount of applause, with some boos mixed in. I ignored the applause and focused on the boos. I recalled playing by myself while chained inside Misty Rose's basement. In my childish imagination I'd start to have fun, or something even more than that, and then Misty Rose would come in with her black hood and flat electronic voice. *No you can't*, said the noise in my head. I needed to be very, very careful to earn my right to survive. Other people could take survival for granted, but not me.

Leanne came over to shake my hand.

"Welcome to the dark side, Ben."

"Gee, thanks."

"Don't worry about LMAC. Underneath it all, she's desperate."

"She is?"

"Certainly. Why else do you think she huffs and puffs? If she had real power she wouldn't be such a kiss ass to the board. You stood up to her, so now she'll leave you alone."

"I sure hope so."

LMAC never attended another faculty event the entire academic year, and communicated with us only through email. She responded to positive messages, and ignored the others. To make herself even more inaccessible, she came to work at the crack of dawn, and left after the evening classes ended. All of her meals were ordered in, and Melinda Joshua took care of other errands. Occasionally Melinda passed along a tidbit about what LMAC said or did, but for the most part, faculty respected Melinda's privacy as the president's administrative assistant.

As for my own survival strategy, I figured out that if I volunteered for as many university committees as possible, I'd be far too busy for Dumont to mentor me. Or pick out his next research assistant, or chair the HBPMRC, or even attend department meetings. I still got a sick, nervous feeling whenever I had to go to my office, but once I closed the door behind me I knew safety. I felt like I crawled out of Misty's basement.

Through an attorney, Leanne got the state court to keep tenure in place until the lawsuit the faculty filed against LMAC was resolved. If nothing else, this bought the faculty time. I continued to build a record that I hoped would be strong enough to award me tenure at the end of my sixth year, which would then protect me from my seventh year onward. I made a promise to myself that once my seventh year started, I'd throw a monster party with my old college friends.

Nonetheless there were days I worried that tenure would be eliminated just as LMAC hoped it would, and I'd be the first person to get the boot. Every day that passed without LMAC calling me into her office became a victory. I continued to feel guilty about Wicki and pissed off at Elmer Butthead for allowing sex crimes to continue as if part of the norm. Even Leanne said that preserving tenure came first, and only after that could we take on other matters.

Alone in my apartment at night, I'd worry and get pissed off and then worry some more. Thank goodness for happy pills. Xanax didn't do much after awhile, unless it got a boost from a painkiller or two. Yeah, okay, or three. And sometimes I'd cross paths with a bottle of Valium. But there was no one drug I did every day, and there were days I took nothing, so I didn't think I had a problem. Sometimes I wondered if everyone who worked at Elmer Butthead popped pills in secret to keep from having a total breakdown. Maybe we were one big zonked out angry bunch of eggheads. Then I'd go to school the next day and act like nothing bothered me, same as everyone else.

Leanne, Janelle and Horace were good company at work, but none of us mingled after hours or on weekends. We shared an unspoken understanding that every spare moment should be spent recuperating from the tension at Elmer Butthead. Far too physically and emotionally drained to have a social life, I either hibernated or worked on a book about my prison interviews. Most of the time I saw myself as a monk or a hermit. I talked to many people in a given day, especially students, yet isolation ruled my life. Even though I avoided my department, or maybe because I did, I felt adrift, without an anchor.

I suppose I'd give my second year a D-, but at least it didn't get an F (or should I say Z-?) like my first year. I had a productive summer, and finished over half of my book. My medicine cabinet seldom got opened. I even had a couple of encounters of the sexual kind.

Then came the first day of my third year.

It began at eight in the morning with an email from LMAC marked urgent. Would I please come to her office at my earliest possible convenience? In other words, would I please pour gasoline over my body and set myself on fire? I felt in equal measure shocked, yet not at all surprised to receive this message. I knew I couldn't get away with smart mouthing the president the way other people did.

Remembering what Leanne told me, I replied to LMAC that she should contact Dr. Moses if she wanted to know what was going on in faculty governance. I knew this wouldn't work, and what a time to be right. LMAC said she wanted to talk about me, and only me.

I enjoyed saying hi to Melinda, but unlike Blankenshit, LMAC didn't keep me waiting. Hers was a swift, matter-of-fact cruelty. She would've considered herself a great humanitarian if she smothered someone to death with a pillow.

After the briefest of pleasantries, LMAC got right to the point.

"Frankly Ah am still furious with you from lahst year. Ah took you into mah confidence, Bentley, and you repaid me by humiliating me in front of the entiyah faculty. Now, it hays come to mah attention thayt you haven't been a participant as you should be in yaw depahment. Dumont is besahd himself. He says you hutt his feelings by not letting him men-ah you."

I did not think it wise to note that while she said she'd only talk about me, she went on to talk about Dumont. Further, I resisted the urge to tell her that she and Dumont could both go fuck themselves. Like she really cared about Dumont's feelings. As if Dumont had feelings.

"Weyll Bentley, what hayve you got to say for yusself?"

"I. . . This is the first I've heard about Dumont being hurt."

"Thayt isn't even the main point. Yaw depahment should be numbuh one on your list of priorities."

I could have said that I thought Elmer Butthead's philosophy was that students came first, but decided against it.

"I'll spend more time in my department," I replied with great care.

"Indeeyd you will. Ah have removed you from awll of yowah university commitments so you cayn concentrate on yowah depahtment. If Ah understaynd correctly, Dumont wants you to work with hiym on selecting his new resuch assistant. And you chayuh a student resuch committee. Thayt should keep you quatt busy, Ah'm sure."

In my imagination, I said all sorts of colorful things. But in reality, caution took control. If I talked back to her she'd can me, maybe even have a local police officer escort me from campus. Plus I had to admit to myself that I didn't have a clear sense of how far to take things with a woman boss. In theory, I knew her gender should make no difference. But in actual practice I knew she expected some good old sexist chivalry.

"Thank you for straightening me out," I said, hoping to disarm her. "And I apologize for what I said last year. I was showing off, and it was rude."

LMAC flashed a big smile. "Ah forgive you, Bentley. Leyt's nevuh mention it agaiyn."

"Thank you very much, Madame President."

"One more thing, Bentley. Since yowah in such good touch with Leanne, you cayn tell huh for mey thayt she bettuh be prepayred for a big disappointment next week. Would you pul-lease give huh this message?"

"Um. . . Sure."

Back in the reception area, Melinda whispered, "I listened in. What a bunch of shit."

I went back to the psych department feeling like the Titanic pulled back up to the surface. A total wreck.

"Are you okay?" Boris asked.

"I'm fine."

I wanted to stall for time with Dumont, so I agreed to meet with him on Friday. In the meantime, I wanted to check in with Leanne, and see if she could suggest any alternatives besides resigning. She couldn't. I passed along the message from LMAC, but Leanne said she already heard it all from Melinda. It seemed to me that even though the department wanted me dead or in a nut house, Melinda and my three faculty friends had genuine concern for my wellbeing.

On Friday Dumont opened his office door to me with effusive welcome. I recognized it as his way of telling me to eat shit.

His office had nothing on its walls, save for dozens of chaotic post-its intended to remind him of one thing or another. They were all the same pale yellow color.

"How are you, Ben?" Dumont asked. Before I could answer, he added, "I'm having a tough time selecting my research assistant this year. Look these folders over, and give me your answer by next week."

They were regular file folders, yet as I touched them I could swear they felt like slithering snake scales.

"I'll see what I can do."

"No, not see what you can do. Do it."

Dumont scared me too much for me to even fantasize sassing him back.

"Okay." But I had no idea how to worm out of committing a student to a life of hell.

Over the weekend, Little Miss Ass Cream died—with her boots on, so to speak, since she croaked at her desk, doing an Internet search for ice cream recipes.

The cause looked to be a heart attack, but with three presidents in a row dying at the start of a new academic year from the same cause . . . Even the clueless local police caught on that this couldn't be coincidence. They began an investigation, though they did not yet make it public

After the boring and phony memorial for LMAC (which I did not attend), I met Leanne, Janelle and Horace for lunch in the faculty's dining hall. As a joke, I said, "It's a goof, isn't it? The way all of us do research about murder, and our presidents keep kicking the bucket, one after the other. Maybe we should co-author a book called *The Power of Wishful Thinking*. Ha-ha."

The three musketeers did not find my attempt at sardonic witticism to be successful.

"Don't even joke about that," Horace said.

"Never say that again," added Janelle.

"We're serious," said Leanne. "Never mention that again to anyone."

"Okay, okay. I get it. Now can I go back to my university committee work?" I went on to share the gory details of my recent conversation with Dumont.

"Poor Ben." Janelle clasped my hand.

Horace said, "No way should you have to go through such crap."

"I agree wholeheartedly," said Leanne. "Ben deserves so much better."

"I worry about our students," I said. "Those poor girls."

Two days later, I met with Dumont. He expected me to have made a decision as to which of our female majors would become his personal blowjob slave for the academic year. Or, as Dumont preferred to phrase it, his new RA.

I knocked on his office door like a convict knocking on the door to the lethal injection chamber.

"Bentley, come on in," he said upon opening the door, gesturing for me to take a seat. "I can't wait to find out who you recommend."

I sat down in the chair farthest away from his.

"I have good news disguised as bad news."

Dumont scowled, which made him look a bit like Hitler.

"I don't understand."

"The good news is that I want you to have the best possible RA. The bad news is, given the good news, I don't find any of the applicants worthy. They're all bad news."

Lame though my excuse may have been, the other possibilities I considered—claiming I lost the files or that I had testicular cancer—were even lamer.

"You think this is funny, something to joke about?" (I remembered sleeping in the dark basement, and Misty Rose woke me up by hitting me over and over with a belt, saying, "I don't even want to look at you. Go away. Everyone leave me alone.")

"Not at all." I forced a smile. "I honestly don't think any of them will work out."

"Ben, what is with your decidiphobia? Damn it, I want you to pick my new RA. Otherwise, I'll report you to the president for insubordination. Which is grounds for dismissal."

What was it about me that crazy people found so much fun to stomp on? They thought possessing my soul should be simple, like finding a nickel on the sidewalk. What made me so easy to oppose? Thousands of other professors got to teach and do research, but I had to be a pimp for a sex felon, and no one cared what it did to me.

"Fine, do whatever you want, Dumont. But I'm done being your scapegoat or threat or whatever I am to you. And FYI, we have no president, not even an acting acting one. Remember? She died."

"Then I'll report you to the BOD. I'm friends with several members. Good friends. They'll believe me and not you."

"I don't doubt it." I stood up and walked to the door.

Just as I turned the key to enter the panic room that was my office, I heard a thud. I wouldn't know until the next day that the thud accompanied Dumont to his death—which was announced as a heart attack.

You see, when the media said we had a murder per year for seven years, it kept things simple yet ominous. But in truth, there were two murders in my third year. Though it was correct that I was the seventh victim in seven years. That much the media got right.

Ghost 12

Taking possession of someone's soul reminded me of riding a roller coaster. It was fun once it was over. Upon finishing with Timmy's body I found myself feeling an unusual calmness, as if I were complete. A day or two later, as the positive sensation waned, I knew I needed to possess a soul again. The urge consumed me, as if I had no choice.

I decided to reuse Timmy. I knew the ins and cuts of his nervous system, so I could avoid the awkward adjustments that might occur with someone else. I found him on the athletic field, his face bruised and bandaged, but still obeying his coach's every whistle. After his workout, he went to the locker room to shower and change. On his way out the door, I saw him pop a pill that I recognized as a Xanax. Small world—Timmy suffered from anxiety, too, though I had no idea what made his life stressful.

For me, taking possession of a living soul was my new Xanax.

It seemed but common sense that if I took over someone's inner essence I might as well make it count for something. I directed Timmy to his car, and he drove us to Misty Rose's old home. The big white colonial house brought back no particular memories, but the pain I felt upon stealing into the basement caught me off guard.

My sorrow turned to outrage upon seeing that the basement had been converted into a rumpus room or TV room or man cave or whatever they called it. The room I lived in for three years no longer existed. In its place was a faux leather recliner and a small refrigerator filled with beer.

I looked around the basement for something to destroy, but my senses did not connect to the newfangled furniture, widescreen TV, or pool table. I instructed Timmy to walk quietly up the stairs. I spied a woman planting herbs in a wooden box at the kitchen window over the sink. She appeared to be lost in the song she hummed, and did not turn to look at Timmy/me. In the next room over, a man worked in a home office on a computer tablet. Even from the back I recognized him as Poindexter Rose. He had the same nerdy glasses as he did thirty years earlier. His hair had gone thin and gray, but he looked as self-satisfied as ever. He wore plaid seersucker shorts, and had ugly, pale, knobby legs. He must have started working from his home. I guessed the woman in the kitchen to be his new wife.

My mind worked fast.

I had us leave the house and drive to Harvey and Madge's place. We rang the doorbell a couple of times and no one answered, so we entered the house. I found the strap-on dildo in the same locked drawer as seven years earlier. Then we drove back to the Rose residence. The round trip excursion took about two hours, but when we returned, the woman still puttered about the kitchen and the man in the seersucker shorts remained at his desk.

Since I knew I could stay put inside Timmy yet extend an invisible arm to unlock a door, I figured I'd see what happened if I tried taking hold of a second entity while still remaining in the first. I once saw a guy who played piano with one hand and the organ with the other, so I figured I should be able to pull off my own two-for-one. We snuck up behind Poindexter. As fast as I could, I scrunched my upper non-torso into his soul.

"Hey, what the—"

I succeeded in silencing Poindexter quite easily. (Timmy for some reason had far more willpower.) We put the strap-on in his hands as we led him into the kitchen. The woman turned to look at us.

"You startled me," she said. "Who is your friend, honey?"

"He's my lover," I had Poindexter say. "See? Here's one of our sex toys. He's the top and I'm the bottom. It's time you knew the truth about me. I want to divorce you so I can marry my sweet Timmy. Don't worry, you can keep the house and all our assets."

He gave Timmy a long, romantic smootcharoo; Timmy responded in kind.

She shoved Timmy aside and pummeled Poindexter's chest with her fists.

"You louse. You no good liar. Our whole life together is a lie. While we're spilling our guts, I suppose you should know I married you for your money. I've always hated you and your spoiled brat kids."

Timmy kissed him on the cheek and said, "See you later, my love."

We left the house to allow them to work things out on their own.

Our next stop was the correctional facility that housed Misty Rose, an eyesore of a mammoth building. Whenever I visited prisons, I felt like I'd left the USA and entered some secret, fascist nation. As we drove into the parking lot, I pointed out the visitor's entrance to Timmy.

"I'm here to see Misty Rose," I said through Timmy.

"Are you friend or family?" inquired the desk officer.

"Family," Timmy said.

We got patted down, and had to pass through a metal detector. A corrections officer walked us to a waiting room that smelled of mildew. The room sat empty except for us.

After awhile a hunched over, unrecognizable elderly woman in an orange jump suit entered the room, accompanied by a guard. The prisoner had chopped white hair, extremely wrinkled skin, and bad teeth. She looked at Timmy with a faint smile of hope. I got the impression people never came to visit. But as Misty Rose walked nearer, her eyes enlarged with fear, and she came to a sudden stop.

"It's him. He's come back to torture me." Her voice sounded crotchety and weak.

The guard took firm hold of Misty's arm.

"It's just someone who wants to talk to you, dear."

"It's the devil, I tell you. Away with thee, Satan."

"She's like this all the time," The guard said. "Please don't take it personally."

I had Timmy say, "That's all right. I'll come back another time."

"You're the ticklish one, not me," Misty Rose hissed.

As we left the building and drove off, I wondered if I'd accomplished anything through this brief visit with my ultimate incubus. Ghosts don't have feelings exactly, but we aren't heartless in a metaphoric sense. Something close enough to human emotion churned inside me, but I found it difficult to label. I felt sorry for her but didn't pity her. While my human mind bore the burden of many complex ideas, my emotions tended to be simple. I either felt good or bad. But Misty Rose introduced me to ambivalence. This disturbed me as much if not more than the fact that she kidnapped and tortured me. In some perverse, unhealthy way, she forced me to grow up prematurely. There is a particular unsettling damage done when someone weaker and stupider than you has control over your life. And the memory of that feeling exacerbated the awfulness I encountered at Elmer Butthead, where even my most refined Misty Rose skills proved useless.

Our next stop could not have been more different. I had us go to my parents' house. They both were retired, and I spotted them in the backyard. Dad had long been the gardener in the family; Mom used to say he spent time in the garden to avoid us. I found him picking a fat red tomato off the vine and studying it, as if its weight and shape were part of a scientific experiment. Mom stretched out on an outdoor lounge, reading from her portable e-device. For a split second, the reading tablet reminded me of Dumont, but I got over it.

"Hi," Timmy/I said. "Is this the Gamble residence?"

Mom used her e-reader as a visor for her eyes.

"Yes, that's us."

"I have a singing telegram for you," Timmy told them. He had about the worst singing voice I ever herd, but I improvised a little tuneless, non-rhyming jingle:

How would you, Mrs. Gamble, like to go to Paris?
With me, your husband, Mr. Gamble, to Paris?
Have I told you lately that I love you?

Mom clasped her hands in rapturous surprise. "I can't believe it. Oh honey, I love you so much. To give us such a gift after losing Bentley—I have no words."

Dad looked thunderstruck, but I hurried over to him and walked us toward Mom, who sat up in the lounge. He kissed her cheek, but she maneuvered him to kiss her lips. I turned away, to give them privacy. Plus it felt icky being so close to my mom and dad kissing.

Timmy dropped me off at Elmer Butthead, and I left his body as if exiting a plane. I assumed he still had the gun I gave him; why wouldn't he?

Since I burned down the president's house, Shuffle-Ass lived with his wife and dog in the campus visitor's suite. His temporary office sat in Lab Hall, where some of the broken windows had been replaced. Melinda spotted me at once.

"Ben, it's so good to see you." She gave me a hug. "What have you been doing?"

"Nothing much."

I made a hushing gesture with my finger to my lips.

"I get it," Melinda whispered. "Have fun, whatever it is."

Shuffle-Ass's temporary office could not compare in size or splendor with the one I burned down. Yet he still had much nicer office furniture than any of the faculty. I barely looked around before I entered into him. His soul did not feel as warm and cuddly as Timmy's. It felt more like entering a trachea filled with phlegm. But I kept my resolve to carry out my higher purpose.

I walked us out to the center green of the campus. Not many students were around over the summer, but five or six were sitting about under shady trees, their shoes kicked off. A boy and girl played with a Frisbee, while another girl played guitar and sang.

"Hi, President Shufflebottom," A boy called out.

As I directed him to do, Shuffle-Ass began taking off his clothes. At first the students thought it a gag of some kind, and there were a few nervous giggles. But as he kept on going, some students looked away, while others got out their phones to film him.

Down to nothing but his underwear, I had him say in a loud voice, "I'd love to show you my pee-pee!"

With that, he stepped out of his boxers and preened about, totally naked.

"C'mon, let's hear it for my dick," he shouted. "Look at my fat ass." He shook his gelatinous butt.

Someone must have called 911, because a few minutes later a cop car arrived. As the officers approached him, I left his soul.

Shuffle-Ass looked at his unclothed self, looked at the students and cops and said, "Oh my God, what's going on?"

The police watched over him as he put his clothes back on. Then they handcuffed him—hooray!—and carted him off. He looked frightened and confused.

If you asked me, I did him a favor. He'd be fired as president and unemployable as his video went viral, yet I may well have saved him from getting murdered.

But try explaining my good intentions to Elaine, who reappeared after the Shuffle-Ass caper. She wore a different designer T-shirt but otherwise looked the same.

She shook her head for her inability to comprehend me. "What does all this have to do with the case? How are you using it to prove that love exists?"

In a defiant mood, I replied, "Well, at least I'm getting people to know my pain."

"And how in the world are you doing that?"

"Shuffle-Ass—Um, Shufflebottom is going to suffer, for one thing. Maybe now he'll look back and think he overreacted to what I did at—"

"But then again, maybe not. What makes you think it's good for others to suffer?"

"Well. . . because it is, isn't it? Isn't that how we become better people?"

Elaine looked at me with an Elvis Presley sneer, as if with each passing second she thought less of me.

"Sometimes, perhaps. But methinks thou art still obsessed with Misty Rose. You can't accept that it happened, so you tell yourself it was good for you or some nonsense like that. You think because you had to go through it, everyone has to in their own way. And they don't."

"Then something is really screwed up. Because on top of Misty Rose, I walked through fire at Elmer Butthead every day for seven years."

She studied one of her dreads.

"You could have left if you wanted to. It would've been hard and a pain in the you-know-where, but you could've done it."

"In theory anyone can do anything. When people take away your will . . . It's like Henry with his rats."

"Come again?"

"If the rat isn't sure it's going to get a punishment or a reward, it flips out. It eats its own tail or something, I forget. But that's what abuse does to people. You don't know if you're coming or going. You don't take enough for granted to change anything."

"If you say so," Elaine sighed. "But I think you need to pay for what you've been doing. I'm sending you to Hell."

"Ha! So what? I don't suffer from hadephobia, which is a fear of Hell."

"I know what it means. Believe me, I know much better than you. Some of the clients I've dealt with—let's just say it wasn't pretty."

"Send me to Hell for all I care. Bring it on." In an odd way, it felt like I told *her* to go to Hell by telling myself to go to Hell. Afterlife consisted of one topsy-turvy thing after another.

"Sweetie, your wish is my command. Live it up."

I got plunked down into the humid hotel conference room where the speaker at the podium clicked on his PowerPoint and spoke in a mumbled voice, so you could not understand a word he said. Yet everyone sat there, saying nothing and taking notes. No one smiled. The thermostat was turned up way too high, but when I tried to lower the setting, everyone shouted at me *leave it alone*.

I sat back down. Slide after slide showed meaningless charts and diagrams. The speaker kept droning on. I sang to myself, I thought about being on acid in the Boy Scouts, I recited my multiplication tables, I wrote a letter to my mom in my mind. Certainly a great deal of time passed. Yet when I looked at the time on the clock, the time hadn't changed. Everyone's utter dispassion felt like stab wounds to my soul.

"Okay, Elaine, I'm outa here," I said.

Then I said it again in a louder voice.

"C'mon Elaine, get me out, damn it. You were right, I was wrong, okay? I can't stand this. I'm going crazy."

The other people made a collective hushing sound.

"Elaine, I'm sorry. Please, come and get me."

I fell on my knees and begged with my hands.

"Anything but this. Please, oh please."

"Will you shut up?" cried the roomful of scholars.

"Please, I'll do anything. Just get me out of here."

Human 12

Department members dealt with Dumont's death with what was meant to be interpreted as restraint. No one said out loud, "Thank God that prick finally kicked the bucket," though this had to be what everyone thought. No tears got spilled, and the most flattering statement anyone came up with had to do with *what a loss for Henry*. Dumont and he were best friends and it's never easy to lose your best friend.

"The one I really feel for is Henry," Phyllis said. "They were such good friends for so many years."

"I hope Henry is taking it well," said Sydney. "Millie, let us know if there's anything we can do."

"Henry is crushed," Millie said, "as you can imagine."

"They were like brothers," said Rayana.

No one had much to say about Dumont's ex-wives, though I did learn he had a kid by one of them that he never saw. I also learned a female student tried to shoot him some years back, but was apprehended before she had a chance.

The most significant aspect of Dumont's death was not Dumont himself. His death solidified the police investigation, and the local cops went public with news intended to startle, though most of the faculty showed no reaction.

Traces of potassium chloride were found in LMAC's stomach, as well as Dumont's. Stinky had been cremated, but Blankenshit's body was exhumed, and it bore traces of the same poison. I dreaded hearing that they discovered traces of my DNA on Blankenshit, but so far anyway this did not happen.

As a forensic psychologist, I found it telling that the killer had no second thoughts about having a woman target. The poisonings appeared to stem from a phobia toward authority figures. Tyrannophobia was the fear of tyrants, which may sound weird. Who isn't afraid of tyrants? That's why they're tyrants. But in a broader sense, maybe someone thinks all authority figures are tyrants. Still, it seemed to me that the last three Elmer Butthead presidents *were* tyrants. You'd be crazy not to fear them. Dumont may not have been our president, but "tyrant" might be the nicest thing he could be called.

Such are the paradoxes of the human psyche.

Since our quaint village cops had no experience dealing with serious crimes, Janelle Waverly and I got invited to help with the police investigation. The board made it clear that as a community service we were to volunteer our time and not accept payment. With Janelle specializing in forensic chemistry, and my background in forensic psychology, the local cops figured they'd have the whole thing solved in a jiffy. But we ended up donating hundreds of unpaid hours to the case.

Complicating matters from Day One of our investigation was the not insignificant fact that I assumed Janelle to be the murderer—with a little help from Leanne, Melinda, and/or Horace. I had no intention of sharing my hunch with the cops. As far as I was concerned, the subversive foursome deserved to be rewarded and not punished for ridding the world of such monstrous people. (There I go again with the behaviorism. Henry would've been proud.)

I also took for granted that their original plan consisted of offing uncooperative administrators, because such despots affected the entire campus. They added Dumont to their hit list to pacify me. My innocuous comments over lunch were interpreted as a way of saying without saying that I knew what they did. Poisoning Dumont, I assumed, became *their* way of saying without saying that if they scratched my back I should scratch theirs in return.

Sergeant Candy MacDougal was the police liaison with whom Janelle and I worked. The Sergeant assumed her role without humor. She called us Doctor and I called her Sergeant. When I found out she did a tour of duty in Afghanistan, I asked her if she knew our secretary, Boris Lang, a fellow vet of the same war.

"I get tired of people asking that," she replied, her jaw set in a grimace. But she never did say yes or no. (A few years later, when she arrested Boris for my murder, she acted like she never met him before.)

Another difficulty in the investigation—beside the fact that the average IQ of a local police officer had to be lower than that of a corpse—concerned a basic assumption I had to make in profiling the murderer. Even if I didn't believe I knew who did it, I couldn't envision this person as having some sort of phobia or mental disorder. Fear of motherfuckers—since when is that abnormal?

With considerable irony, I made myself central to the investigation. I did as much as I could with smoke and mirrors to keep the hapless homicide detectives from sniffing around my friends. I had to get murdered myself for them to arrest someone at long last. And Boris didn't have it in him to do something so dishonorable, regardless of his low opinion of me.

Early on, a couple of police detectives asked me what I thought of Janelle as a suspect.

"She's on Faculty Governance," one of the dummy detectives pointed out. "And they have a terrible relationship with administrators."

"She's a forensic chemist," pointed out some other detective dimwit, as if having discovered top-secret information.

"Janelle doesn't have it in her to be a murderer," I replied. "And anyway, what about Dumont? She had nothing but respect for him." (Total bullshit of course.)

"Then what about the other Faculty Governance leaders?" asked the first detective.

"They're just as unlikely as Janelle. Even more unlikely."

"And why is that?" asked the second detective.

"Well, they. . . they're good Americans. They work through the system. They respect due process. We're looking for someone with no regard for law and order."

"You mean like a socialist or something?" asked the first detective.

"Precisely."

"I bet whoever did it burned a flag," offered the second detective.

"You sure are a smart guy, Doc," said the first detective.

"No, just patriotic."

Yes, they made it that easy for me to fool them.

They never mentioned Melinda Joshua as a suspect, and I did not bring up the possibility. However, I made a point of wondering aloud about Henry Zwieback.

"He's pathologically competitive," I said. "He wants to be president of our college"—I couldn't bring myself to say EBCLA—"and was intensely jealous of those who were. Especially since his father sits on the Board of Directors. Even daddy couldn't make Henry president. And Dumont— talk about an archenemy. As the two old time guys in the department, they never let up on each other."

"But he's not a commie left-winger," protested the first detective.

"Ah, but that's where you're wrong. He wants you to think he's a good American. But he's been poisoning our students with his radical commie propaganda for years."

"Why would he wait such a long time to start murdering people?" asked the second detective.

I extended my hands in a questioning pose. "Who can say why crazy people do what they do?"

Of course, as a forensic psychologist I was supposed to know the answer to my own question, but what good is logic anyway? It pleased me no end to learn that Henry got interrogated on numerous occasions, and spent money on a criminal defense attorney just in case he got charged. I imagine Millie knew about his problem, but Henry did not otherwise mention it to the department. Yet he had to know that I knew.

We got permission to do a job search for a replacement professor, though Henry pontificated on several occasions that Dumont could never be replaced in our hearts. However, we managed to try nonetheless, and narrowed the search down to two candidates. We were split down the middle with three votes for each of them. Henry, Millie and Rayana liked Candidate A, while Phyllis, Sidney and I liked Candidate B. Candidate A had a better publishing record, while Candidate B gave a better teaching demonstration.

"The boys and the young women will learn so much more with our candidate," as Sidney put it. Everyone discussed our collective misfortune in not being able to combine the research of A with the teaching of B and construct a brand new person, as if people consisted of nothing more than their job qualifications. The biggest tragedy in each of our lives was that none of us were Dr. Frankenstein.

In our email deliberations, Sidney told Rayana she had Borderline Personality Disorder, while Rayana called Sidney a paranoid schizophrenic.

After weeks of no one budging, I suggested—or rather, Henry did—that we consider our third choice, whom we all liked. But that candidate took a job elsewhere, so we were back to our split. Both of those candidates also took positions elsewhere before we could decide. Given budgetary constraints, the BOD thanked us for having the foresight not to hire anyone, since Elmer Butthead deserved nothing less than perfection in its hires.

In the meanwhile, I met Janelle for coffee in the Elmer Butthead faculty lounge. I told her how the cops thought she might be the guilty party, given her forensic chemistry acumen and her contentious history with all things Elmer Butthead.

"You're not telling me anything I don't already know." She took a tiny sip of her espresso. "It makes perfect sense they'd suspect me."

As I stirred half-and-half and sugar into my regular cup of coffee, I thought it best not to mention my own suspicions.

"Dumb question, but are you worried?"

"Certainly not. You know how stupid the cops are."

This wasn't the answer I hoped for, so I tried again.

"Janelle, please don't take this the wrong way, but I need to know if—"

"You think I did it, don't you?" She burst out laughing.

"Um . . . no. And I said as much to the cops. But I have to admit it's crossed my mind."

Janelle struggled to catch her breath.

"Well, why stop with me? What about Leanne or Horace? Or Melinda?"

"Leanne and Horace have been mentioned. I said they were innocent, too. Melinda hasn't come up. At least not yet."

Janelle finished her espresso, and set the small cup aside.

"As long as you don't change your story, its sounds like I'll be fine. Guess I better not get on your bad side." She laughed some more.

I stared at her, not sure what to say.

"Lighten up, Ben. We both know I didn't do it, so there's nothing more to say."

I disagreed, and spent many an evening alone in my apartment rehearsing how I'd bring the topic back up with Janelle. But I never did. Maybe I didn't want to know the answer—not the best attitude when you're expected to solve a murder. Yet it's also true we were kept more than busy as the corpses continued to pile up.

The board decided it was better not to tempt fate, and did an outside search for a permanent president. Though no one came right out and said this, people hoped that a non-in-house hire would be better received. Or at least not get bumped off.

In the end they hired Dr. Lizabetty Woodbead as our new president. She came to us from a university in the lower Midwest, where, as a public policy professor, she studied patriarchal inequalities in waiting list preferences for community-based summer recycling programs. Lizabitchy, as she was soon christened, eventually served her old college as a VP for Academic Interface before coming to Elmer Butthead.

In her first semester with us, Lizabitchy laid off all first-year faculty, put a salary freeze into effect, and had a hot tub built next to the swimming pool at the president's house. The Faculty Governance trio raised holy hell, but I think many faculty believed like I did—that one should be patient, and let the cookie crumble when it saw fit. Sure enough, my fifth year proved Lizabitchy's last, both figuratively and literally.

The cause of her death? Potassium chloride poisoning meant to mimic a heart attack.

The killer gave the impression of being a one trick pony, so to speak. But why spoil a perfect winning streak?

The police made little progress on the case. I kept shoving Henry down their throats as the murderer, but they hadn't any evidence to arrest him. I thought about planting potassium chloride in his office, but to do that I needed two things I didn't have. The first was a key to Henry's office. Boris had copies of all our keys but he protected them with the dedication of a guard at Buckingham Palace.

The second thing I needed was potassium chloride. I considered finding a way to order it online, but decided the cops, even our cops, could trace the sale back to me. Janelle had access to it, and I dropped a subtle hint for her to give me some:

"Hey Janelle, howsabout giving me some potassium chloride so I can plant it in Henry's office and they think he's the murderer?"

"Ben, I'm surprised at you. Jokes about planting evidence are not my idea of a laugh fest. I went into forensic chemistry because it got my uncle out of prison for a crime he didn't commit."

Curses, foiled again. But hope dies a hard death.

When you're in a small department, the addition or subtraction of even one person can change the dynamic. Compared to a mound of possum droppings, Dumont was found lacking, yet with his absence the department grew worse. Henry decided he had to work twice as hard at destroying my spirit since Dumont could no longer assist in this important campaign. Declaring himself my new mentor, Henry made me report to him on everything I said or did. He might as well have been a walking and talking giant red pen. If I said or did it, it sucked, period. I did not have to pick an RA, but Henry had me clean his rat cages just to make sure I didn't get a swelled head. Knowing I hated every minute of it, he treated me to extended private lectures on behaviorism and statistics. If he could've pulled my heart out of my body and run over it with a Mack truck, he'd have done so, and done it with a shit-eating grin on his face.

With Dumont gone, the women grew ever more boisterous. The battle between Sidney and Rayana escalated into World War III. Phyllis played both sides of the fence with greater relish. At times I wondered if she saw Sidney and Rayana as her parents having a fight. Millie made even longer speeches. She tried but failed to quit smoking.

When in doubt—and there would always be plenty of doubt—I functioned as the all-purpose scapegoat. I might as well have been one of those inflatable Bobo dolls that remain vertical after you punch it, its frozen smile intact. My having stated that Wicki got murdered became a perennial source of putdown. When I hadn't done anything new for them to dissect, people ragged on me about Wicki.

"Any students get murdered today?" Henry would say.

Phyllis liked to joke: "There he is, our resident Sherlock Holmes."

"How are you coming with your delusional paranoia?" Sidney queried.

If I disagreed with Rayana, she might say, "What do *you* know? You think we murder our students."

Once when I looked at Millie while she smoked, she said, "I'm trying to kill more students with my secondhand smoke."

The drug company that manufactured Xanax had me to thank for its sizeable increase in sales. I had a recurring dream in which Misty Rose and I were picking wildflowers together on a sunlit hill near the sea.

Leanne, Janelle and Horace—along with Melinda, whom I saw less often—expressed their concern for me, but I didn't see how they could help.

I began my sixth year with the enthusiasm of a swatted fly. Henry greeted me the first day of class by saying, "I expect much more out of you before I recommend you for tenure." In a pure objective sense, he had a point. My teaching became listless and frightened as my defeatism and panic increased. I got my book on convicted murderers published, but it got a bad review from a leading journal—though the reviewer astutely noted that the first half read much better than the second. I'd be the first to admit I felt so disconnected from life that the second half could've been written by shutting my eyes and hitting letters on the keyboard at random.

But fate did not forsake me.

Henry called me in to his office that first day to tell me that he wanted to set up a meeting with me later in the day. Of course he could've emailed me, but calling me into his office was the bigger mind fuck. I didn't bother to ask him why.

I knocked on Henry's door at the appointed time, and he did not answer. After trying a few more times, I checked the front office and men's room. I asked other people if they'd seen him that afternoon, and no one had. Boris unlocked Henry's office to find him with his face lying in his lunch—an extra long Italian sausage slider, which food selection I tried not to find amusing.

Yes, he was dead. Yes, they found potassium chloride in his system. No, they did not find who did it. The cops told Janelle and I that we had to work harder than ever on solving the case. I nodded in agreement, but I reflected on how cheated I felt. I did not get to see Dumont or Henry die.

Watching them take their final breaths might have returned to me my sense of empowerment.

The women in the department claimed to be crestfallen, so very concerned over Millie's loss, but it looked to me like they loved every minute of it. No one could possibly be sad that Henry died, but his death gave them so much to worry and complain about. For Phyllis in particular the occasion must have been a peak experience. I wondered if in actuality Millie missed Henry at all. It must have been disgusting to let him touch her body.

Phyllis emailed Sidney, Rayana and me her opinion that Millie should be our new chair. We all agreed. I didn't like Millie, but she hadn't been as awful to me as the others, and maybe underneath it all she shared my contempt for her late husband.

At Henry's memorial—which I attended—our creepy new president, Kingsley Shufflebottom, made a long, pompous speech about Henry's dedication to Elmer Butthead. Though new to Elmer Butthead, Shuffle-Ass made it sound like he'd known Henry all his life. Millie managed to maintain composure as she told us highlights of her life with Henry both at and away from Elmer Butthead.

I heard Phyllis whisper to Sidney and Rayana: "What a role model. She's so courageous."

Kingsley asked if anyone else wanted to speak about Henry. My hand went up, and despite the deeply creased frowns of Phyllis, Sidney and Rayana, I walked to the podium.

"Good afternoon," I said into the mic. "Henry considered himself my mentor, so I'd like to read just a few excerpts from emails he sent me over the years. I will treasure them always."

"That's so kind of you, Dr. Gamble," Millie interjected. "But really, I'm sure these conversations were quite personal between the two of you. We are running out of time."

With a reassuring smile, I said, "This will only take maybe five minutes." Then, before Millie could interrupt me, for once I got to speak over her as I launched into Henry's messages:

Bentley,

You say you are sorry for interrupting me at the meeting, but go suck shit. I know you don't mean it, because you think only of your putrid, gangrene self. You are worthless to the department and if I ever catch you trying to undermine my authority again I personally will cut off your cock and balls and make you eat them. I wish you were one of my rats so I could fuck your brain to death, assuming you have one.

Fuck you,
Henry

I heard gasps in the audience as I started to read another email, but the mic got cut off. Leanne, Janelle and Horace rose to give me a standing ovation, but other people booed me, especially the gleesome threesome from psych. Cecilia Puff ran over to Millie to comfort her, as well as scream into my face, "Shame on you."

"He was a flasher, a sex criminal, and every one of you know it. Dumont forced his students to perform fellatio. They both should rot in hell."

People looked at me with disgust and incredulity. A lot of them booed and threw their memorial service programs at me.

Kingsley Shufflebottom took out his cell phone, and called 911 to have me removed from campus. I began to walk away, but Shuffle-Ass told me to stay there and wait for the cops. I glared at him with contempt, my head held high.

"Sure, why not?"

The cops arrived within minutes. I'd like to say I strode out with as much cool as Clint Eastwood as Dirty Harry, but I got a Misty Attack. I didn't anticipate that they'd cuff me.

"Come with us," said a cop I happened to know from working on the case, as he held out the handcuffs. They reminded me for some reason of teeth. Sharp, smiling teeth.

I socked the cop in the nose. The other cop tazed me, and as I squirmed on the ground with convulsions, I screeched out, "Go fuck yourselves." Everyone formed a circle around me to hiss and call me names. I got tazed a second time.

"This is a memorial service," someone said. "Where are your manners?"

"Where is your professional decorum?" asked someone else.

"You're getting what you deserve. You're always such a loudmouth."

"Fuckers!" I shouted. "Dirty rotten stupid bunch of motherfuckers."

They took me to the local jail. I made bail within the hour, thanks to Leanne. The charges against me were being a public nuisance and disturbing the peace. I acquired a lawyer, who threatened a lawsuit. Kingsley Shufflebottom dropped the charges, but he told me he'd never seen anything like me in his life. "Imagine reading such filth at a memorial service," he said.

I got a certified letter from the BOD president informing me that I would not be awarded tenure, but I could stay on the remainder of the academic year. The grounds for denying my tenure were listed as "refusing to be mentored," and "disrespecting colleagues."

I called my lawyer, who threatened another lawsuit. A few days later, I got a certified letter from the president of the BOD stating that the last letter he sent should be disregarded, and the Board had already met and decided to grant me tenure. It was official upon my receipt of the letter, and would go into effect in the fall.

Some people get tenure because of their academic records. I got it because I threatened to sue. Still, I experienced it as a victory after a long, merciless battle. I emptied my newest bottle of Xanax into the toilet. Before flushing, I pissed on the pills as if pissing on Elmer Butthead and his entire legacy. I sent the remaining members of the psych department all of my emails from Henry and Dumont, and composed a lengthy analysis of each remaining individual, emphasizing how fucked up and pea-brained they were and how much I hated them, adding that they were more boring than staring at a blank white wall.

I mentioned a few choice specifics to show how hypocritical they were, such as Sidney the Commie crowing about what a profit she made selling her summer home on the Great Lakes, or Rayana the Feminist deciding to resign and lose her career because her latest boyfriend wanted to move to Alaska. Another great feminist, Millie, kept excusing any error she made by reminding us that she lost her husband (Henry the Sex Criminal) only a year or however long ago. I told Phyllis she was the most insecure person I'd ever met.

"Sitting in this room right now makes me not want to live," I said once, at a department meeting, as they went on about something or another that made no difference. A bit of an exaggeration perhaps, or maybe the gift of prophecy, but at least it shut them up.

"I'm going to go flash my thingie and bully a student into giving me a blowjob. Let's see what you do to stop me," I added.

After all, I had tenure. What could they do to me?

There was a search to find a replacement for Henry. Millie emailed me that she thought it best I not serve on the search committee, and I agreed with her. Other than necessary communications with Millie as chair, none of the women spoke to me. I felt myself getting my life back a little more each day. I got a good night's sleep for the first time in years.

The four members of the search committee never reached an agreement on what the search ad should say, so once again we had no new hire, and once again the BOD thanked us.

One thing bugged the crap out of me: Now that Henry died, he could no longer be hassled as a suspect. I thought about staging evidence that would show he did it, so that his posthumous reputation would be tarnished.

Ghost 13

My spirit guardian planned for me to stay in Hell for quite some time, but when even the residents of Hell said they couldn't stand me she removed me. Besides relief, I felt more than a little proud. How many people do you know who've been kicked out of Hell?

Elaine made a huge production out of telling me I had what she called a third chance to redeem myself. The first had been my life—and we all know how that went—then came pre-Hell ghosthood and now I found myself in post-Hell ghosthood.

"No more goofing off," she told me. "You are to work on the case as if. . . as if. . ."

"As if I cared about something?"

"That's not what I meant, but fine. Just get busy."

It took me awhile to get into it, but I thought some more about affectphobia, and how fear of emotion could be related to murder by design. Yet after possessing people's souls and what have you, I acquired new knowledge of the human endeavor. I wondered if I had it wrong. If someone plans out a murder in a painstaking, calculated way, it seemed to me they may well be feeling a great deal of emotion. I know I did as I took possession of Timothy Whatshisname and the others. So in terms of homicide theory, where did this leave me? The algebra of aggression? Thrill kill? Labeling theory?

I'm sure you can relate to my dilemma.

Cecilia's sudden presence never made my day, but I found it particularly annoying for her to pop up now, with Elaine on my case for being a bad little boy.

"I'm still abjuring you," she said.

"I don't care. In fact, ignore me even more. I like it."

"You're pathetic. You act like you're such a victim of misfortune, but you're not. We create our own fortunes. There are no victims, only participants."

I could all but see the light bulb go off above my head.

"Say that again. What you just said."

"I said there are no victims, only participants."

My mind clicked and clacked more rapidly than it ever had before, like a new computer that makes other hardware look like the Model T. What Cecilia just said is called Denial of Victim, and it's part of neutralization theory, my original second choice. People drift into criminal behavior by denying that they are causing any harm. This process manifests in five different ways: There is a denial of responsibility, injury, and victim. There may also be an appeal to higher loyalties, and the condemnation of condemners. I know this sounds fancy-shmancy, but a perfect example was what Cecilia said to her colleague about me moments before tripping, hitting her head and dying:

"Why would I feel guilty? I don't control other people's destinies. [denial of responsibility] From what I understand, it took him all of a minute to die, so it's not as though he suffered. [denial of injury] I'd say he got off easy, considered how he treated other people. [denial of victim] We faculty need to stick together, and it's hard to do that when people like Bentley Gamble are among us. [appeal to higher loyalties] Really, if the worst thing you ever did is wish someone dead, look at what other people do to make life as miserable as possible. [condemn the condemners] It was his time to go. There are no accidents in life. [additional BS]"

Moreover, these denial mechanisms signaled a fear of emotion. Witness Cecilia.

Then I remembered something else Cecilia said: That no one in my department killed anyone. I gave her a hard time for saying this, for how could she know this for certain? Yet on the other hand, the gay husband who left her was a medical doctor. She said she supported him through med school to give something back to the world . . .

Cecilia re-tightened her ponytail and stared at me.

"Did your husband, or rather ex-husband give you the potassium chloride willingly? Did you blackmail him to get it? Or did you steal it?"

Cecilia wore a haughty expression, as if I should kiss her ass for bothering to answer me.

"Now what are you ranting about?"

"That you're the murderer. You murdered me, you motherfucking piece of shit. And you murdered all those other people. I think you stole the potassium chloride. You knew he was gay when you married him. You just wanted access to the poison. All that's missing is a little something called motive."

"Bentley, I have seen firsthand what you put your department through all those years. No wonder they hated you. You come up with these ideas, but what you don't see is what a bad judge of character you are. You attribute qualities to people that are 180 degrees off base. People are good. People are kind. And you just don't see it. I have no idea why."

As Cecilia blabbed away, I remembered something else she said: How her parents were alcoholics who essentially killed her, and that such people deserved the death penalty.

"It started with your parents, didn't it? How did you kill them?"

"What the heck are you talking about? I loved my parents. Why would I kill them?"

She started crying. A deluge of tiny diamonds poured from her eyes.

"Your father molested you, didn't he? And your mother didn't believe you? So when Blankenshit and Stinky raped you, as I imagine Henry and Dumont did, it brought you right back there. So Emily and Lizabetty—did you just throw them into the murder pile to even things out? To keep the focus from yourself? Or were they substitute mother figures? Mothers who betrayed you?"

"I didn't kill my parents, I swear. But I wanted to. I *needed* to, can't you understand? Didn't you want to kill Misty

Rose? In your mind, didn't you kill her every day of your life?"

"Then why kill me?"

"Because you were such a jerk. The way you said those awful things at Henry's memorial—it crossed the line. It just wasn't right."

"Henry molested you, remember?"

"I believe a modicum of decorum should be maintained at all times. And incidentally, I would've stayed married to my husband if he wanted to. I didn't mind him seeing men. It's not like they were other women. I hated being lonely. You think you know everything, but two people can love each other in all kinds of ways that have never occurred to you."

"Why did you sneak the potassium chloride into Boris's desk? Why pick him?"

Cecilia gnawed a few strands of her hair.

"He was a war monger. Two tours of duty in Afghanistan—give me a break. He deserves to go to prison for what he must've done over there."

"Then what about—"

Cecilia vanished.

She didn't choose to go away like she'd done before. Her spirit self no longer existed. I could feel the absence, my new aloneness. It made me think of a power outage during the middle of a TV show.

Elaine tapped me on the shoulder.

"You'll never see her again."

"Gee, how sad. She went to Hell, right?"

"I am not at liberty to say. But now you know what her unfinished business was, and why I had nothing to do with her. Major conflict of interest."

"So I had ghost sex with a mass murderer—my murderer. Thinking about it creeps me out."

"We all do the best we can. Now all you have to do is free Boris."

"How do I do that?"

"You'll have to contrive a way to break into a hospital and get some potassium chloride and then put it in Cecilia's office, and enter into someone else so that they find it and call the cops."

"But her office has been cleaned out. There probably aren't even any molecules left inside."

"Ah, but her apartment hasn't been."

I took a deep anti-breath. "Sounds like a lot of hassle, but I'll do it."

"You know Boris hates you."

"Yeah, but he's innocent."

Elaine smiled with her whole face; rainbow prisms shot out in all directions.

"You did it. You passed the test. I was only kidding about having to do all that nonsense. I can take care of everything from here on out."

"How?"

"Why is everything everyone else does any of your business? Boris will be set free by tomorrow at this time, and leave it at that. It's also high time the world got up to speed about Wicki's murder. But don't you see? You have a genuinely kind feeling toward someone who doesn't like you. For all of your pain that no one notices, you committed an act of love."

"I did?"

Elaine laughed.

"I'm sure you must be extremely disappointed with yourself. But the answer is yes. You wish nothing but kindness upon someone whose imperfections should bother you, but they don't."

I felt embarrassed. Like I was just some regular shmuck.

"There's one thing I still don't get. Why did you have me start with my original department when I could've started with Cecilia?"

Elaine frowned.

"Why do you think, dummy? Because you needed to relive all that pain to understand Cecilia's."

I thought that sounded lame.

"Fine, if you say so."

"I think you're ready now for the next phase."

It looked exactly like it did when Elaine gave me a sneak preview—heaven, that is. The lush green hill, the bluest mountains and waters and sky, warm weather with a light breeze. There were a bunch of laid-back, righteous people eating endless plates of brownies and listening to Zeppelin, followed by the Stones and then Metallica. The marble statue of John Lennon seemed to watch over us. I wondered how anyone could possibly suffer from Uranophobia, the fear of heaven. Who wouldn't want to spend eternity in such uninterrupted bliss?

I'd soon find out.

Hard as it is to explain, heaven, for me, got old pretty fast. Before long I was back on my knees, begging Elaine to rescue me. I missed the rough edges of existence—the passion, the intensity, even when it's rage over something stupid spurring you on. I wanted that vitality again.

"Elaine, please. Can't I go back to Earth? I promise I won't hate or even get pissed off at anyone, just to be alive again."

After pleading my case for quite some time, heaven went away. But I wasn't back on Earth, exactly. I was a ghost again.

"I can't bring you fully back to life, so this will have to do." She sounded irritated with me, like I was this ungrateful slob or something.

"So what do I—"

"There have been others like you. I can't be bothered. Good-by forever."

And so my spectral existence continues. However, I am no longer confined to one location. I travel every which way, even crossing oceans during storms at sea so I can blend in better. I spend my time looking for people whose souls look like fun to possess. I go inside them and create earthly chaos. My achievements are necessary destructions. I peel away a little more of the lie each moment. I crawl into people's sleep until there is nothing left but the truth.

Human 13

With my tenure in place, I no longer sucked up to people or pretended to agree with them. The people in the psych department knew how I felt about them courtesy of my nasty messages and remarks. I think all concerned felt relief when I attended departmental meetings and social functions as little as possible. I overheard Phyllis telling Sydney that I'd become as bad as Henry or Dumont, if not worse. Sidney replied that all men were the same.

It upset me to be compared to those two monsters, especially since, whatever my shortcomings, I did not commit sex crimes or figure into the murder of students. But the fog of denial had not lifted from the department. I believed that Phyllis, Sydney, Rayana and Millie were also victims of a sort. They spread poison, at times they thought this their major task in life, but they didn't start out that way. Years of pretending that sexual abuse and other offenses did not exist at Elmer Butthead, while trying to live up to their feminist ideals had warped them, perhaps permanently. None of them became any more self-reflective or any less defensive.

I saw a few movies over the years that featured an innocent person sent to prison who turns into a hateful, hardened criminal—exactly the kind of person he or she feared when first sent to prison. Elmer Butthead functioned as a different sort of prison, but its effects were about the same. It happened to me, and I came to realize it also happened to the women in my department. When good people tolerate the intolerable, it changes them.

I still liked Leanne, Janelle and Horace. But having reached my threshold of tolerance for bullshit, and with many faculty avoiding me because of my behavior at Henry's memorial, I went from being the apple-cheeked young recruit to that high-strung, crazy weirdo who offended people whenever I opened my mouth—or even if I didn't. Melinda

Joshua became about the only person with whom I felt secure, though our paths had little reason to cross.

Back in Misty Rose's basement, I'd sit there in the dark and long for human companionship. I missed my parents beyond words, but I also wanted to get into the thick of things, to be involved with lots of people performing a wide range of human pursuits. Popularity mattered to me even as a small child. I daydreamed about my high school yearbook picture, and how I'd have more activities listed under my name than anyone else.

Savoring my alone time in my office or at home, I thought about the active life I dreamed of having versus the isolated one I lived. I imagined that as I aged I'd be regarded as the crazy old man who lived upstairs. Though fate spared me that destiny.

Contrary to what some people assume about tenure—that it makes teachers lazy—it made me much more dedicated to my classes. No longer having to worry over course evaluations or the department pouncing on my every idiosyncrasy, I became an inventive and lively professor. I let me be myself with students, starting with telling them about my kidnapping, and it worked.

"Do you hate that woman who kidnapped you?" A student asked.

"If only it were that simple."

Several students laughed in recognition of complicated, messy emotions, and I felt a genuine connection to them. By not talking down to them, they no longer saw me as an ogre or a bore.

I did not yet know how Boris felt about me, and as secretary he got paid to act nice to everyone. I did not confide in him, but I assumed a certain good will between us that did not exist. Even when I said nothing to other people in the department—or they to me—I chatted with Boris for a few minutes every day about something a student said or something I read in the news. He seemed to enjoy these mini-chats.

One day I told him some especially stupid story in the news about a man who accidentally set himself on fire by trying to launch a firecracker through his mouth.

"It takes all kinds," Boris said, shaking his head. "I almost forgot—someone left a piece of banana nut bread in the break room for you."

"Great, I love banana nut bread," I said. "I still can't get over that guy. Let's face it. Life is wasted on the living."

A Note to the Reader

Cognitive dissonance is what happens when you realize the inconsistent or illogical nature of something you think or believe, compared to your behavior. For example, you believe junk food is bad, you even say junk food is bad, but you eat it anyway. Should you realize that you are contradicting yourself, you will feel cognitively dissonant, or mentally uncomfortable. According to social psychologist Leon Festinger, people will try to restore cognitive consonance (mental harmony) through one or more of the following three strategies:

Change either your cognitions or your behavior so that the two are consistent. Stop eating junk food or stop believing and saying it is bad.

Find new information that makes this dissonance seem consonant. You read an article that says junk food helps you live longer.

Forget, ignore or avoid the dissonance so that it no longer bothers you. Enter a state of denial in which you keep eating the junk food and continue believing and saying it's bad.

This is a novel about Number Three.

Ph.Dead is fiction. I have never been a psychologist, or for that matter a ghost. And there is no such college as EBCLA, or the characters who populate it. However, there is nothing fictional about the very real problem of sexual assault on our nation's campuses. Check out *http://www.futureswithoutviolence.org* for more information.

ABOUT THE AUTHOR

JP Bloch is a novelist and Ph.D scholar interested in alienation. His novels explore how damaged anti-heroes seek and reject connections to other people. He has appeared on TV and radio numerous times. JP's novels include *Shadow Language, Deadbeat Dad* (Pegasus books) and *Identity Thief*, a #1 Amazon bestseller. He hates bigots and enjoys people who have gained wisdom from hardship and ask questions more than they assume answers.

A gargantuan thank you to Christopher Moebs and Marcus McGee of Pegasus. Big thanks also to the many fine professors who made me a better person, as a college student and as a student of life.

·